A Heart in the Right Place

by Heide Goody and Iain Grant

Pigeon Park Press

Published by Pigeon Park Press
www.pigeonparkpress.com

Finn selected her café table carefully. She sat where she was able to easily scan the Arrivals lounge crowd, access all exits, and read her Facebook posts without being overlooked. The Starbucks cup in front of her was scrawled with the name *Hellebore*. Her Facebook account was in the name of *Celandine Dogweed*: a twenty-nine year old retail manager and mother of two from Hull who liked stylish functional clothing, sharing videos of life hacks, and changing her profile picture to show solidarity with the victims of this week's atrocity. Whatever it was. Finn was none of those things; apart from the clothes.

What Finn liked was control – having it, taking it, removing it from others. She liked to be in control of any situation; even if it was just picking someone up from the airport. Picking people up from airports was not something she liked. Airports were fine: they were functional and anonymous, Liverpool John Lennon no different to Glasgow, or Leeds, or Bristol. It was the people aspect she found distasteful.

The very best thing about her current job was she never had to meet colleagues. She received instructions and was paid electronically. Meeting people nearly always ended up badly. For them, especially. She had a low tolerance for idiots, and the world was full of them. Her tolerance for other people was very low, and it suited her to avoid them unless absolutely necessary. Once upon a time there were a few people (a very few) she had been fond of, but they could now be variously catalogued as incarcerated, hiding or dead.

Adam Khan walked towards the café. He was thirty-something, slender, a haircut straight out of a boy band and a skin tone which could have signalled mixed race, Muslim, or a two-week holiday in the Canary Islands. She instantly found that irritating. She liked pigeonholing people, and would have to ask for clarification later. Despite the self-consciously sculpted hairstyle, he dressed like his mother had chosen his clothes. He walked with an inefficient, somewhat fussy gait. Gay? she wondered. She would ask him that, too.

She hadn't been given a picture; just a fair description and told he would be carrying an over-shoulder boxy fabric bag like an old video camera case.

She stood, her Muubaa leather biker jacket creaking. "You are Adam Khan," she said, holding out her hand to shake because that's what people did.

"Finella?" he said. His handshake was firm but brief.

"Finn," she said.

"I was told I was meeting a Finella." He had flown in from Dublin but didn't have an Irish accent.

"Finn."

"Your cup says Hellebore," he said. He pronounced it *Hell-boar*.

"It's *Hell-e-bore*," she corrected. "I'm working my way through a seed catalogue."

"I see," he said, but clearly didn't.

"For aliases. I'm looking forward to the vegetable section." She wanted to test the credulity and politeness of the people she met with names like Cardoon, Chicory and Courgette.

"Shall I call you Finn or Finella?" he asked.

"It's Finn."

"I prefer things formal." His face twitched as he looked at the smart watch on his wrist. "I was delayed in baggage reclaim." He patted the bulky fabric bag.

"What's that for?" she asked.

"For the heart." He checked the smart watch again. "We are on a tight schedule."

Finn took her Polaroid camera out of her pocket and took a photo of him. He grimaced unhappily. The instant print rolled noisily out of the front slot.

"So what's *that* for?" he said.

"It's a camera," she said, like it was the most obvious thing in the world. Biting the top off her black Sharpie she wrote on the drying photo. "Adam. A – D – A – M."

"But why did you take it?"

She looked him in the eye and blew the photo dry. "You were saying we're on a tight schedule."

"I'm booked onto a six o'clock flight. The donor?"

"Oz Bingley. I have an address in Liverpool and a photograph." She showed him the photograph. It was one she'd been emailed, not one she'd taken himself.

"You can barely see his face," he protested.

"It's recent. A grey-haired dude called Oz who owns a huge and hideous sheepskin coat. It's enough."

"Does he know we're coming?" said Adam.

"We're going to steal his heart. Course he doesn't fucking know. Ready?"

Adam nodded and pointed at her. "Finn," he said, as though reminding himself. "Oz Bingley. Six o'clock flight." He looked at his watch again.

The man was a weirdo, Finn decided and tucked both photos into the lapel zip pocket on her Muubaa.

"Oz Bingley? Who on earth is Oz Bingley?" Nick asked of no one in particular. There was no one to ask. He was alone in his house.

Which was sort of the point. All morning he'd waited at home for the parcel to arrive. He should have been at work at the ChunkyMunky offices in Birmingham city centre but he'd taken an official duvet morning (they only got three a year) and waited for the parcel he knew was arriving.

He'd paid for next day, timed delivery. An extra twelve pounds it had cost him, but he couldn't afford to miss this delivery. He'd been on high alert all morning, not daring to put on the radio or turn up the television in case he missed the knock at the door. He even went to the toilet in the dark so the noise of the extractor fan wouldn't mask a particularly stealthy approach. That had been a mistake, on reflection. He'd been so worried about not wiping properly he'd been completely unable to go. He'd come out, walked past the front door on the way to the kitchen and there it was:

WE HAVE A PARCEL FOR YOU...
SORRY WE MISSED YOU. YOUR ITEM IS:

There was a ticked box.

WITH YOUR NEIGHBOUR:
OZ BINGLEY, 42 LANGOLLEN DRIVE, BRANDWOOD END, BIRMINGHAM

Nick fumed. Not as much as he would have done if they had ticked the box for *BEING HELD AT OUR DEPOT, READY TO COLLECT THE NEXT WORKING DAY*. And at least it wouldn't be a repeat of when the postman had left the parcel *IN YOUR SAFE PLACE*. Said place being his bin. His actual wheelie bin rubbish bin. On bin day.

Nick still fumed.

Being forced to stay in, like a housebound oldster or a sickly child, even for a few hours had driven him near stir crazy. He could have been at work already, trying to fix the shitstorm which was the

Kirkwood account. He could be at the gym, lifting weights and making a start on the New Year's resolution he'd made five months ago. He could be in town buying an apology gift for Abigail. Or just getting drunk and leaving inappropriate and remorseful messages on her voicemail. Anything but waiting for a parcel which was apparently delivered by stealth ninjas.

How had they achieved this in complete silence? Why didn't they knock the door or ring the bell? Nick went to the door and, looking past his beloved, imported Cadillac on the driveway, scanned the street for signs of the courier. Nothing. Maybe the slip had been there for hours.

He checked the address and crossed the street. Number forty-two was a large, detached house with a big brass knocker on the front door: a gurning lion's face with a ring in its mouth. He banged it hard as the postman should have done at his house. It made a thunderous racket, which pleased Nick. There was nothing worse than knocking or ringing a door and being unsure whether it could be heard.

The noise set a dog barking inside. Nick listened intently. There was a low whining sound as well. No one came to the door.

He wondered what the appropriate time was to wait before knocking again. Knock too soon and it would appear rude. Wait too long and you were just waiting on someone's doorstep doing nothing. He counted down from thirty to zero and then waited another minute before knocking again.

The barking dog set off again. He waited. Still nothing.

He looked at the card. *OZ BINGLEY. 42 LANGOLLEN DRIVE.*

Nick didn't know his neighbours well. Tall fences made good neighbours and all that. He tried to recall seeing anyone coming in or out of that house. Was Oz a man's name? He had a vague recollection an old woman lived there, but he hadn't seen her for a while. Maybe she'd moved out.

He went back to his house and sat at the window, hoping to see Oz returning from some small task – like posting a letter. He checked the time and turned the TV on. He'd go and check again in an hour, and then he'd have to go into work.

7

3

Finn led Adam to the multi-storey car park and the Volkswagen hatchback she had acquired for the job. She liked Volkswagens. They were reliable, good in tight spaces and were faster than they appeared. If she ever bought a car, actually paid her own money for it, she would buy a Volkswagen.

He went to put his bag in the boot.

"Boot's full," she said.

"With what?" he asked.

She didn't answer. He hesitated before putting the bag on the back seat. He got in the front.

As they drove out, Adam produced a phone and scrolled through windows. "What's the address we're going to?"

"Flat fifty-three, Estuary Tower, Conway Street. Just up the river from here."

"Thirty minutes on the sat-nav."

"I know where I'm going," she told him.

He took out a notepad and pen and scribbled. "I'm just factoring in delays and contingencies. Have you read the schedule document?"

She had seen an e-mail and read what she'd needed to.

"I've left a one hour window for your part of the ... procedure," he said. "Can you give me details?"

She glanced down at his pad, then at him, and then back to the road. "You don't need details."

"I want to know how it fits into my plans."

"This is my mission; you are coming along for the ride. I don't need a planner, I'm more of a doer. I don't even know why you're here."

"I do logistics for Mr Argyll." He looked genuinely confused. "Surely your handler told you that."

"Handler? I just get texts and e-mails."

"But do you not wonder who from?"

She shrugged. "Not if they pay. So you're the postman, or whatever."

"And I need to know how we're going to do it."

"We're going to do the job," said Finn. "Simple as."

"But how are we going to—?"

"We locate the mark. We take his heart."

"And you know how to do that?"

"I watched a video. We just start from the outside and work in. Like that sculptor."

"Which sculptor?"

"Cut away anything which isn't a heart until all we're left with is a heart."

"That's not a plan," said Adam. "It's not even an approach."

"What's the difference between a plan and an approach?"

He sighed and put his hands in his lap. "The importance and difficulty of logistics is often overlooked. There are so many things to sort out. It's a human heart we're talking about: you can't just pop it in a jiffy bag and put it in the post. It has to be prepared and transported extremely carefully. You and I both know how important that is in this case, yes? We need to cross borders too, which is a complicating factor. Without me, you have a very low chance of achieving all of this, believe me."

"So you're the man with the box. Got it."

"Logistics," said Adam. "It is essential the heart gets to Dublin within twelve hours of removal. We must get it straight into the box, which will maintain a temperature between two and six degrees. The heart must also be securely double bagged in the special solution I have. If any part of this goes wrong, then the mission has failed."

"Fine," sighed Finn. "The plan is: we locate the mark, we take his heart and *then* you can do whatever you need to do with your double-bagging and your special solution."

"That's still not a plan," he said. "There are so many unknowns. If I were you I'd have a dozen questions."

"I do have one question."

"Good," he said enthusiastically.

"Are you black?"

He stared. "What?"

"Black. Racially. Are you? You've got brown skin. Not very brown, but brown."

"I don't see how..."

"Or are you Muslim?"

9

He blinked and shook his head as though he'd just tasted something bitter. "Are you being ignorant or—"

"I am ignorant. That's why I'm asking."

He looked away out of the window. She thought he wasn't going to answer and then he spoke with deliberate calm.

"As it happens, I am a Muslim. It's my religion, not my skin colour."

"Yeah, but you know what I mean."

"What you're perhaps asking is if I'm Indian or Pakistani or—"

"Right, right. That."

"Lebanese. British Lebanese. My parents are from Lebanon. Does that answer your question?"

"Yes, it does."

"And is my ethnicity or my skin colour going to be a problem between us?"

"No," she said, surprised. "I just wanted to know."

"Fine," he said, letting his emotions go in a loud exhalation. "And are there any more questions?"

"Are you gay?" she asked.

"For fuck's sake," he muttered and looked out the window.

"Is that a yes or a no?" said Finn.

4

Hi Oz, you've got my parcel and I really need it ASAP.
If you get this note before I come back,
maybe you could pop it in my porch so it's out of sight?
Nick (number 37)

Nick had posted the note shortly before 1 pm after hammering on the door for the fifth time that day. The dog had barked, as he'd barked the previous four times. The whining sound he'd heard earlier on had still been there. He'd flicked open the letterbox and called through, but he got no response; saw nothing.

There had been no movement at number forty-two. Nick had watched. There had been no sign of the mysterious Oz. And now Nick, going into work after the most disappointing duvet morning of his life, was consumed with what to do next.

What he should do was sort out the rampaging clusterfuck that was the Kirkwood account job; what he wanted to do was to get his parcel. What he didn't need or want was a phone call from his mom as soon as he sat down at his desk on ChunkyMunky's Digbeth offices. There was a pile of papers on his desk in the supposedly paper-free office. Memos and notes from others, the folder for the Kirkwood job, a dozen Post-Its. And underneath, a phone was ringing. He didn't look at the caller ID before answering: too preoccupied with a Post-It note from the Kirkwood job copy writer asking if the presentation went okay.

"No, it bollocking well didn't," he said to the note as he put the phone to his ear.

"Is that Nicholas?" said his mom, Diane, in the tones of one who hoped the speaker of such vulgarities wasn't her darling son.

"Oh, hi," he said, realising it was too late to pretend he wasn't there. "Hi mom."

"Am I calling at a bad time?"

Every conversation with her started with those words. They could be read at a number of levels from *I know you're busy and I don't want to intrude* through *There never seems to be a good time to call you* down to *It's like you've forgotten us and no longer need us in your life.*

"No, not a bad time," he said, screwing up the Post-It and tossing it away.

"*Not too busy.*"

"Not at all," he said.

"*Because Simon is always busy.*"

Of course, he is. Here, there and everywhere. "Where is he this week?"

"*Scuba diving in Mauritius. I did tell you.*"

"Hardly sounds busy."

"*He's saving the planet by counting bits of plastic in the sea. Don't you watch his vlog?*"

Aside from the annoyance of hearing a septuagenarian using the word *vlog* proudly, unironically and correctly, Nick couldn't think of anything worse than watching his stronger, braver, smarter, older brother prance about the world and show off how much he really, really, *really* cared about the environment. Nick was snidely aware Simon's planet-prancing was confided to sun-kissed paradises with western hotel facilities. Simon would not be found crawling through the rubbish tips of Mumbai or dragging Saga Ullansdottir into the chemical wastelands of the former Soviet Union.

Saga – Scandinavian, bred from pure Aryan stock, as sleek, as tall and as much fun as an IKEA wardrobe – was Simon's life partner. Not girlfriend; not wife. The pair of them were too damned on-message for that kind of patriarchal nonsense. Saga and Simon: fit, bronzed, existing on a gluten, lactose and cruelty-free diet, living a life so bloody pure and carbon-neutral they practically hovered above the world; too fucking amazing to taint it with actual footprints.

As his mom filled him on all the details of his brother's life he had so assiduously avoided, Nick searched through the piles on his desk for the picture boards to the Kirkwood presentation, so he could either destroy the evidence, or work out what he could salvage. He was sure he'd flung them down here yesterday, after the fiasco of the presentation—

He realised his mom had stopped and there had been a question.

"Sorry?" he said.

12

"I said, how is Abigail?"

He swept a pile of papers onto the floor in the hope this one final dramatic act would uncover the Kirkwood picture boards, but no such luck. He swivelled round on his chair.

Abigail was stood on the other side of the glass partition to his office, one of the Kirkwood picture boards pressed up to the glass with one hand, holding her belly with the other as though rocked with uncontrollable mirth. It was the *Nice Bangers, Missus!* picture board. It was embarrassing to behold and wasn't even the worst of them.

"Great," he muttered.

"Is she?" said his mom.

ChunkyMunky Marketing had always praised Nick's out-of-the-box thinking, had trusted him with some big clients and let his judgement lead the way; soon forgotten when words like *inappropriate* and *completely unprofessional* were being bandied about after his latest presentation.

The Kirkwoods were looking to expand, and make an impact on the national market after moving their base of operations from a small farm business in some backwater place called Dalwhinnie to a bigger facility in the Scottish Lowlands. Expansion or not, selling sausages was not an easy job. No one had been excited by sausages since the Seventies. Any advertising campaign would have to be a bit lateral, a little bit edgy, even a little controversy baiting. Greggs had drawn a lot of media attention with their nativity scene featuring a sausage roll in place of the baby Jesus. Poundland's captioned photo of an Elf on the Shelf teabagging a Barbie doll (with an actual teabag) had courted outrage and amusement in equal measure.

Nick had decided to tap into a bit of that. He'd done a load of work (browsing internet memes) and commissioned a photo shoot. Somehow, the copy writer had taken his light-hearted commission and turned it into a pornographic horror; presumably reacting to her own relationship problems. Nick had fallen victim to one of his own worst habits: a tendency to leave things until the last minute. Instead of having the captioned photos a week ahead of time, he'd left it so late he didn't see them until the morning of the presentation. As he reviewed them he knew in his heart of hearts the tone was wrong; very wrong. As he saw it, he was faced with only two options. He could brazen it out and risk losing face, or he could postpone the presentation and definitely lose face. It seemed worth a shot. Mistake number one.

Mistake number two, with the benefit of hindsight, was failing to research the people involved at Kirkwood. The most rudimentary internet search would have revealed Mary Kirkwood was an old-fashion Presbyterian, founder of a women's refuge and a staunch anti-pornography campaigner. Had Nick known this, he might not have presented her with a picture of a woman raising a fat sausage to her red glistening lips and captioned:

SHE ALWAYS ENJOYS MY SAUSAGE IN CIDER.

He was in such a hurry to get it off the board when Mary Kirkwood gasped her outrage, he'd clicked on to the next slide showing a man holding a sizzling Kirkwood sausage, very clear at groin height with the words:

YOU CAN'T BEAT MY MEAT. YOU'RE WELCOME TO TRY.

Nick's feeble protests that the Kirkwood's wild boar sausages were clearly visible in the photos really didn't improve things. He'd screwed the pooch, jumped the shark and shafted the sausage account good and proper. And Abigail pinched the evidence from his desk to have a good laugh. That her silent laughter was clearly not meant as mockery only made Nick more irritated.

"Yes, mom, Abigail is fine," he said. Still no longer my girlfriend, still coping with it far better than I am, but still fine. "Just fine."

He turned his back on Abigail, giving her the finger as he did. He intended it as a cheeky gesture, as jokey and in-jokey as her window-gurning, but it immediately felt mean and miserable. He instantly regretted it.

"*She going with you this weekend?*" asked his mom.

"No, no. It's just me and dad."

"*Thought I should check. Your father wanted to know.*"

"And how is he?"

The pause on the line struck Nick like a physical blow. *How is he?* was the wrong question. Nick's dad only had his own imminent death to worry about, and good old Tony Carver regarded that minor inconvenience with the same pragmatic stoicism he viewed every unavoidable event. Diane, on the other hand, was having to contend with the loss of her husband, the loss of – Nick balked at the phrase, knowing nonetheless it was true – the love of her life.

"And you?" he added lamely.

"Yes," she said, simply. *"And everything's sorted for this weekend?"* There was now a note of worry, a lack of trust. Nick was prepared to bet she didn't ask Simon if he'd brushed his teeth or pack clean undies before jetting off to the Seychelles or wherever it was he'd gone.

"Yes, yes, all sorted," he said. And then, the walls of his own worry gave way, involuntarily added, "I've got one thing to sort."

"What?" she asked, not exactly tutting but with a *tut* definitely built into that one syllable.

"The present. I just wanted to buy him something nice. I ordered it on-line but..."

"You didn't leave it to the last minute, did you?"

"I most certainly did not," he replied passionately. "The blasted post office have—"

"Well, you should call them."

"It's not so simple."

"Is there a phone number?"

"Um. Um." He cast about his work desk as though a phone number for the post service was going to conveniently materialise. "I did knock."

"Knock?"

Nick didn't want to go into it. He swivelled round in the chair.

The incriminating Kirkwood picture was propped at an angle between glass and carpet. Abigail was gone. He didn't know where.

"I'll sort it," he said to his mom. "I'm sorting it right now."

As Nick stared at his phone he wondered if there might be something else he could do. He went to the Brandwood End Facebook forum and wrote a quick post.

HI, DOES ANYONE KNOW THE PEOPLE AT 42 LANGOLLEN DRIVE? I'M TRYING TO GET IN TOUCH. IT'S URGENT.

Unleashing the local busybodies. Why hadn't he thought of it earlier?

5

At the Conway Street tower block, Finn watched Adam picking carefully through the bits of litter and mysterious stains in the stairwell.

"We still don't have a plan," he said, not for the first time.

"No," she agreed. "You said I'm supposed to use a particular tool for this job. Do you have that?"

Adam handed her a slender knife in a leather sleeve. It was silver, shiny and very sharp. It wasn't a surgeon's scalpel; not quite.

"And I've got to use this why?"

"Because those are the instructions," said Adam. "You have any medical training?"

"No," said Finn, slipping the knife inside her jacket.

Adam huffed irritably. "Tell me one thing then: who's going to speak when we go to the door?"

Finn stopped at the turn of the stair and looked at him. Was this stuff important? "Do you want to speak?" she asked.

"I can."

She gestured ahead. "By all means, take the lead."

"Right... Right." He stepped past her. "Yes, I will."

The flat was on the fifth floor. There was the ammonia stink of stale piss in the hallway. Finn looked at the door: it was shabby, with a piece of chipboard nailed over the upper panel. Paint was peeling from the bottom edge. She ran her foot along it; more paint and damp wood came away on the toe of her Moncler boots. The piss stink briefly intensified.

Adam gave a firm knock, brushing at his knuckles with a look of distaste. "I can speak," he said to himself.

A few moments later the door was opened. The man on the other side was short and unshaven, wearing a grey hoodie and jogging bottoms; the kind Americans called sweatpants. He probably did more sweating than jogging. It looked like his four main food groups were lager, cigarettes, porn and Jeremy Kyle. He probably supplemented it with cheap cider as one of his five-a-days.

This was not Oz, Finn could see. Adam had reached the same conclusion. "Oh, hi. We're looking for Oz. Is he in?"

The man shook his head and was closing the door even as he was mumbling, "No, man. He's gone down the Asda, like—"

Finn stepped into the gap, slammed back the door and shoved past the fat scruff.

"Eh! Eh!" he exclaimed. "You can't do that. You the bizzies? The social? You need a warrant."

Finn ignored him and checked the flat. There were two bedrooms, unoccupied. She had to fling wide the scrappy curtains in one to be sure there wasn't someone hiding beneath the crusty mound of duvet on the bed.

"This is my home!" protested sweatpants.

She turned to him, held up her Polaroid. "Name?"

"What?"

She took his photo. "Name?"

"Wait, man. I'm Shaun."

"Where's Oz?"

"I need to see some ID."

She ignored him, pushed out into the cramped hallway as she shook the photo to dry it. Adam was checking the bathroom.

"Some people," he muttered. "You should see the state of the toilet."

She ignored him and went through to the lounge. It was less a lounge and more of an Aladdin's cave; one from a version of the story where Aladdin uncovered a hoard of stolen electronics, tanks of exotic pets, and the remains of a month's worth of takeaways. A large cage sat in one corner: a dog crate for the world's biggest dog. It was empty. The room stank. Piss, alcohol, rotting food, Shaun's reeking body odour, and the musk of a dozen animals all fought for dominance.

"Where's the dog?" said Finn.

"What?" The man looked at a ginger cat sat in the doorway to the kitchenette. It licked its paw, making it abundantly clear this shithole had nothing to do with him.

Finn kicked the cage. "The dog!"

"He's gone."

Shaking her head, Finn casually inspected the stacked boxes of electronic white goods.

"It's all legit!" whined Shaun.

Finn flipped a box open. Down the side of a plastic toaster was a silica gel sachet, usually included to absorb minor quantities of moisture. This sachet was filled with methamphetamine. She didn't get involved with the distribution side of the business, but she knew this was one of the ways they shipped the drugs over from Ireland.

"Oz," she said, simply.

Shaun had a bottle of vodka in his hand. He took a mouthful. He was nervous and jiggled like he had the DTs or was going to piss himself. "Who the fuck are ya, eh?"

In a plastic vivarium behind his head, a bearded dragon pawed at the side.

"You said Oz has gone out somewhere?" said Adam, stepping inside the lounge, blocking the exit.

"I have nothing to say to you," said Shaun. There was a slur in his voice: a note of drunken bravado. That would need sorting out, quickly. "But you—" He gave Finn a wet-lipped leer.

She reached down and gently took the vodka bottle from his hand, maintaining eye contact as she lifted it to her lips. She took a swig, unimpressed by its quality, before smashing the bottle over Shaun's head. He slumped against a wall of boxes, barely staying upright.

"I cannot believe you did that," said Adam.

"Chair."

"Seriously, you drank from that filthy bottle? This whole place is disgusting beyond words!"

"Chair," she repeated, pointing to a dining chair. It had one splintered leg repaired with parcel tape. A tape gun, which had been used to reseal some of the open boxes, was on the threadbare seat. Adam handed it over. Finn hauled the semi-conscious Shaun into the chair.

She went into the kitchenette. The cat leapt aside. Finn opened the drawers to see what knives Shaun had in. It was the lucky dip of wet work. Crap kitchens were better than fully stocked ones: more pleasantly challenging with dope heads than, say, well-to-do rogue accountants. A cutlery drawer in a place like this would have a very limited selection, an invitation to get creative. She once had to do a four hour torture session with nothing but a plastic spatula and a potato masher. This cutlery drawer— Her hand hovered between a short fruit knife, a lever-armed corkscrew, and a fork with a bent tine. Of course, she could use the blade Adam had given her to extract Oz's heart, but Finn enjoyed variety in her work.

A toaster on the counter matched the ones in the boxes in the lounge. A white kettle clearly came from the same range. Shaun and Oz had been sampling the goods. Further along the counter was a chopping board on which were a pile of open sachets, a razor blade, a tube of glue and two pots of white powder. Someone was clearly in the process of exchanging *silica gel* for silica gel.

"Put the kettle on," she told Adam.

He tutted, looking through cupboards for clean mugs. "I'm going to have to wash up if we want a drink. Not that we have time."

Finn ignored him grumbling about the filthy dishcloth, taking the corkscrew and toaster back into the lounge. Shaun was mumbling groggily. Finn took Shaun's left hand, inserted it into the toaster and strapped it in place with a dozen circuits of the tape gun. Shaun wasn't waking, not quite yet. He was like one of the giant insects or slumbering toads in the translucent tanks by the wall. Not aware; not focussed.

The kettle came to the boil. Adam rinsed a trio of cups, rubbing them gingerly with his fingertips under the tap, all the while pulling a face. Finn picked up the kettle, carried it over to Shaun and poured the contents into his lap.

His screaming made Adam drop the mugs. "For fuck's sake!"

"Awake now?" Finn asked. "Focused?"

Shaun screamed, tried to stand, to pat and waft his parboiled groin. He saw the toaster taped to his hand and screamed some more. Finn pushed him back into the chair with ease.

"Shush, now," she said.

Shaun grunted and yowled and cried. Finn opened up the corkscrew. "Be quiet or I'm going to have to cut your tongue out."

The screaming immediately subsided into a terrified mewling. The ginger cat jumped onto a stack of boxes and watched with interest.

19

"Are we actually having a cup of tea?" said Adam. "I've cleaned cups now."

Finn paid him no mind. "You are a naughty man, Shaun," she said.

Shaun's mouth was an unhappy rectangle, the freeze frame of a toddler who had just let go of its balloon. "Is this about cutting the meth?" he sniffled.

"I bet Mr Argyll doesn't know about that," she said. "Yet."

"Shit." Adam noticed the chopping board of drugs on the kitchen side and began taking pictures with his phone.

Finn took out her black Sharpie and wrote on the latest Polaroid. "Shaun. S. E—"

"H," said Shaun, keen to please. "S. H. A—"

"U. N," finished Finn. She blew on the drying ink and sniffed. The scalding water had brought out the stink from his filthy sweatpants. She went to the large lounge windows and threw them wide. A cold city wind blew in, but did nothing about the smell.

"Where is Oz Bingley?" she asked.

"Oz?" said Shaun. "I thought this was about the drugs."

"It's not about the drugs," said Adam.

"*You* don't get to know what it's about," Finn told Shaun. "You're low life. You know, from a philosophical and scientific point of view. I'm deeply into my science. I have no evidence you are even a conscious being."

"What is she on, man?" Shaun said to Adam, pleading.

"Is that a yay or nay on the tea?" Adam asked Finn, ignoring him. "Our schedule is already slipping dangerously."

"In times gone by," Finn continued conversationally, "people didn't believe animals had thoughts. Or even feelings."

She picked up the cat and threw it out the window. The cat yowled, and flailed, and vanished. Shaun yelled something and tried to stand. Finn punctured his shoulder with the tip of the corkscrew and pushed him into the seat again. The toaster taped to his hand clanged against the chair leg.

Adam went to the window and looked out.

"You fuckin' bitch!" sobbed Shaun. "What d'you do that for?!"

"Are those words?" mused Finn "Or just the noises made by a robot. A meat robot."

20

"Ya fuckin' threw it out the window!"

"You did," agreed Adam. "You threw the cat out."

"How can we know I'm not the only thinking and feeling being here?" Finn said, inspecting the creatures in the tanks. "How can I get to the heart of what you are, Shaun, and know we're—" she waved the corkscrew in front of his eyes "—communicating?"

Shaun was snivelling and blubbing. His face was variously wet with blood, vodka, tears and spit. "What do you want?"

Finn gave him a tired smile. "We want to know where Oz Bingley is."

"He's in Birmingham, man."

"You said he had gone to the shops," said Adam.

"You're going to tell us where he is," Finn said gently.

"He's in Birmingham."

Finn plugged in the toaster, using a socket on the wall behind Shaun. "He could be anywhere. He could be in Manchester. He could be in Leeds."

"He's in Birmingham!"

"You will tell us eventually." She took a plastic tank down from the shelf. "This is a tarantula, right?"

Shaun nodded miserably. "Don't hurt her. Don't throw her out the—" He stared at his hand, jammed into a toaster. "I don't know what's going on."

"Where's Oz?"

"Birmingham, man! I told you. Birmingham!"

"You can't hold out on us."

"He said Birmingham," said Adam.

"Yes!" shouted Shaun. "Birmingham! He's visiting his mam. She's sick. Birmingham!"

Finn sighed and glanced at Adam. "He'll tell us eventually."

She put the tank on Shaun's lap. "You're going to eat the tarantula."

"What?"

"Let's say, two legs."

"What?"

"Bite off and eat two of the tarantula's legs, see if it can still walk. As a special favour, I'll let you choose which legs."

He stared at her, his mouth unable to form a response. His eyes darted to a movement behind: Adam had returned to the kitchenette and was focused on making two cups of tea. He hadn't found any tea bags, but that wasn't going to stop him. He didn't want to watch? Fine, thought Finn.

She slid down the toaster's release button. The spring inside went *sproing*. Shaun whined.

"So, it's on *dark brown*," she said. "That's normally about three or four minutes by my reckoning. Eat two legs, I'll let your hand out, and you tell me where Oz is."

"Birmingham!"

"You'll tell me."

The man keened loudly and turned to the tank, sobbing *Birmingham* over and over. He knocked off the lid one-handed and lifted out the spider, gentle fingers under its fat belly. He looked at the creature. His hand in the toaster twitched.

"Please," he mouthed.

"Two legs," Finn said. "Your choice."

He thrust the big spider to his mouth and ripped at it with his teeth. The animal spasmed like a hand caught in a car door. Finn had never heard someone scream with a mouth full of spider before.

"No. You spat that one out!" she said. "Doesn't count. You need to do two more. Quickly."

The next scream was more animal than human, more machine than animal. He threw the spider down, stamped on it and mashed it with his toaster hand before grabbing two twitching legs and stuffing them in his mouth.

"There! *There!*" he yelled, a hairy joint still poking out between his lips. "Birmingham! He's gone to his mam in Birmingham!"

"His mom does live in Birmingham," called Adam from the kitchenette. "Mr Argyll covers her care bills."

"Oh," said Finn. "You should have said."

Shaun was making a noise which was off the chart: a weird feedback loop, high and horrible. The smell of cooking meat was fighting its way through the flat's general stink.

"Off to Birmingham, then," Finn said. She gripped the corkscrew between second and third finger and rammed it into Shaun's carotid artery. Yanking it out smartly, she danced to one side. Shaun bled out rapidly against the wall, screaming all the while.

"Classic arterial spurt pattern," she said. "Adam, look. Do you see how you can pick out the rhythm of the heart just before it stops? Look, at the pattern on the wall, like a wave form."

She looked around: Adam was already on his way out of the door. Finn went to the kitchen, rinsed her hands under the tap. She stopped in the lounge on her way out, looking at the smashed and ripped remains of the tarantula.

"Fucking savages some people," she said, and followed Adam down to the street.

He was standing beside the ruin of her Volkswagen.

"Well, this is a nuisance," she said.

"You think?" He looked at his watch.

The car no longer had its alloy wheels. In fact it no longer had any wheels at all, and rested on piles of bricks. It also had something like paint poured over the roof: running down the windscreen and onto the bonnet.

"This is logistics, right?" Finn said to Adam. "You can fix this."

He was already making a phone call.

She looked around for the perpetrator, but there was nobody. Just a ginger cat on the wall, curled up tightly. It watched her.

23

6

Nick flipped over the SORRY WE MISSED YOU card from the postman and tapped in the reference number as directed by the excruciating automated system. Precious minutes ticked by as he established who he was, what he wanted and answered a number of security questions which seemed to serve no purpose at all.

"Hello?" he said, when finally connected with a person. "I haven't received my delivery."

"*I can see it was delivered yesterday, sir,*" came the melodious reply. Nick groaned inwardly. It was a Geordie accent; he was a sucker for women with a Geordie accent. He steeled himself to be assertive.

"It wasn't delivered to me. I still haven't got it."

"*It was delivered to a neighbour. Would you like the details?*"

"I have the details, but they aren't there."

"*They aren't there?*"

"I've been round to the house on eighteen separate occasions, and the person just isn't home." Nick could hear a peevish note creeping into his voice.

"*You must be very frustrated, sir,*" came the voice.

"Yes. Yes I am," said Nick. "There's a lot riding on this delivery, a hell of a lot. It's for a special weekend I've organised with my dad."

"*Oh, I see.*"

"Do you know why it's special?" It was a churlish and offensive question. Of course she didn't know.

"*Do tell me sir.*"

"It's special because my dad's got cancer. Throat cancer, yeah? This weekend might be the last chance I get to..."

"*I understand, sir.*"

"I just want it to be special."

"*I see, sir. It sounds as if this is very important to you.*"

"It is!" Nick agreed. "It's a bottle of thirty year old Talisker. That's whisky. Single malt. It's supposed to be part of the magic, part of the special moment. Can you picture it? A view over the loch, a whisky in hand, maybe a fire roaring in the open grate."

Nick could have gone on. He could have said, *My dad had this amazing picture on an old tobacco tin when I was a kid. It had a grand old guy sitting there: whisky, fire, loch, full Moon rising, dog at his side, a shotgun broken over his arm. The man looked as if he was the king of the world. I always associate my dad with that picture, always carried in his coat pocket. I don't know what he kept in the tobacco tin but it's the one thing I really associate with him and the one thing I know I'll have of him when he's gone.* He could have said it but didn't; his voice was cracking with emotion as it was. What he did say was, "I owe my dad the best weekend I can possibly give to him and this package is part of that. He said he always liked Talisker and if I don't have it before we leave for our weekend together then I'm finished. Do you understand now how important this is?"

"I understand you are upset about this, sir. Can I suggest you continue to try the house? If you are denied access for seven days then you can make a claim for the cost of the package. We will, of course understand if you choose to buy a replacement in the meantime."

The gentle Geordie accent made this sound so very reasonable Nick was almost lulled into agreement. Almost.

"Where on earth am I going to buy a replacement from?" he shrieked. "I can't just go down to the offy and buy a bottle of Bells. It has to be perfect! Like the tobacco tin."

"Of course, I can raise an internal investigation for you. Would you like me to do that?"

"What? Why would I do that? Will it get me my dad's bottle of whisky?" he demanded. "I paid for next day delivery, does that mean *nothing*?"

"An internal investigation might help if you feel the courier has behaved improperly and wish to raise a claim to recover—"

Nick slammed the phone down. He was wasting valuable time. Was there another way? He called up a map of Scotland on his phone. Their destination was a cottage near Inverness. The whisky distillery was on the Isle of Skye. Was there any chance at all it was on their route, or somewhere they could detour to? He checked the internet. Inverness was on the east coast of Scotland. Skye was off the west coast. Scotland was a thin country but not that thin. There was a lot of wibbly-wobbly, uppy-downy bits in the middle, and his Cadillac, beautiful though it was, didn't like wibbly-wobbly, uppy-downy bits very much.

It would be a seven hour diversion at best. Seven hours of extra car travel on a weekend of long car journeys. Seven hours of sitting side by side with his father's silent disappointment.

Nick grunted with frustration. He could handle all sorts of problems, in fact he excelled at solving them, but there was one thing he absolutely couldn't face, and that was his father's disappointment.

Finn watched Adam chatting to the girl at the car rental. Specifically, she watched his hands. He was half-clicking his fingers, flicking one fingertip with the nail of another, as though trying to dislodge a speck of dirt.

Things were not going to plan; not his anyway. Adam backed away from the desk and pulled out his phone.

"Just need to make a call. There's been a mix up with the vehicles. I have a man who can get the right one out to us in thirty minutes." He suddenly looked ill. "Thirty minutes. Doreen Bingley is in the Avebury nursing home in Stechford, Birmingham. That's still a two hour drive."

"There are cars outside," said Finn. "Why can't we take one?"

"All pre-booked."

Adam walked across to a small seating area to make his call. Finn went to the door and looked outside at the parked cars, then she walked back to the counter. The woman – her lapel badge said *Megan* – was fiddling with her phone.

"We need a car," said Finn.

Megan didn't look up from her phone as she spoke. "I explained to your boyfriend. We don't have any cars at the moment."

Finn stared at the top of the woman's head. "Is that one of the new iPhones?"

Megan held it out casually. "No. Old model. Just had the screen replaced."

Finn plucked it from her hands and stepped back. "Never had an iPhone." She swiped through Megan's social media feed. "Looking at your horoscope, huh?"

"Could I have it—"

"Taurus. *With Pluto moving through Capricorn, expect upheaval in your career.*" Finn made a show of looking round, making it clear she couldn't imagine much of a career in a dockside car rental place, never mind an upheaval.

"Can I have my phone, please?"

Finn nodded, returning to the counter. Before Megan knew what had happened, Finn had the woman's hand flat on the counter, an opened up staple gun pressed gently into it. Megan stared, her mouth working like a goldfish.

"Scream if you want," said Finn with a shrug. "Who's this?" She held up the phone to show a picture.

"My husband," gasped Megan, as though air was suddenly in short supply.

"He looks like he works out. What's his name?"

"Kai."

Finn flipped to the phone's contacts and scrolled through the call log. "Kai," she repeated, and read out his number.

"Yes," said Megan. "Please. My hand..."

"Have you got any Volkswagens out front?"

"No. None."

Finn bore down a little on the stapler, wondering if the prongs were beginning to pierce Megan's skin. She held it a half centimetre away from punching out a staple.

"We've got a BMW," whispered Megan, the words tripping over each other. "Very sporty."

"And we can take it?"

"I'll sort something," said Megan, her voice reduced to a squeak.

Finn let go of the stapler and tossed the phone back to Megan. "Adam!"

"What?" His own phone was still attached to his ear.

"She's got a car for us." Smiling at the pale Megan she repeated her husband's phone number, just in case the woman thought she'd forgotten it.

8

Nick rushed home.

He had spent the afternoon staring. He'd stared at a Google map of Scotland. He'd stared at options for buying Talisker. He'd stared at the visual car crash which was the Kirkwood photos.

While he stared, Inverness and Skye didn't move any closer together. Bottles of whisky didn't suddenly become available for delivery in the next few hours. The pictures didn't mystically become any less horrific.

No inspiration had been forthcoming on any front. He'd been so preoccupied with the whisky problem – a mere dozen yards from his house and wholly inaccessible – he'd been unable to put any thought into resolving the Kirkwood job.

Perhaps some calming downtime with his dad would stimulate the killer concept he needed to get back in the sausage peoples' good books. So, as he returned to Birmingham's suburbs, he decided the way to fix all problems was to fix the weekend.

Get the whisky.

Meet up with his dad.

Have a once-in-a-lifetime fairy-tale father-son weekend in the Highlands with his old man.

Make those magical memories.

Fix everything.

As soon as he was back in Langollen Drive, he went straight over to Oz's house and banged loudly on the knocker. The dog barked again. If anything it sounded even more frenzied than before. If it had been left alone the whole time it was hardly surprising. It must be hungry. How often did dogs need feeding? It was animal cruelty, wasn't it?

He looked up a number on his phone and made a call. "Council dog warden? Hello, I'd like to report a neighbour's dog that's barking a lot."

"You'd like to make a complaint of animal nuisance?" came a woman's voice.

"No, it's not causing a nuisance," said Nick. "More like it's been unattended for the last two days, as far as I can tell."

"You'd like to report possible animal cruelty then?" she asked.

"Yes. Yes, I would," said Nick, hoping the dog warden would break in to rescue the dog. If he could just tag along then maybe—

"The best organisation to deal with cruelty complaints is the RSPCA," said the woman. "If you give me the address, I can get one of our wardens to call by and assess the situation. How would that be?"

Nick gave her the address and hung up gloomily. He had expected a little bit more from the council dog warden: maybe not SWAT teams and helicopters, but at least something with flashing blue lights and the power to break down doors.

His phone pinged with a text from his mom confirming his dad was packing his things and would be round in the morning at eight o'clock. It was a simple message, barely a dozen words long but the subtext was deeper than decades: *You haven't forgotten your dad is coming over tomorrow and you're taking him away for the weekend? Please don't mess it up as I suspect you will.*

He sent her a reply that simply read, YES. LOOKING FORWARD TO IT, which he hoped said nothing more.

He flicked to the Brandwood End Facebook forum.

There were a number of replies from people saying no, they didn't know who lived there. Nick wondered why people felt the need to provide such redundant information, but was soon distracted when he saw a fuller answer.

I BELIEVE HE WORKS IN SALES OR SOMETHING. HIS GIRLFRIEND DUMPED HIM A MONTH OR SO AGO AND HE'S ON HIS OWN NOW. A BIT OF A NUTTER. I'VE HEARD HIM SINGING SHOW TUNES WHILE HE WASHES THAT RIDICULOUS LIMOUSINE OF HIS. NAME'S MICK OR SOMETHING LIKE THAT.

Unbelievable. Nick was momentarily stunned. He banged out a reply:

ACTUALLY THAT'S NUMBER 37. HOW DO I KNOW? BECAUSE IT'S ME YOU'RE TALKING ABOUT, DUMBASS. AND IT'S NOT SHOW TUNES I SING, IT'S THE CLASSICS FROM THE RAT PACK. AND IT'S A CADILLAC FLEETWOOD SIXTY SPECIAL, NOT A LIMOUSINE. AND I WASN'T DUMPED. IT WAS *MUTUAL*!

He deleted his words, suspecting the insult would get him thrown out of the group, and he wanted to read the rest of the replies. He scrolled down and found a reply from a user called *AshleysNan*.

I LIVE NEXT DOOR. A LADY CALLED DOREEN USED TO LIVE THERE BUT SHE'S GONE. I SEE HER SON LOOK IN FROM TIME TO TIME TO SORT OUT MOLLY. CAR IS ON DRIVE WHICH NORMALLY MEANS HE IS THERE.

Nick's hopes rose. A car was on the driveway; it had been there all day. Maybe Oz had been at home all the time. Maybe he had been in the garden, or was profoundly deaf.

There'd be no harm in taking a peek through some windows.

The windows around the front door were frosted glass, he could see nothing through them. There was a bay window at the front with net curtains up. Nick pressed his face against the glass to see whether he might be able to see through. Only vague shapes were visible through the fabric. There were the vertical struts of metal bars just inside the window. The owner clearly took their security seriously. Beyond that, Nick saw something tall like a bookcase, and an easy chair. Certainly no movement. He banged on the glass to check.

He walked around the side of the house. There was a gate to the rear access. He tried the latch but the gate wouldn't open: bolted from the other side.

"Hello? Oz?" he called over the gate. There was no reply.

He tested the top of the gate. Nick was no acrobat. He had never stepped beyond the bottom rungs of climbing frames as a child and was a complete stranger to chin ups and other favourites of the gymnasium narcissists. He would never normally contemplate vaulting over a six foot fence; but a bottle of thirty-year-old Talisker, his dad's happiness and his entire future was hanging in the balance.

The gate appeared strong enough to support his weight, so at least it meant he was only likely to break his bones rather than shatter the gate and impale himself on the wreckage. With a grunt he jumped, surprising his arm muscles by commanding them to support him above and beyond the normal call of duty. He got one leg over before his muscles could make any formal complaint, and rolled to the other side. He snagged his shin on a nail, suppressing a yelp of pain. He really didn't want to attract attention from the nearby houses. "I'm just trying to get my parcel," might not wash if he got arrested for breaking and entering.

At the back of the house there was an untidy and poorly tended garden, another bay window and a back door. Beneath the window was a large flower bed. It was overgrown and untidy. Evidently, Oz hadn't been in the garden today, or for some time. Nick walked towards the window, pushing aside a snaking bramble which threatened to snag his trousers. He peered inside.

Again, there were bars set in the window frame, running top to bottom. This room was full of furniture, cluttered with books, magazines and papers. There was a high-backed armchair near to the window. He edged forward, trying to look down on it, and tapped his head on the glass. A dog leaped up from the seat, paws creasing the antimacassar. It came face to face with Nick. Its intelligent brown mongrel face stared at him for a second before it burst into a fresh fit of frantic barking and jumping.

Nick staggered back in surprise, the bramble caught on his trouser cuff and he ended up sitting in the flower bed. He prised himself out of the mud, scratching his hand on the bramble, and got back on his feet.

The dog continued its alarmed barking: running circuits of the room so quickly Nick half expected it to zoom up the wall. Cursing himself, the filth on his trousers and the dog's incessant noise, Nick went back to the window. Just inside the shadow of the curtain, on the narrow windowsill, was a package. It was so close he could read the address label.

"That's my Talisker!"

He felt ready to burst with frustration: close enough to touch it, but on the wrong side of the glass. The dog's lunatic travels jiggled the chair each time it bounded on and off, knocking against the windowsill, rattling the package. Could the whisky survive a fall – even if it went via the chair? Nick banged on the glass. All that did was send the dog off on another wall of death routine, and smear blood down the glass from his hand. It was, he realised, bleeding copiously from the bramble scratch.

What if he just smashed the window and took his parcel? It was so tempting. The flower bed was edged with bricks – it would be a simple matter to throw one through the glass. The bars would prevent a burglar climbing in, but wouldn't stop him simply reaching through and taking the bottle. But it was big window; destroying it seemed excessive.

He looked sideways at the back door. It had tiny panes of glass, just like his own back door. He took a closer look. After crouching down and squinting from every angle, he could see there was a key in the lock, on the inside.

What was the point of heavy duty bars if someone could smash the tiny pane and unlock door? It was very tempting. Nick could just...

He shook his head at himself. "You're not breaking in. Seriously?"

He sighed. He was bleeding, he was dirty, he was not going to stoop to burglary even if it was to retrieve his own possessions. Even if it was possibly the key to a perfect weekend with his dad, the essential seal to their uneasy relationship in the twilight of his dad's life...

He gazed longingly at the parcel before tearing himself away and returning home for a perfectly miserable final evening before the father-son trip.

9

Outside the Avebury Court nursing home in Birmingham there was silence. At one o'clock in the morning it wasn't a huge surprise.

"How will we find Doreen Bingley?" whispered Adam, scanning the large, mock-Georgian frontage.

"What details did you find out?" asked Finn, not bothering to whisper.

"Mr Argyll pays her bills, so we know she's a resident. I haven't got a room number or anything."

"Well, we can either hope they are prepared to come to the door and let us in," said Finn, picking up a brochure from the covered porch, "or we make them all come outside."

"And how might we do that?"

"We set off the fire alarm."

"The fire alarm?"

She rolled up the brochure and pulled a lighter from her pocket.

"Oh. Right, that's a bit..." He pulled a face. "A place like this will have their alarms linked to the fire brigade control room, you know."

There was a garage attached to the side of the sprawling house: a brick structure with wooden doors, built in an age when cars were far narrower. A shoulder barge broke the wood around the lock. Thirty seconds later Finn re-emerged with a squeezy bottle of lighter fluid, a hi-vis workman's tabard, and cobwebs all over her Muubaa.

She threw the tabard at Adam. He caught it and held the mouldy item gingerly in disgust. "What's this for?"

"Looks authoritative," she said. "Now: back door."

She doused the edge of the brochure with lighter fluid, lit and carefully posted it through the front door.

They waited on the back lawn. It took three minutes for the alarms to go off: a shrill shock of a noise in the early morning. Lights came on almost immediately. It was another two minutes before the first people emerged.

"This way," said Adam, waving them over. "Everyone assemble here."

The residents shuffled onto the lawn, some with the aid of Zimmer frames. Most of them were wet as well. Obviously the building had a sprinkler system.

"Ladies this way, men over there," Adam called. The hi-vis did indeed give him an authoritative air. "Doreen Bingley?" Adam asked each lady as they passed. He received a variety of responses, from a polite "No" through sleepy (or dementia-fuelled) confusion, right up to shocked outrage from the more security-conscious oldies.

"Who are you?" demanded one feisty old biddy.

"We're here for your safety," said Adam.

"Has Audrey signed you in?"

"Everything's fine."

"We know what elder abuse is. I'm not afraid to call Esther Rantzen."

"I'm sure you're not," said Adam.

Finn left him to it and moved through the crowd. "Where's Audrey?" she asked. A damp and scowling crone pointed out a stout woman in a towelling gown, pushing a white-haired man in a wheelchair.

"Audrey?" called Finn.

"Yes?" The woman squinted. "Who are you?"

"You see this?" asked Finn. She held up the lighter fluid so Audrey could read the label.

"I struggle without my glasses," said the woman, squinting. "I—"

"You see this?" repeated Finn. She squirted a good quantity of fluid into the white-haired man's lap.

"My pyjamas are leaking again!" he declared.

"See this?" Finn pulled out her lighter.

"You're crazy," said Audrey, finding her voice. "The police are on their way."

"Not soon enough. Where is Doreen Bingley?"

Audrey's brow creased. She was having trouble understanding.

Finn flicked her lighter. The little flame brought the woman's attention into sudden focus. "Doreen's dead."

"Dead? When?"

"Been a week or more now. It was her heart in the end."

"Oz? Her son?"

"Yes?"

"Seen him?"

"He's been in a couple of times to sort out her stuff. He said he was staying at her old house. Please put the lighter down. Rob here hasn't done anything to deserve this."

"I need new pyjamas!" announced the old man.

"Where is he?" asked Finn.

"Who?"

"Oz."

"I don't know! I think he's staying in his mom's old place. You know, making arrangements."

"Do you know the address?"

"Yes, it's Langford Drive or something like it. I—"

Finn took her picture; Audrey blinked at the flash. She tried to rub her eyes, but Finn grabbed her wrist, twisting it in a subtle but wonderfully agonising way, and marched her round to the driveway and their car. Finn whistled and waved for Adam.

By the time the blue lights of the fire engines appeared along the road, they were accelerating away, a discarded hi-vis tabard left on the pavement.

On Friday morning, Nick put his bag in the boot of his red Cadillac before crossing the street.

He rapped the lion's head door knocker violently even though he knew it was hopeless. The knocker echoed through an obviously empty house. No lights had shown during the night and there had been no movement around the house all evening. Nick had watched it near constantly from his living room window, fuelling his vigil with a plate of three-day old chicken from the fridge, and a party tub of twiglets.

Now, with his guts churning in protest at last night's poor dinner offerings, Nick stood outside number forty-two, shuffling from foot to foot. Inside, the dog was still barking. It was almost certainly hungry; starving even. There was also the strange background noise: a machine buzz he could hear through the front door.

He looked at his phone. Seven twenty. Forty minutes until his father arrived.

He considered his options. He could nip to the Londis round the corner, buy a bottle of generic whisky (or, worse, whiskey) and try to pass it off as a superior blend. The end result would inevitably be the look of disappointment on his dad's face. Not displeasure, no – that would be easier to contend with – but the everlasting disappointment a father felt for his second and second-best son.

The alternative was a little light burglary. A quick in and out. He might leave Oz a note with an apology and an offer to pay for damages. He could even feed the hungry dog, which would surely count in his favour in whatever skewed system of karma ruled the universe.

No contest really.

Nick went round the back of the house, through the now unbolted gate and selected a loose brick from the edge of the flowerbed. He whacked it end-first into the back door's little glass pane nearest the lock. It smashed first time. He used the brick to knock out the jagged pieces of glass remaining, reaching through and unlocking the door.

He was inside the kitchen – it was that easy! He hurried through the kitchen, pausing by the table. There was a half-eaten bowl of cereal and a hand-written letter. Oz must be an older guy – who received hand-written mail these days?

He opened the door to the next room, and the dog barrelled into him. A split second of fear followed by relief as the hairy mutt nuzzled and licked his hand.

"Hello there," he said in his best talking to dogs and babies voice. "You been left on your own, huh?"

It jumped up, placed its paws on his chest, unsuccessfully tried to lick Nick's face before dashing into the kitchen. Nick heard something sounding very much like a dog jumping onto the table and slurping the remains of breakfast cereal from a bowl, but chose not to investigate.

The parcel was still in the window, just behind the armchair. Nick picked it up, feeling its wonderful weight, the rich heritage and supposedly delicious flavour of a high-end Scottish whisky. He was Indiana Jones holding a golden idol; he was Carnarvon in Tut's tomb; he was Pickles the dog recovering the stolen World Cup. He held the parcel in both hands, knowing he was grinning like an idiot, and turned to go.

The dog was back again. It pawed at the room's other door, barked and spun in a circle.

"What's that, Pickles? Has Timmy fallen down the well?" grinned Nick.

Another bark, another pirouette.

"No, don't try the Lassie routine on me. I've got to go."

The dog whined and fixed Nick with expressive, soulful eyes.

"What? Is your dinner through there?"

Nick sighed and opened the door. The dog barged past, into the hallway, pushing the door wide.

Nicked looked out into the hall. He stopped breathing for several long moments, and closed the door again.

He wasn't sure exactly what he'd just seen. He stared at the white paintwork of the door. Pure white, like he'd pressed the reset button on his vision.

He opened the door again and stared. He didn't know what to think. He was *very* sure he was in terrible trouble.

In the middle of the hallway was a Black and Decker workbench. He recognised it because his dad owned one just like it. There were several power tools clamped to the workbench. Nick wasn't sure what they all were, but knew his dad would not only know what each was called, he'd also know how to operate them and what sort of job they'd be used for. Nick was pretty sure the scenario in front of him was not one recommended by any of the manufacturers. Each of the tools had its gouging, drilling, sawing bits turned upwards, and the mutilated remains of a man's body lay face down on them. The whirring sound Nick heard from outside was made by several tools which were running. Some of them stuck out from the back and side of the man's body. There was even a lengthy drill bit, still spinning, poking out through the skull.

"Oz?" asked Nick. He felt like an idiot. He felt sick.

Oz was in no state to confirm or deny his identity. Chunks of his body had splattered the walls. Blood had pooled on the hall rug, seeping through and spreading to the skirting boards. The parts left on the bench juddered with the tools' movements, as if Oz was having sex with his workbench. The dog was licking at the dead man's dangling hand. Perversely, Nick thought this was particularly wrong.

"No. No. This isn't right?" he heard his mouth say.

The tools were plugged into a multi-socket extension lead. Hurriedly – like acting swiftly would make any difference to this scene of butchery – he reached under the workbench. He grabbed a cable and pulled the extension lead towards him. As he closed his fingers around the socket strip, something tugged at the body, shifting its weight. Both body and workbench toppled sideways and onto Nick's legs; dragging him down, entangling him.

"Fuck! Fuck no!" he yelled. He flailed. If he ever recalled the moves which got him out from underneath and across the floor, he'd have invented a new swimming stroke. As he lay panting a few feet away from the tangle of workbench and body, Nick realised two things: he was plastered from head to toe in Oz's blood and brains, and his churning guts had, during the crisis, made a unilateral decision to order a complete evacuation. Nick had shit his pants. In fear. He had no idea people could actually do that.

He stood on wobbly legs and wondered what he should do. Actually, he tried to marshal and gather any thoughts at all: he currently felt as brainless and insensible as poor dead Oz.

Obviously, the correct thing to do would be to call the police, tell them everything and rely on justice finally prevailing. He pictured how that might go. It didn't make a pretty picture, from the trail of evidence he'd left outside, to the breaking and entering – obviously done by him as he'd left blood on the window yesterday and probably elsewhere. The police were good at finding spots of blood. They'd go all CSI on his ass.

The incriminating icing on the guilt cake was him standing over the corpse, dripping with Oz's blood. Could he seriously imagine anyone not thinking he'd done it? Even the power tools and the extension lead now bore his finger prints.

He needed to get out of there and somehow get rid of the evidence. All of the evidence.

The dog bounded up to Nick, capering joyfully. Why did it look so pleased? It had blood on its muzzle.

It was chomping on something. The dog's jaw worked. It looked like a sausage. It wasn't a sausage. Nick didn't need to do a digit count on Oz to know it wasn't a sausage. Nick reached out to take the finger from the dog. It growled at him in an amiable enough manner and trotted away again.

"This all needs to go away," he said firmly, as though a helpful genie might be passing and offer to magically fix things. "This needs to..."

Nick was finding it difficult to concentrate with the load in his pants. Even the slightest movement squirted it sideways, upwards and out. He needed to get rid of the appalling mess.

He slipped off his trousers and removed his sticky, heavy underpants. The smell was overpowering. He searched for a clean corner to wipe himself with, but every inch was thick with the stuff. He looked around; there was only one thing available. In a piece of decision making which would give him cause for some serious introspection later, his need for cleanliness completely overrode any squeamishness he felt.

"Sorry, Oz," he said as he backed up, felt behind him and pulled out the tails of Oz's shirt from his waistband. Don't think about it, just do it. He could put his trousers back on with no pants. Or he could get another pair from somewhere. His eyes slid over to Oz, and he briefly considered whether he might be able to remove and use Oz's, but a thought tugged at him. Did people shit their pants when they died, or was it an urban myth? He decided today was not the day to find out and put his trousers back on. The stink seemed to rise up from everywhere. With a brief yipping bark, the dog ran past and grabbed his pants, whipping them away with enough force to send a backsplash up the wall.

"No! Jesus! Pickles!"

Nick chased after the dog. It ran into the front room, the one with the net curtains. By the time Nick got there, the dog had run round and coated nearly everything with smears and daubs of poo. Still the pants sagged heavily in its jaw. There was a lot of stuff to go around. Nick lunged in desperation and grabbed the pants. He needed to get them out of here. He went to the bay window. He fumbled with the latch on the upper pane. He lobbed the pants outside, lobbed them far and hard, and shut the window. He stepped back and saw he'd managed to get streaks down the net curtains.

Nick imagined a forensics team coming into this house. The place had become a smorgasbord of forensic fun. There were enormous amounts of DNA, both Oz's and his own. What would they make of it all? It didn't matter, it was not a trail left by an innocent man. He saw the dog had spread footprints around the carpets and furniture. And so had he.

"I'm sorry, Oz." Nick went back the way he'd come, squeezing past the body. Oz's face had been resting downwards on something like an electric-powered cookie-cutter; the effect was a cross between Munch's *The Scream* and a butcher's window display.

"I need to sort this," Nick said, not knowing what he meant by it.

He felt a deep physical urge to make the situation go away. It needed to go away. He needed it to vanish. He looked at his phone. Seventy thirty-one.

Yes, he needed to sort this out. He needed to *tidy*. Oz and the power tools and the workbench. Disassemble, tidy, hide.

He grabbed the feet of the fallen Black and Decker workbench and hauled it away from Oz's corpse. It came with various slicing, sucking and grinding noises he'd didn't want to think about and would never forget. He looked at the workbench and tried to remember how they folded. He remembered if he got it wrong there would be pain and squashed fingers in his near future. A little lever *here* and a spring-loaded gizmo *there*.

The workbench snapped together and crashed at his feet. He lifted it, all of the clamped-on tools dragging in its wake, and shoved it into the cupboard under the stairs. That left Oz, currently slumped in the hallway, half-on and half-off the rug. There were little pellety things on the floor, among the gore. Nick prodded one with his foot and it cracked open. White powder spread, soaking up still-drying blood. Pills. Maybe Oz had dosed himself up before embarking on his last DIY project.

Rolling the body up in the rug seemed sensible, inevitable even. Nick debated which way round. If he rolled Oz up from the short edge, then his feet and head would stick out. If he turned him round and rolled from the long edge, he suspected the rug wouldn't go around properly. With a sigh he rolled from the short edge. He'd need a bag for Oz's head.

How practical I'm being, he thought. An inappropriate surge of pride swept through him, as though he'd just put up a shelf or remembered to put down dust sheets before painting a wall. Clearly some part of his brain thought neatly disposing of a body was worth ticking off in the entirely imaginary book of *Top Skills to Master as an Adult*.

When Oz was neatly rolled up, Nick surveyed his work. The hall still looked as if a bloodbath had taken place. He tried to imagine how long it would take to clean up. Even if he spent the entire weekend with a full set of cleaning supplies, there was no way he could make this house look normal. The thought of the weekend made him check his phone. Seven forty-eight.

He had twelve minutes until his dad arrived. And Tony would be on time; always on time.

Nick took a deep breath. Problem solving – he could do this. His thoughts went to the cottage he'd rented. One of the reasons he'd chosen it was its isolated cragginess. There were warnings for parents on the website, saying the site was not suitable for those with small children, as the grounds contained a deep and ancient well—

"Coo-ee!"

A shrill female voice came through the letterbox, close enough to make Nick jump.

"I just wanted to make sure you're all right. I thought I heard breaking glass and screaming. Someone on the internet was asking about you, so I thought I'd check. I'm from next door."

Next door? Was it AshleysNan? Nick froze, silent. As the dog came bounding past and Nick managed to grab hold of its collar.

"Shh." He gave its ears a tickle, hoping it would stay quiet if he distracted it. The dog barked loudly. Bloody traitor. The dog wagged its tail and barked some more.

"Are you all right in there?" shouted AshleysNan. "Shall I call someone?"

Nick couldn't risk that. He looked at Oz's head, poking out of the edge of the rug. Much of it was a bloodied pulp, but there were clearly some grey hairs among the wet red, plus a few wrinkles here and there. He reckoned Oz would have been fifty-something, sixty-something. Maybe even the same age as his dad. He cleared his throat and did the best impression he could manage of his dad.

"All fine here," he declared throatily. "No need for alarm. Just doing some DIY."

"Oh, I see," said AshleysNan. "There was a man looking for you."

"Yes. Yes. I'm ... I'm in the middle of something so I can't come to the door. Bit of a mess in here."

He looked at the dog and thought it was laughing at him. He didn't care about, he just needed AshleysNan to be convinced.

"I think you splashed some paint on your curtains," she said.

Paint? Oh. "Yes. Yes, that's right... Twiglet brown."

"Oh. Yes," she said after a pause. "Can I help with anything?"

"No thank you." Why on earth was he being polite? She would just keep chattering. "Can you go away now?" he added.

A few moments later, he heard the sound of her footsteps receding down the path and sighed with relief. He let go of the dog, went into the lounge and peeked through the window, and watched her go up the drive of the house to the left. When he returned to the hall, the dog was gnawing hungrily at Oz's raw face.

"For God's sake!" he hissed. "That's gross. Show a bit of loyalty to your former master. That's a total cat move." Nick meant for his words to sting.

The dog gave him a hurt look and continued to eat, more daintily.

"But it would be helpful if you could eat the whole thing," he pondered out loud. He didn't want to overlook an obvious way to dispose of the corpse. "How long would that take?"

The dog was about a quarter the size of a full grown man; he obviously wasn't going to manage to eat him in a single sitting. Nick checked the time again. It was probably unworkable, even if the dog was willing.

No, the best option for body disposal was Scotland. Wide, wide, expansive Scotland. So many places to dump a corpse. A zillion miles away from the crime scene. The body: faceless and unidentifiable.

He still needed a way of getting the body to his car without attracting the attention of the nosy neighbours.

"Wheelie bin," he said to the dog. "That's what we need."

It took him a few minutes out the back of the house to locate the wheelie bin, tip the rubbish out onto the borders and drag it into the house.

He set the bin down next to Oz's body. All he had to do was lift the wrapped corpse and pop it in the top. He reached around the middle part of the rug and tried to lift. It was enormously heavy. Oz wasn't a huge man, but Nick was beginning to realise a human body weighed a lot, and he wasn't in prime body-lifting condition. Not for the first time, he cursed himself for not keeping up with (or not even starting) his New Year's resolution to work out.

"Bend at the knees," he told himself. "Keep your back straight."

He heaved at Oz's middle, unable to lift him so much as an inch off the ground. He needed to work smarter, use some sort of natural lever. What if he worked him up the wall? Nick pictured how that might work. He could drag Oz to a sitting position, propping him up on the wall, then somehow nudge him up a bit at a time: toppling him into the open wheelie bin when he was high enough. It was a convincing picture.

A few minutes later, he had Oz sitting up. Nick had been able to get him into position by a hug-and-shuffle kind of a move. He could use the same technique to get him further up the wall. He grabbed Oz around the middle. It was way too intimate, but he had to get it done. He tried to shunt him up, just a little bit. Oz's head fell forward; they were briefly face to face in a sort of horrific smooching session: red seeping wounds pressed to Nick's cheek. He shrieked and fell backwards. By the time he'd crawled back, Oz was lying on the floor again.

"Fuck my life," he panted, on the verge of tears. He took a moment to collect himself.

He explored the cupboard under the stairs to see if there was anything which might help him. He found a length of strong rope: a new washing line. Interesting. He backed out of the cupboard, looking up at the staircase spindles. He tied the rope around Oz's chest, armpit to armpit, and threaded it through the spindles, above the wheelie bin. He took a deep breath and hauled on the makeshift pulley. Woodwork creaked as the rope tensed. He hung on and glanced down. Oz's body had lifted, not as much as he'd hoped, but he was off the ground. He looked like a seriously creepy butterfly emerging from its rug chrysalis now. Nick had tugged the rug down to get at Oz's armpits, and it was slipping away.

Nick tied the rope around the broom cupboard's door handle so he could change his grip without losing the progress he'd made. He reached over his head and dragged the rope down. Oz was lifted to his knees. He lurched forward, closer to the wheelie bin. Nick had to swallow his fear, especially when one of Oz's arms came loose from the rug and swung about. Nick repeated the manoeuvre, hauling Oz to his feet. As soon as the body was off the floor, Nick knew his plan was going to work.

As Oz swung lazily, the haft of a knife still wedged in his chest nearly poked Nick in the eye. The dog reappeared and snatched at Oz's left slipper, dropping it and going for the right. A moment later the dog turned its attention to the rug flapping like a terrible superhero cape. It dragged the rug off and down the hall, worrying it back and forth. Nick shook his head. At least it was a little bit less weight on the end of the rope.

As Nick braced himself to haul a few more inches of rope, the dog leapt up to grab something else hanging from Oz's pulverised front.

"Ew! I thought we had a deal? You can't eat his – ah what *is* that?" Once again Nick reflected his father would know the name of whatever organ the dog had grabbed in its mouth. It certainly came with extra gore attached. The dog flung it from side to side, splashing blood up the walls before dropping it and adopting a fake good boy pose.

Nick sighed and pressed on. Six more hauls on the rope, the slack belayed around the spindle, and Oz was above the level of the wheelie bin. This was surely tougher than any gym workout. Nick carefully lined the bin up, directly under Oz's bare feet, and released the rope as slowly as he could manage. The body successfully lowered, he grinned with relief and let the rope slide from his hands. The lid wouldn't shut completely, but it wasn't obvious what was inside.

Nick wondered briefly about putting the bin out and hoping the bin men would just hook it onto the back of the dustcart. What were the odds of them not noticing the corpse dropping into the mashing thing? Fairly slim. No, he needed to get rid of the body himself. He'd completed step one and felt absurdly pleased with himself, given the circumstances. His foot squished on something: he'd trodden on the unidentified organ the dog had dragged out. It gave him the germ of an idea. One of the problems he faced was the wealth of evidence to indicate his presence at the scene. What if he obscured it with a whole load of *other* evidence? If he could create footprints and evidence trails leading away from here, it might buy him a bit more time.

Nick pictured himself creeping out of the front door: the oozing organ in his hand, visiting several neighbouring houses, running along their drive to the front door and back, leaving trails of gory footprints, replenished with blood from Oz's organ. Oh, how he'd fool the police! Oh, what a mystery he'd create! The street a confusing mess of footprints, evidence of a little army of killers...

"No." That was a bit too fanciful. He should be attempting to destroy the evidence, not just fling it about. Oz's house was detached from its neighbours. If, *say*, there was an enormous, evidence-destroying conflagration, it was unlikely to hurt anybody.

Burn the house down to destroy the DNA evidence.
Take the body away.
Dad, whisky, magical weekend, love and laughter.
Result.

Nick set about setting a fire.

He went into the front room and piled cushions onto the floor – they were sure to burn well. He found matches in the broom cupboard, good. How long would it take the fire to get hold? He positioned the wheelie bin by the kitchen door so he could make a rapid getaway. A thought struck him. The bin looked innocuous enough, and would raise no eyebrows on the way back to his house, but he was covered in so much blood he looked as if he'd been swimming in it. He rinsed his face at the kitchen sink and went in search of something to wear. He found Oz's big coat on a hook near the door and fastened it over his clothes. It was a giant sheepskin coat with enormous horn buttons. He'd melt if he had to keep it on for long, but hopefully he'd have time to change his clothes.

He ran back to the front room, struck a match and threw it onto the piled cushions. It went out as soon as it hit the first one. He lit another and crouched more carefully, putting the blazing match to a tasselled corner. The tassel smouldered briefly, and went out. Nick repeated the same thing several times with no success. He considered the match box. It was a large one, and nearly full. He built a small pile of matches nestled inside the cushion pile and lit the bottom one. For good measure, he dropped the box and remaining matches on top. He smiled as he saw flames licking up the side of the box.

He retreated into the kitchen. If he spread out paper or something, it would be sure to catch. He grabbed the kitchen roll, picking up the letter from the table at the same time. He stuffed the letter in his pocket and kitchen roll under an arm, and turned on the gas hob. Adding a bit of gas to the mix would help things along a bit. He only turned one ring on: he wanted a good old cleansing fire, not a sudden explosion.

He went back to check on his bonfire and was staggered to see it had gone out. All that remained was a blackened tower of burnt matches. No! He went back to the broom cupboard, but there were no more matches.

"Bugger!"

He would have to come back and light the fire after moving the body. Back in the kitchen the dog was sitting next to the wheelie bin, lead in its mouth.

"What? *Really*? Well I guess I can't leave you here." Nick clipped on the lead and grabbed hold of the wheelie bin. He was about to leave when he remembered the whisky. After all of this he did not want to leave without it. He fetched the box and wondered how he'd carry it. There was a small rucksack on the hook where he'd found the coat. He put the precious gift inside.

As he crossed the kitchen he realised there were two dog baskets under the island worktop. Two?

"There's not another dog here, is there?" he asked the dog.

Its only reply was to cock its head, one ear up, one ear down. There was definitely only one dog. Maybe the other one was in kennels or something. Maybe this mutt was a dog of means, the owner of two baskets. There was no time to dwell on it.

"Right, come on then," he said to the dog. He managed to get the wheelie bin down the step from the kitchen, which wasn't easy with a dog lead in one hand. Especially when the dog was desperate to go and sniff everything just out of his arm's range. They went up the side of the house.

11

"Left here," said Finn, reading from her phone. "Langollen Drive."

Adam yawned. "I sincerely hope it's this one."

"Langford Drive. Langley Close. We're running out of Langs," said Finn.

"I'm fairly confident it's this one," said a tired and terrified Audrey from the back seat.

"You said that about the last one," said Finn.

"I struggle without my glasses."

"You don't need your glasses to remember a street name." muttered Adam.

Finn took the printed photograph out of her lapel pocket. The photo of Oz Bingley provided little more than a profile shape and an indicator of Oz's taste in clothing.

"Number forty-two," she reminded him.

"I remember," said Adam. He sounded testy. "I remembered it the last fifteen roads we tried."

He pulled up on the opposite side of the road and several dozen yard further back. "There."

Their target appeared from around the side of the house. "Look, he's got to be our guy. He's wearing the same ridiculous coat he's got on in the photo."

Finn considered the man from where they were parked and scrutinised the photo. He looked younger in real life. Where was the grey? But his hair was slicked back, wet. Hair looked darker when wet.

Oz was struggling with a heavy wheelie bin, twisting, pulling, failing to steer it.

"Audrey, is that the man?"

Audrey leaned forward to look between the front seats. "I struggle without my glasses," she said eventually.

Adam picked up his notepad, and the remains of his ruined schedule. He looked at the many crossings out and notes in the margin. "You're not making things easy, Audrey," he muttered.

"What's so fun about easy?" said Finn. "If I only took easy jobs I'd get the hell out of here the second a police car turned up, wouldn't I?"

"What?" said Adam.

She smirked and hooked a thumb at the white van which had pulled up behind them. A woman in dark combats stepped out.

"Oh, shit," groaned Adam.

12

As he reached the front of the house, a woman in a dark uniform approached.

"Morning!" she said brightly.

And that's it, Nick thought. My life of crime over in less than an hour, door-stepped by a copper.

Except she wasn't a cop. The uniform, black combats, utility belt, hi-vis vest, looked very police-y but it wasn't.

"Council dog warden," she said.

"Oh, thank fuck!" he exclaimed and then coughed. "I mean, good morning."

"Indeed," she said. "We got a call about this house, so I need to check up on things."

Nick gave her a wide smile. Perhaps it was a little bit too wide, because she backed away slightly.

"I have a dog," said Nick, indicating. "He's perfectly fine and he's on a lead." He edged away from the wheelie bin as he spoke.

She crouched down to look at the dog. "He has a lot of blood around his muzzle," she observed. "Is he hurt?"

"No, definitely not," said Nick. "He's been chasing wotsits."

"Wotsits?"

"Badgers?"

"Badgers?" She looked horrified.

"I mean squirrels. Squirrels. In the garden."

She shook her head and turned the dog's head from side to side, checking for injuries.

"He's very fond of raw meat," said Nick. "He won't leave those squirrels alone."

"I'm just going to take some details," said the woman, rising to her feet and producing a book of forms.

Nick really wished she would go away. "I wonder if it's next door you're after?" he said. "I saw a dog running round there and making a mess." He pointed at AshleysNan's house.

"What sort of dog?" asked the woman.

"A big one. With a stomach complaint. Look!"

The woman's gaze followed Nick's finger. A trail of excrement was clearly visible going across the shared border between this house and next door. Happily, the underpants which had held the poo were hidden in the foliage.

"Oh dear," said the dog warden. "Although, it will be a civil matter, of course, given it's on private property. We're more pavements and footpaths."

"Well, maybe you could just go and tell her off a bit?"

"Tell her off?"

"Some people are just a bit thoughtless or, you know, ignorant. In need of educating."

The woman gave Nick a sideways glance before turning to look at next door. "I'll pop round, *but* I'll be popping back to see how you're all getting on." She scratched the dog behind the ears. "Can I suggest you get your dog a nice bone from the butchers in future?"

Nick nodded and smiled before wheeling the bin, dog in tow, over to his own house. He unlocked his car and put the dog on the backseat with the rucksack as he worked out a way to transfer Oz's body to the boot. He was dimly aware of raised voices drifting across from AshleysNan and the dog warden. Good. If they were arguing with each other they were leaving him alone.

His car was parked facing the street, so getting the body into the boot could be done discreetly, although Nick berated himself for his slovenly habits. If his garage wasn't so full of useless clutter he could have reversed his car inside and been completely unseen. He popped the boot and wheeled the bin round. He experimented with the idea of tipping it over the sill and just dropping Oz into the boot. He didn't think he had the strength. He had an idea if he did a fireman's lift, he could get Oz out. If only he knew how to do a fireman's lift.

He heard the sound of a car slowing down just beyond the driveway. He looked fearfully at his phone. Eight o'clock, on the dot.

With speed and strength fuelled by outright fear of his dad catching him in a compromising position with a corpse, he grabbed Oz by the armpits, yanked upright and hit his head on the open boot lid. With a cry of pain he stumbled forward, somehow taking Oz with him. Behind him the bin tipped over. He kicked it away.

Blood trickled into the garden borders. There were splashes of it on the Cadillac, but the hot rod red paintjob hid them well.

"Is that you, Nick?" called his dad from the road.

Oz now leaned halfway into the boot, legs trailing over the sill. Nick poked his head round the car. Tony Carver, in sensible cords, a no nonsense shirt and a wouldn't-suffer-fools-gladly raincoat stood on the pavement. Tony Carver, the unstoppable dad machine.

Throughout Nick's life there had been a number of things he could count on. He knew, for example, his enthusiasm for a project was not always matched by his technical ability or his patience. One reason the garage was filled with half-painted junk shop finds and planters with mysterious twiggy dead things in them. He also knew this would never stop him from launching, half-baked, into the next new and exciting thing. When he'd caused *actual* damage to the house, like the time he'd put a house brick into the cistern (a simple, water-saving measure), and dropped it so hard it cracked the thing and created a flood, he'd always relied on his dad being there to help. His dad: always knowing how to do things and knowing how things worked.

But disposing of corpses was well beyond Tony Carver's remit. He couldn't be allowed to see the body. He just couldn't.

"Dad," said Nick, needlessly.

Tony jerked his thumb over his shoulder at the kerfuffle going on across the road. "What's that nonsense about?"

"I think that woman's been letting her dog do its business all over people's gardens."

Tony tutted. "Should be a criminal offence."

"I think it is," said Nick.

"Ah." Tony gave a sharp upward nod of his head as though his own views were being confirmed. "Here come the boys in blue now."

"What?"

Tony pointed, beyond the front hedge, where Nick couldn't see.

"Maybe you should see what they're up to," suggested Nick.

Tony pulled an interested face, nodded and wandered off. Nick hurriedly began tucking splayed limbs into the boot.

53

13

"Now, that's a police car," said Adam.

"I can see that," said Finn.

The police officer ambled towards a woman resident and the council dog warden. It was unclear from this distance what they were arguing about, although the resident appeared to waving around what Finn could only think of as a shitty pair of pants.

Finn leaned back in her chair. "Audrey..."

"Yes?"

"You're thinking you could jump out of the car and run over to that copper, screaming for help, and he could keep you safe."

"I wasn't," she said. "I'm just going to sit here and—"

"It wasn't a question," said Finn. "I just want you to be aware if you so much as touch that door, I will kill you, the cop, the dog warden and that woman waving— That *is* a pair of pants, isn't it?"

"Would appear so," said Adam. "Here comes another man. Is he one of Oz's known associates?"

Finn watched the older man approach the policemen with a well-practised amble of his own. His contributions to the pavement conversation were unclear but they didn't seem to be helping.

"Don't know," said Finn. "It's unimportant. Oz is still on the driveway. I can see movement. We just observe for now."

14

"That's a rum to-do and no mistake," said Tony, sauntering down Nick's driveway.

Oz's dangling body bits had been pushed into the boot. Nick was in the process of turning the sheepskin coat inside out so the fresh splashes of gore he'd suffered in packing Oz were on the inside and he could present an almost passable exterior to the world. Things rattled and crinkled in the coat pockets.

"Rum to-do?" Nick slammed down the lid.

"Even a fracas, one might say," added Tony. He held out his holdall and approached the boot.

Nick slammed his hands on the lid. "Ah, no. You can't go in there. The catch has gone."

"What? You were just in there as I walked up the drive."

"Yes. Yes I was," agreed Nick. "I was fixing it. With glue. We can't open it again now, the glue's setting."

"You can't fix a thing like that with glue," said Tony with an impatient shake of his head. "Let me have a look, you don't want to gum up the mechanism, or you'll never get it working again."

"It's fine, dad. I booked it in first thing next week. The garage gave me special temporary glue. Just put your bag on the back seat and we'll get going."

"Temporary glue?"

"Yes. Or wax, maybe it was wax. They said to keep it shut anyway. We don't need the boot when there's only two of us."

Tony gave him a sceptical look but stepped up to the rear door. "And why's there a dog in your car?"

Nick cursed his own stupidity. How could he have forgotten about the dog? "Yeah. Funny that. I've, um, got a dog. It was a fairly recent thing. Just fell in love with him."

"Great stuff!" said Tony, reaching in to fuss the dog. "Joining us for the ride, huh? What's your name then, pooch?"

"Pickles," said Nick instantly. "He's called Pickles."

"Really? Well unless I'm very much mistaken, this is a bitch."

"Yes," said Nick. "And *her* name is Pickles. It can be a girl's name."

"But you called her *he*. Is this one of those gender things I hear them going on about."

"Probably that. Exactly that," said Nick. "I don't want to put labels on things. He. She. Pickles can be what she wants to be."

"Trannie dog," said Tony.

"I think the preferred term is trans or transgender," Nick corrected gently.

Tony gave Nick a weary dad look.

Pickles' contribution to the discussion was to spit something out of her mouth onto the back seat.

"What's this?" said Tony, leaning across. "Good Lord above, it looks like a wedding ring." He held up a gold band for Nick to see. "Where do you suppose she got that from?"

"She's a bit of a devil for picking things up," said Nick. "Um, I'll hang onto it and see if I can find the owner. Let's set off, eh?"

They got in. Father and son in the front. Dog, luggage and a whisky presentation gift on the back seat. A dead guy – most of him – in the boot.

Nick glanced across the road at Oz's house. The policeman was talking to AshleysNan, who still seemed to be embroiled with the dog warden. He had no idea who had called the police. Perhaps the dog warden; or more likely AshleysNan had phoned about the screaming and smashing noises. He hoped nobody decided to go and have a look next door. If only his fire lighting skills had worked out better. He'd feel so much better if he didn't have to leave the exuberant display of bodily fluids he'd created. It occurred to him his dad would have known how to light a better fire, or why his own efforts had proven so ineffectual.

Nick drove the car off the drive and turned right. He accelerated towards the junction at the end of the road, not turning his head to look at AshleysNan and the rum to-do (or possibly fracas) centring on his discarded underwear as they passed.

"So, here's a question for you, dad," he said. "Er, a friend of mine let their cigarette burn against one my cushions at home."

"What friend? You let people smoke in your house? That kind of thing affects property re-sale value."

"Point is," said Nick. "Point is, it didn't burn the cushion, and I was just wondering what the stuff in them was that ... didn't burn."

"I had no idea any of your friends smoked."

"It was Abigail, all right."

Tony made a very dubious noise, although Nick wasn't sure what about. "Most likely polyester stuffing," he said eventually. "Maybe wool or feathers if it's an old-school cushion. Of course, interesting thing about natural fibres—" Tony settled into his favourite role of dad-style lecturing "—they are naturally safer. It's quite hard to set fire to wool, did you know that? Often it will just smoulder. Of course all upholstery has to be fire resistant anyway."

"What? Like it's the law?"

"Fire regulations." Tony gave him a stern look. "Don't they teach you anything in school?"

And like that, their old roles were established for the journey; the father and the child. The fire regulation thing did explain why his bonfire had been unsuccessful though. If only there had been some minor smouldering...

There was a loud boom from behind them. In the rear-view mirror Nick watched glass, upholstery and splintered woodwork billow out into the street on a ball of flame, peppering a BMW which was doing a three-point turn.

"What the hell was that?" declared Tony, trying to turn in his seat.

"Nothing, nothing," said Nick, pulling onto the main road. "Car backfiring. Or something. Probably something."

15

The blast rattled the windows of the hire car. Audrey gasped. Adam slammed on the brakes, mid turn. Flames were visible in the downstairs windows of Oz's house, thick black smoke billowed out of the shattered glass.

"You stopped," said Finn.

Adam looked at her and did a double take. "The house...! The house just exploded!"

Finn pointed down the road. "Oz is leaving."

Adam did his own pointing: at the windscreen. Scraps of net curtain and charred window frame littered the glass. "The house...!"

Finn reached over and flicked on the wipers. "There."

The copper ran to his car, presumably to radio for help. The dog warden stared, dumbfounded, at ruined iron bars bent outward from the windows, like crooked teeth.

"Time to go," said Adam.

The rear door slammed. Finn turned. Audrey was gone: gone and hurrying towards the copper. Finn put a hand on the door handle, but Adam was already accelerating. She touched the lapel pocket of her Muubaa. She had the woman's name and face; she'd be able to find her again. The cop and the dog warden ... they'd be a little trickier to track down, but life was all about challenges. Finn was always adaptable.

Adam turned onto the main road, cutting up a transit van in the process.

"You know," he said, "this looks a lot like he's on the run and covering his tracks."

Finn nodded. The assignment just got a whole lot more interesting.

16

The chafing of Nick's trousers was beginning to get annoying. As a younger man he'd questioned the point of underwear. Why wear an extra layer? Surely it just meant more laundry? He laughed at his naivety. Underwear was surely the basis for civilisation. Without it, there could be no way to avoid grinding his unfortunate genitals into the clinging remnants of poo he could both feel and smell. He hoped his father couldn't smell it too. There was a good chance the heavy sheepskin coat was shielding Tony from Nick's private, stinking ecosystem. The coat was extremely hot, but Nick couldn't possibly take it off, given the blood-soaked state of his clothes. He turned the car's heating down a little. He would have to put up with it for a while, until he could find an opportunity to change into clean clothes.

"There's some sucky sweets in the glove box," said Nick as they turned onto the motorway slip road.

Tony pulled open the glove box. "You want me to pass you one?"

"No, I'm fine," said Nick.

"Oh, right."

"They're barley sugars."

Tony took out the tin and looked, holding it at a slight distance to focus. "Yes, they are."

"Your favourites," Nick prompted.

"Maybe later." Tony closed the glove box.

They drove onto the motorway, and immediately hit queuing traffic. Nick jiggled his mobile out of his pocket, wiping it on the coat in case it had somehow been splattered with blood or, God forbid, crap. He cradled it in the Satnav holder on the wide American dashboard.

"Ok, Google. Directions for Rosemarkie, near Inverness."

The Satnav app whirled and thought.

"I think we can get to Inverness without the need for that," said Tony sourly. "It's M6 for the first two hours at least."

"I know, dad, but it's nice to see how far we've got to go. And maybe if there's traffic..."

"M6, M73, M80, M9, then the A9 for over a hundred miles. Just point the car north."

"Ah, but where's north, eh, if you don't have a compass?"

Tony stuck out his left hand decisively. "North."

The Satnav app concluded much the same. Four hundred and fifty miles to go. Eight hours travelling time. And north was indeed that way.

"Shall I tell you some of the things we've got in store for us this weekend?" asked Nick, shuffling in his seat, eager to share the excitement.

"Yes?" said Tony.

"So, the cabin's got gorgeous views over the Moray Firth. And I've even ordered us a hamper of goodies for when we get there."

"Nice," said Tony. "Saves us having to go to the shops, I guess. If it's self-catering I did think we'd need to pop to a Londis, or something. Pick up a loaf of bread and maybe a couple of Fray Bentos pies, or something."

"No, these are proper goodies. Not quite a Fortnum and Mason hamper, but fine cheeses, patés and I think there's some of those cracker bread with the—"

"Can you still get Fray Bentos pies?" said Tony. "Haven't seen them in the shops for edges."

Nick glanced sideways. His dad wasn't sharing his enthusiasm for fine food treats. "You like cheese and paté and that, don't you, dad?"

"Spam," said Tony.

"Sorry?"

"Not seen that in the shops for ages either."

"I couldn't say," said Nick. "But we won't waste time going to the shops because we have some serious fun to pack in this weekend. We're going to be doing some clay pigeon shooting, did I tell you that?"

Tony frowned. "No, I don't think you mentioned it. Do you like shooting?"

Nick had never fired a gun in his life.

"I just never realised you were a fan of shooting," said Tony.

Nick tightened his grip on the steering wheel. This wasn't about what *he* was a fan of. This weekend was all about his dad,

60

surely that was obvious? "I haven't got to the best part yet," said Nick, unable to contain his glee any longer. "You'll never guess what I've got a bottle of? Something special to sip as we watch the sun go down."

Tony looked up at the sky and down at the slow moving traffic. "The sun will have gone down by the time we get there."

"Or while the Moon rises," said Nick peevishly. "There's a full Moon this weekend. Guess."

"Guess what?"

"The drink? Go on. Guess!"

Tony puffed out his cheeks in thought. "Don't know. Horlicks?"

"I said something special. Guess. We're going to Scotland," he added helpfully.

"Some sort of whisky?"

"Talisker! Dad, I've only got us a bottle of Talisker!" Nick slapped the steering wheel for emphasis.

He looked away from the road, wanting to see the expression on his dad's face. Tony gave a gentle nod of his head and murmured something sounding like "That's nice. Mind if we turn the heating up a notch?"

Nick adjusted the heating, feeling a droplet of sweat run down his back and into his trousers as he moved.

17

Finn rode in the passenger seat while Adam drove. "I think we can assume they're not just going to the shops," she said. They'd been on the road for forty five minutes.

Adam scowled. Before he could reply there was the warbling of an incoming call through the car's sound system.

"It's our handler," said Adam.

"We have a handler?" asked Finn.

"Let me do the talking, right?"

Finn wasn't sure what a handler did, but it sounded way too personal for her liking. This was becoming far more involved than her usual jobs. They amounted to Instructions, Execution and Payment, and certainly didn't require any *handling*.

Adam answered the call. "Hi Col. I'm on loudspeaker in the car. Finella's with me."

"What the hell's going on, Adam?" came an amiable and lilting Irish tone. *"You weren't on the feckin six o'clock flight."*

"No. We tracked the target to Birmingham, but he's currently in a vehicle, heading north on the M6. He might be heading back to Liverpool."

"We're not interested in all that shite. When you going to get the fecker?"

"We are in pursuit and will intercept when possible."

"Which means feck all. I don't need to remind you about the schedule. You don't have much leeway here, you see. Be sure you don't lose him."

"No danger of that," said Adam. "He's driving a bright red Cadillac with a flag on the bonnet. It's probably the only one in England."

"Good God, I don't want to picture it!"

"I'm staring at it."

"Get the job done, Adam! ASA-feckin-P. Call if you need further support."

"Won't be needed."

"Just feckin get on with it, yeah?"

"Sure Col, speak later." Adam killed the call. He glanced at Finn. "Don't you just love the way the Irish make swearing sound so musical?"

Finn had no idea what he was talking about. "Who was that?"

"Col."

"So he's guy's in charge, yeah?"

"He's our handler," said Adam.

"You said that. Is he the boss of you?"

"What? Why does it even matter?"

"I'm being paid. I have a job to do. I need to know who to listen to. Especially if the two of you say something different."

"We're not going to say something different," protested Adam.

"You already did. Col said we're to fucking get on with it and yet you're waiting around until it's possible to intercept them."

"How is that different?" said Adam.

"Well, we could do it now if we were fucking getting on with things."

Adam closed his eyes a moment, which Finn thought was a strange move for someone doing eighty miles an hour in the fast lane. "We're on the M6. Three full lanes of traffic. We could force them off the road so you can get busy with your knife, true; but the chances of not being observed are slim, wouldn't you say?"

"Depends if we care."

"Adam sighed. "Sooner or later they are going to have to stop and we will take advantage of it. I'm keeping a careful eye on the time, you can be assured of that. You take your orders from me, yes? Col and I are very much aligned, so there will be no problem with you getting paid if you listen to me. Are we clear?"

"Yes," said Finn.

18

"Have you noticed the number of Dacias on the road?" said Tony, pointing at one as they overtook it. "Sign we're living in leaner times. A more affordable car, stripped of luxury."

Nick nodded. "A soulless choice."

"Soulless? It's noisy, rolls on corners and looks like it's made from recycled Renault parts but ... what does *soulless* mean?"

"You know, there's no love there," said Nick. "You've got to feel something for your car. I mean: who buys a car based on purely utilitarian reasons?"

Tony laughed.

"What?" said Nick.

Tony stared at Nick. "What? I thought that was a joke."

"What was?"

"Surely it's a joke? Everyone buys a car for utilitarian reasons. It's a car. Why would you do anything different?"

Nick smiled affectionately at his father. "Emotion is at the core of most of our choices, dad. People surround themselves with things which reflect the image they want to present to the world. Car-buying's often an aspirational choice."

"Jesus, Nick. Really?"

"Yeah. If I want to tell the world I'm important, I buy myself an important-looking car."

Tony shook his head. "The thing you're overlooking here is a good many people don't have the money to go around buying aspirational choices. You don't know how lucky you are you've never had to buy a car based purely on whether it will pass its next MOT ."

Nick thought back to childhood journeys in rusty saloons with window winders which no longer worked. "Yes, that's true. I accept certain demographics work with severe constraints."

"You mean some people are poor."

"Yes. Let's just pretend the people on this motorway don't have severe financial difficulties and bought their cars because they liked them. You can tell a lot about a person based on their choice. Like the Audi over there. Who do we think it belongs to?"

"You could just overtake so we can see," suggested Tony.

"We could..."

"Go on, tell me what you think."

"Well," said Nick, warming to the game, "it's a cabriolet. So it's most likely a woman. She's asserting her independence by choosing something with a high social status, so perhaps recently divorced. It's not a cheap car, so she's more likely to be forty plus."

Tony shook his head, smiling. "Is this what they teach you in marketing school?"

"Pretty much, yeah," said Nick.

Tony scoffed, not unkindly. If anything he sounded uncharacteristically tolerant. "Maybe it works sometimes," he said. "But I think a lot of people buy cars for their features. Practical things. Like modern heating. You and I could have different heating settings in a lot of newer cars, did you know that? Save you wearing a thick coat while you're driving."

"I like to wear it."

"Really?"

"It's a fashion thing," lied Nick. "But that's sort of the point, don't you think? Most modern cars all have the features you want. Very little to choose between them in terms of features."

"I'm not so sure about that. If a car manufacturer came and asked me what I wanted, I would have a few things to say to them. If I'm honest, I think sometimes they get a bit carried away with their own cleverness; they go backwards in terms of features I *actually* want."

"Like what?" asked Nick.

Tony counted off on his fingers. "Let's start with cup holders. I used to be able to put my cup up there, on the dashboard, where I can reach it while I'm driving. Now I have to scramble around down by the gearstick. Who decided to put a cup holder there, where I can't even reach it if I'm looking where I'm going? Worse is all the nonsense they put in modern cars like refusing to start the engine until I've got my seatbelt on, or I'm pressing on some pedal or other. I liked it much better when *I* was in charge of how I drove, and not the car."

"Ah, that would be safety by design," said Nick. "There's a Japanese word for it, *poka-yoke*."

"That's those little cartoon things people chase around on their phones."

"Not *Pokemon*. *Poka-yoke*. The idea is to prevent behaviour which could cause an accident."

Tony rolled his eyes. "See, the idea of someone wanting to *prevent* me behaving how I want to behave makes my blood boil. If I start my car and I need to reverse out of a space, I want to do it with my seatbelt off. Perfectly legal, and the safest way to do it in my opinion."

Nick nodded, acknowledging his father's words, but wondering if there was a generational problem. Research had proven older people were more resistant to change. "Eyes sharp. Audi."

They pulled past the car and turned their heads to look at the driver. A bearded man glanced across with a scowl. Tony and Nick both looked quickly away.

"Have you ever killed someone?" asked Finn.

"No," said Adam.

"Have you ever hit someone with the intention of killing them?"

"Not a realistic intention, no."

"Stabbed anyone?"

"No."

"Smashed someone's head in with a bottle or similar."

"What? Like you did to that guy in Liverpool? No."

They had been driving north for nearly two hours and were almost back in Liverpool. If Oz was heading back to his grimy flat, he'd find an unpleasant surprise inside, and get another when Finn got hold of him.

"Kicked someone in the balls?"

"No."

"Have you ever had fight with anyone?"

"Yes."

"Really?"

"When I was eight. My friend Karim broke my Lego car and—"

"Shit. Are you gay?"

He cast a sharp glance at her. "What?"

"I asked, are you gay? This is the yes/no game. You said it would be a way of getting to know each other a bit better."

"I'm more concerned you asked me if I'm gay because... Is it because I owned Lego or because I've not had a fight since I was eight?"

"It's just a question."

Adam cleared his throat irritably. "Listen. Can we change the rules of this game? The answers can be *yes, no* or *stop asking offensive personal questions.*"

"Fine," said Finn. "Are you gay?"

"That was one of the offensive personal questions I meant. What's wrong with you?"

"And that's not a yes/no question. So, you never killed anyone?"

"No."

"But you work with people who deal in death?"

He stared at the road. "I guess."

"Doesn't that make you a bad Muslim?"

"For fuck's sake. Right. Stop it, seriously. My turn to ask you some questions."

Finn shrugged. "Fine."

"Are you gay?"

"No," she said after a pause.

"You hesitated."

"I was thinking."

"If you were gay or not?"

"Yes."

Adam looked the ceiling of the car in exasperation. "Have you killed people before?"

"Yes. You know that."

"How many?"

"Directly or indirectly?"

"Does it make a difference?"

"Of course it does. Just by living in a Western country, we're part of the system which causes all those Africans to starve, and those people in the Middle East to get blown up in wars. Indirectly, I've probably killed fewer people than the average person."

"How so?"

"Never had kids," said Finn. "Do you have any idea the kind of environmental damage just having kids does?"

Adam chuckled. "I never had you down as an environmentalist."

"I'm not. You just asked me how many people I've killed. In my entire career, as a killer I'm saying, I'm probably going to cause less pain and suffering than a woman who selfishly pops out three sprogs the world doesn't need. I'm actually behind everyone else on the kill-count."

"Really?"

"Really."

"Does this mean you don't see anything wrong in the things you do?"

She grunted. "No one cares about right and wrong these days. People whinge about their rights and they get a right bee in their bonnets if you do something illegal. But when was the last time someone said you were doing something wrong. Not *illegal,* or *inappropriate,* or *unfair,* but actually wrong? No one cares about that kind of crap anymore."

Adam seemed to take a time to digest this. "Weren't you brought up in a faith?"

"A faith?"

"A religion."

"We had to go to church on Sunday at the school I was in as a kid."

"You were in school on Sundays?"

"Boarding school. I was privately educated. Why are you laughing?"

"I was smiling," said Adam. "Just trying to picture it."

"We had church on Sunday. Well, chapel is what they called it. It was a cold place. Hard wooden seats and people trying to stop you having a proper look around. Sit up straight, face the front. Why would you trust a deity when you're not even allowed to look underneath his altar cloth?"

Adam's brow knitted.

"The first person I killed was a vicar," said Finn, thinking back. "Indirectly."

"How do you indirectly kill a vicar?"

"He had a heart attack in his... What do you call the little room in the back of the church where the vicar puts his robes on and stuff?"

"You're asking the wrong guy."

"He was having a heart attack. I was the only one there. I could have gone to get help. I could have run and told a teacher." She unzipped the lapel pocket of her Muubaa and pulled out a thick pile of Polaroids. She always kept that particular photo with her. She sorted through and pulled one out. It was old now: the colours drifting towards yellow and brown. She held it up to show Adam.

"Don't show me a picture of a dead priest while I'm driving! Jeez," he muttered. "What is it with you and that camera? And why did you have one on you when the priest – vicar, whatever – had his heart attack?"

"I didn't," she said. "It was his."

"It was..." Adam fell silent. His lips worked silently and his face twitched. For some reason Finn couldn't understand, a grim expression came over him. "How old were you?" he said, quietly.

"Hey," she said. "These are meant to be yes/no questions. You're cheating."

Adam swallowed, nodded, and returned his full attention to the road.

"I've a yes/no question for you," said Finn.

"Yes?"

"Do you realise we've gone past the turning for Liverpool?"

"Yes."

"Where's Oz going?"

"I wish I knew," said Adam.

20

"So tell me," said Tony, "if a car says so much about the person who chose it, what on earth does this weird car of yours say about you?"

"Weird? Why would you say that?" asked Nick, caressing the Cadillac's steering wheel: green to match the rest of the interior. "It's a design classic, and yet relatively unusual here in the UK. A win-win."

"So, parts are easy to come by, are they?"

"No," said Nick, remembering some of the car's lengthy and difficult repairs. "No, parts can be a bit of an issue, but this car gets admiring glances wherever I take it. I like to think it speaks of someone who does things a little bit differently."

"Oh, it definitely does that," said Tony. "It speaks of someone who likes to take public transport instead of driving while his car's off the road. It speaks of someone who stumps up more money for fuel in a week than most people would pay in a month. If you ask me, I want a car which does great mileage, one I can fix without the aid of one of those computers they have at the dealership, and for which parts are readily available."

"Why would you ever need to fix your car yourself, dad? There are people for that."

"When all else goes to pot, you've got to be self-reliant. You can keep your *pokey-dokey* designs and your emotional purchases. I want a car which will last for years and which, push comes to shove, I can maintain myself."

"I had no idea," said Nick.

"No idea?"

"That my dad was Mad Max."

Tony laughed.

"It's a great ride though, isn't it?" said Nick. "Amazing interior." He ran his hand over the quilted velour upholstery.

Tony gave a begrudging nod. "Yes, your mother and I had a sofa like this years ago. The green colour was all the rage for a while."

"Maybe that's why I like it so much," said Nick. "I have fond memories of that sofa."

"You really remember it?" said Tony, surprised.

"Saturday mornings, Simon and I would flip up the cushions and wedge them along the front, to make a wall between the two arm rests and we could be inside. Like it was a castle or a boat."

"I don't remember that," said Tony.

"You were always at work on Saturday mornings."

Tony grunted and tilted his head, side to side. "Okay. This car's got some charms. Nice solid chassis. Won't crumple like tinfoil in a crash like modern cars." He looked round at the dog on the back seat. "Nice legroom. Big boot too, I guess?"

"Massive boot space. Or trunk space as our American friends would say." Nick glanced at his dad. "You'd have no problem transporting a body with a car like this." Nick wondered if he could possibly have an entirely hypothetical conversation about the disposal of a body. Hypothetical. Betraying none of the horrible truth. Oh, his dad would have lots of good, practical ideas about body disposal.

"Well it's big enough for a body," Tony conceded, "but the catch has gone, remember? You'll be in trouble if you find yourself suddenly in possession of a body to transport."

"I'm sure that won't happen," said Nick with a nervous laugh.

Tony turned to stare at Nick. "Wait a second. Is this...?"

"What?"

"Is this about the cancer? Are you planning what to do if I pop my clogs while we're away?"

"No!" said Nick, unable to stop his voice sounding high and squeaky. "I was – no! I mean it was just a joke, you know?"

"Joke?"

"You've got plenty of time left. Well, some time, I guess. Oh, God."

21

"I'm just saying," said Finn.

"You've been *just saying* for the last twenty miles," said Adam irritably.

"You are a Muslim and work for criminals."

"You are Christian and work for criminals," he retorted.

"I'm not a Christian," she said.

"Were you christened?"

"Yes."

"Did you go to church?"

"Chapel. Yes."

"Sounds pretty damned Christian to me, Finn."

"But you're a Muslim."

"That's as much a cultural thing as it is religious. Have you seen me getting out my prayer mat today? No."

"So, you're not really a Muslim?"

Adam made a weird growling noise like he was trying to show how angry he was. "Right. I am a Muslim. I believe in God and the Prophet. I believe we are judged for what we do in this life. But I'm not compromised by the work I do. The job I'm doing here is one I'm happy with."

"The job you're doing here is cutting someone's heart out. Your religion's fine with that?"

"Islam is fine with organ transplants."

"Against the person's will."

"Not exactly; but my own personal principles are fine. It's a deal all parties entered into willingly."

"The guy in the car has *agreed* to have his heart cut out?"

"That's exactly what I'm saying. He might be regretting it now, but he signed a contract with Mr Argyll." He chuckled. "You know who that guy is?"

Finn nodded ahead. "Oz Bingley."

"But *who* he is? See, Oz was Mr Argyll's top killer, back in the day."

Finn shook her head.

"Code name was Lupo," said Adam.

"Lupo. I've heard of him." Finn tried to recall. "He was an animal. That explains the job he did on the house. Have *I* got a code name?"

"No," said Adam, too quickly. Finn figured he was lying. "Anyway, Oz retired, and Mr Argyll pays him an extremely generous monthly retainer on the condition that, when requested, he will donate his heart for Mr Argyll's research. He even paid for the care home for Doreen as well."

"Research. Cool," said Finn. Mr Argyll sounded like someone with interests very similar to her own. "So he didn't want to wait until Oz just died? I get that. What's the research?"

Adam shrugged. "I'm not sure. But we have instructions on what to do with the heart, once it's extracted."

"So, how much longer do we wait to extract it?" asked Finn. We're what – somewhere in the Lake District now? We could—"

"We wait," said Adam firmly.

22

Nick had been trying to find a way to unravel the uncomfortable atmosphere in the car. It wasn't all in his trousers, although that was becoming almost intolerable. Theirs was not a family which indulged in emotional exchanges, but he wanted to show his dad he cared about his illness, and wasn't just freaked out by the ghoulish possibility he might drop dead while in Nick's care. Actually, he realised, he was *extremely* freaked out by the ghoulish possibility his father might drop dead while in Nick's care. How likely was that, exactly?

"Dad?"

"You want one of your sucky sweets now?" said Tony.

"No, dad. Can I ask you about your, um, condition?"

"What about it?"

"What have the doctors said? How much do they know?"

Tony looked at him. "Son, they're doctors. They know as much as anybody because they're the experts on this stuff. They don't have a crystal ball, though. Nobody really knows how things are going to play out. No point in dwelling on it either. I'm a firm believer in not giving something headroom if you don't want it taking over your life."

"Yes," said Nick, who recognised the signs of his father terminating the conversation, "but I wasn't sure if there's anything I should look out for. Like if you might get symptoms I should tell you about, or something. You know?"

"Symptoms?"

"There have been studies which say people on their own are more likely to die because they don't notice things, or act on them. It's particularly bad for men, because we just don't tell people when something's up. Suffer in silence and all that."

"Nothing wrong with suffering in silence," said Tony.

"I just want to know what to look out for."

Tony growled. "Heaven help me. Right, listen up and don't bug me anymore about the cancer after this. Apparently, I might meet my end in any of the following ways. You ready?"

Nick gripped the steering wheel tightly and braced himself for the details. "Ready."

"I have throat cancer." Tony pointed helpfully at his throat. "Where the tumour is located means it's possible my lungs might be affected and cause me respiratory problems; although I expect I'll notice I can't breathe *way* before you do."

"Right."

"If it decides to infiltrate one of my major blood vessels then I expect I'll just drop to the floor and bleed out, dying almost instantly. A much more likely scenario is I will simply lose the ability to swallow as my oesophagus closes up."

"Shit."

"Again, I think I'll notice before you."

"That's ... that's..."

"Bloody awful, yes," said Tony with fierce simplicity. "Whatever happens, I don't need you mothering me. Understood?"

"Yes," said Nick in a small voice.

"Mind you," said Tony, "nobody ever mentioned olfactory hallucinations."

"What, smelling things that aren't really there?" asked Nick, afraid he knew where this was going.

"Yes. Smells like something crapped in your car. Tell me you can smell it too?"

Nick was trapped. Under any other circumstances he would have denied he could smell anything. Having it presented as a possibly worrying symptom, he didn't have that option. He did the only reasonable thing.

"I smell it too. I think Pickles has farted."

His dad glanced sceptically back at the dog, snoozing on the back seat. "Get that dog to the vets when you can. I'd be worried if that was my guts. Seriously. And I'm dying."

Nick glanced at his father. Tony was grinning to himself. Nick was torn between smiling and crying. He tried smiling.

"We're on the news," said Finn as she checked her phone.

"What?" Adam said, his eyes wide.

"An unexplained explosion destroyed a house in Brandwood End, Birmingham today. There are no reported fatalities, but a neighbour is being treated for shock. Police are keen to track down the drivers of two vehicles which left the scene, in particular a blue BMW, thought to have been hired in Liverpool. The police are not saying if this incident is terrorism related."

"Shit, that means they've got our registration," said Adam, thumping the steering wheel.

"I expect Audrey's told them all about me," said Finn, pulling her Polaroids out of a pocket and flicking through until she found Audrey's picture. "She might come to regret it."

Adam looked across at her. "Would you seriously go back and mess her up?"

"Of course," said Finn, surprised by the question. "I intend to."

"It could put you at risk. It could put Mr Argyll's entire operation at risk."

"I'm not sure you understand how I work. There's only risk when I don't have control of a situation. I always have control of a situation."

Adam smiled. "You can't control every situation. Something will always happen which you can't anticipate."

"Oh, I'm very adaptable," said Finn. "It's when I do my best work."

"Welcome to Scotland," said Tony, pointing at the giant blue and white saltire on the road sign.

"*Fàilte gu Alba*," read Nick, not knowing or caring how badly he was mispronouncing the Gaelic. "Nearly there."

"We're in Scotland," agreed Tony. "Still bloody miles to Inverness."

Nick looked at the landscape to the sides of the motorway. It didn't look particularly Scottish. It just looked English: grassy, green and dull. No mountains, no heather-strewn valleys, no bonnie lassies skipping through the glen in tartan kilts. Maybe it would get a bit more Scottish further up.

"Gretna Green," said Tony. He pointed at the sign for the border town. "I guess it doesn't carry all that much significance for your generation. I don't hear about anyone eloping anymore."

"Can't imagine many sixteen year olds nipping over the border to get married," agreed Nick. "But I think people still like to elope; just for different reasons. They sneak off to Vegas to get married because it's cheaper, or they can't bear the family bickering."

"I wonder what your mother would make of it if you and Abigail decided to do that?" Tony chuckled. "If you haven't already, of course!"

"No, we haven't," said Nick. He immediately felt like a complete lowlife. Every single sentence about Abigail coming out of his mouth which did not include the fact they were no longer together was a hideous lie by omission. One he knew would only get worse as time went by. He needed to man up and put his father in the picture. If he could spend the morning rolling in the blood of a dead man then he could tell his father the truth about his relationship status. "The thing is, we decided to take a bit of a break from each other."

"For the weekend, you mean?"

Nick realised the term was not in his father's vocabulary. "No, dad, I mean we've split up."

"She dumped you? Oh, what a shame. Nice girl Abigail. Really nice. Should have kept hold of that one."

Nick bit down on the urge to protest it was a mutual split. In truth she *had* dumped him. He was annoyed at the unspoken implication Abigail was too good for him and he'd simply failed to do what was needed to keep her. He cast around for a scathing retort, but he had nothing. The truth of the matter was he had failed to do what was needed to keep Abigail.

"Well the journey wasn't going the way I thought it was. I did a fair amount of research on it too, but I guess I had it wrong."

Tony turned in his seat and fixed Nick with a stare. "What journey? Your mother and I had some of our most blazing rows when driving."

"Not that kind of journey."

"Then what on earth are you on about?"

"I'm talking about the emotional journey; the narrative stages."

"Is this that marketing thing again? There's a difference between selling ... whatever it is you sell, and a relationship."

"That's what she said," muttered Nick. He was silent for a long time, thinking about the awful scene in John Lewis. It had started as a simple enough task: buying a dining table so they could have friends round for dinner parties. Abigail had been saying something about not wanting to cook, or not liking to cook and he'd shushed her. A few Jamie Oliver videos and they'd be fine, surely. Having dinner parties was what people did when they got to a certain stage, wasn't it? The style magazines featured endless photos of cool urban interiors, geared up for entertaining friends. He'd been pondering what sort of a centrepiece would work most effectively when he'd turned to see Abigail sprawled across a table, stark naked, yelling "*I am not a customer journey, I am a human being! If I stick a candle in my arse and call myself a centrepiece will you listen to me then?*" He'd wrapped her in a table runner and hustled her out as quickly as he could, although he had to go via the tills to pay for the runner once he realised he'd forgotten to pick up her clothes.

Nick wondered why he still had the table runner when he didn't have anything to put it on (neither a dining table nor an Abigail). He sighed. "I didn't pay her enough attention. I thought I was doing the right things, the things we should be doing; but I didn't spend enough time listening to what she wanted to do."

Tony looked disappointed. "Well it explains why you're in such a state, I suppose."

"I think I'm holding it together quite well."

"Not emotional state, Nick. It's not the dog's farts at all, is it? You're in some sort of a filthy mess under that coat. You stink to high heaven."

"The coat has got a bit of an aura, it's true. The salesman told me they use buffalo urine to cure the leather—" Nick clamped down on his words. Sometimes his enthusiasm for bullshit got the better of him. Just because he could spout moderately plausible lies at will, didn't mean he should. It was a lesson which eluded him surprisingly often.

25

By the middle of the afternoon, they were off the motorways and on the one dual-carriageway which ran up Scotland's eastern side. Traffic was light but constant, the white-peaked mountains rose ahead of them. Finn itched to kill something.

"We need to fuel up," said Adam.

"We're not losing them," Finn told him.

"I think that car of theirs must have an enormous fuel tank. I can't believe they're still going. We're going to need to stop at the next place."

"We're not stopping."

"It could be fifty miles to the next petrol station."

Finn looked at her phone and tried to get a signal to bring up a map and list of petrol stations. She was operating on zero bars of data.

Adam glanced at her mute phone. "There aren't many garages on these isolated roads."

Finn rolled her eyes. "Isolated roads, more opportunities. If I was driving we'd have rammed them off the road by now."

"That's why you're not driving. If we're fast, we'll soon catch up with them, this Beemer will go a lot faster if we need it to."

"As long as we don't get stuck behind something."

"There's a place coming up in a couple of minutes. Pitlochry. I'll put fuel in the tank, you can go in and pay, yeah?" Adam paused. "One thing. Do you think you could just give them the cash and not kill anyone? Please?"

"Why so squeamish all of a sudden?" asked Finn.

"No, it's not that, but I can go quicker if I'm not, you know..."

"Worrying about what I might be doing?"

"Yeah, that."

"Fine. Don't worry about what I might do." Finn was careful not to commit fully to any no-killing rules. She liked to remain flexible.

26

Tony reached into the back of the car. "Got some bacon sandwiches here, courtesy of your mother. I reckon it's about time we dug them out, don't you?"

"Mm, yeah!" said Nick. A bacon sandwich would be a welcome distraction from the growing irritation in his groin. What sort of disease would you get from sitting in poo-stained trousers for hours on end? He couldn't come up with anything better than nappy rash. There was sure to be something more serious and grow-up sounding. What was that blood disease you got from infected bed sores?

"Pickles, you'd better not be chewing the upholstery," said Tony.

"Probably bored," said Nick, half-looking round. "Oh cool! You've got the tin!"

Tony was piling things from his bag onto his lap to retrieve the sandwiches. "What? This?"

He lifted the old tobacco tin. It was scuffed. Almost all of the lithographic print's colour was gone, but the details of the picture were just as clear.

"That picture there, that's us this weekend," said Nick.

"It's—?"

Tony turned it over in his hands. The picture oozed manly nostalgia. It could have come from a Boy's Own adventure thriller, with its rugged solo male in his fisherman's sweater. He was sat on a boulder on the shore of a wide body of water. At the far side, black against blue, were forests and a zig-zag mountain range. Just to one side, on the edge of the vignette was the edge of a veranda and the wall of a log cabin. A faithful hound sat at his side, picked out in the light of the campfire. The man sat with his back to the viewer, shotgun over his arm – he held it with such casual cool – and a tumbler of whisky in the other. This man, this *uber-mensch* figure, looked like he was merely relaxing for a moment before sailing away across the dark lake, or going to hunt majestic stags in the wood. Nick thought it looking fucking gorgeous.

"This is us?" said Tony.

"Yep."

"This ... this scene?"

"Yes."

"So, the business with a log cabin in the Highlands?"

Nick waved his hands at the mountains surrounding them. "Inspired by that."

"And the whisky?"

"The Talisker. Yes."

"And the clay pigeon shooting?"

"Yes."

"And the dog?"

"The dog was sort of a last minute thing. But, yeah, I look at that tin and I think of you."

Tony looked thoughtful. "I have had it a long time."

"It's not just that. It's the essence of dadness. A bit old-fashioned, but in a good way. A man who taps his barometer and knows about tools. A man who likes the classic tunes of yesteryear but can't stand the noise of modern music. A man who likes meat and two veg—"

"Are you talking about me or the guy on the tin?" asked Tony.

Nick paused. That was an unexpected question. "Er, both?" he ventured.

Tony shook his head. "The man on the tin is not me."

"I know that."

"Are you sure? You only think in stereotypes, like we're all walk-ons in one of your adverts. You've got a little box in your head which says *mom,* and mom goes in there. Little box in your head which says *dad,* and I go in there."

"I care about you very much," countered Nick meaninglessly.

"But do you know what it is you care about? Do you really know who I am, apart from this *dad* thing." Tony actually drew air quotes and he didn't usually hold with that kind of nonsense, so Nick knew he was angry. "Do you know anything about mom and me?"

"Of course, I do!"

"Go on then."

"What?"

"Go on. What do you know about us?"

"Um. Well, your birthday is on the tenth of September. Mom's is the fourth of April. You were born in nineteen forty seven, mom in nineteen forty eight."

"That's just dates. You've probably got a reminder on your phone for that."

"You were born in Knowle. Your parents were George and Charlotte Carver and—"

"When did we meet?"

"Shortly after you were born, I should think."

"Not my parents. Your mom and me."

Nick stared at the road ahead. "At a dance?" he hazarded.

"A dance?"

"Some sort of village disco?"

Tony scoffed. "May twenty-second, nineteen seventy one, Birmingham Town Hall. King Crimson were playing in concert."

"Who?"

"King Crimson! *Court of the Crimson King*? *Twenty-First Century Schizoid Man*?"

Nick had no idea who or what King Crimson was or were.

"Prog rock!" said Tony.

Nick only had a vague concept of what prog rock was. In his mind, it was just music which had been fed into a shredder and stuck together again with drum solos; from some distant era when they had discovered LSD but had yet to discover actual tunes.

"You're into prog rock?"

"Yes! All those records I used to listen to. Van der Graaf Generator. Kansas. Uriah Heep. Frank Zappa and the Mothers of Invention. Jethro Tull."

"Okay. And these are bands you're listing? You're not just having a stroke?"

"You don't remember?" Tony was incredulous. "That's a part of me. That's your dad. *That's* who I am."

"And mom liked that music too?"

Tony laughed: a release valve laugh. "She had gone there with her boyfriend."

"Mom had a boyfriend before you?"

Tony's eyebrows rose and he gave Nick a fixed look. "Your mom didn't just settle down with the first bloke she met. She shopped around until she found the ideal man."

"Shopped around? Ugh! Dad!"

"What?" Tony shrugged, amused. "She was there with some pillock called Alistair. That kind of music wasn't her scene. She went to the bar to get a drink. It was soft drinks only, but I'd snuck in a couple of bottles of my homebrew beer."

"I remember your homebrew. The airing cupboard stank of fermenting yeast when I was a kid."

"That's right," said Tony. "Anyway, a bottle of homebrew and a few charming words from yours truly and I don't think your mom saw Alistair ever again. We left before the final number, your mom came back with me to my digs in Olton and—"

"Okay! Enough already!" Nick rested his wrists on the steering wheel and made a frantic *Time Out* gesture.

Tony sighed, not unhappily. "You are aware your mom and I had sex?"

"La la la. Not listening. Oh, mental image!"

"Well, it's a blasted sight more realistic than this mental image!" Tony tapped the tobacco tin loudly.

There was silence in the car for a while (apart from some canine growling and mumbling in the back seat).

"So, let me get this straight," said Tony, staring out to the brown and grey slopes crowding the road on both sides. "This Scotland thing...?"

"Yes?" said Nick.

"It's because of the tin."

Nick shrugged. "Yeah. I guess."

"Because the man on the tin loves Scotland, you think *I* love Scotland?"

"You do like Scotland," said Nick.

"I don't. I really don't."

"What? No! Mom said you were keen!" Nick had the feeling his grip on the situation was slipping.

"She said I should go to keep you happy."

"It's not about keeping *me* happy."

"Sacrifices I make to keep the peace. Scotland! Midges all over the place, roads with no passing places and the whole fetishizing of whisky."

"No, no, no. You like whisky."

"Since when?"

Nick thought. In truth, he'd never seen his dad drinking the stuff. He'd never really seen his dad drinking anything, except maybe a bitter shandy with his Sunday dinner. At most, a pint of beer at the end of a country walk. But...

"You said Talisker was the finest whisky there was!"

"You asked me about whisky one day. I'd heard someone go on about the stuff on Radio Four. Frankly, I couldn't taste the difference between whisky and turps, Nick. I don't like it. I don't like Scotland. I've got zero interest in shooting."

Nick's head was spinning. "What? Surely you want to do the shooting?" He cast about for the reasons why and found himself reaching for the same flimsy set of reasoning which had led him down this path the first time.

"No. I really don't feel comfortable with guns," Tony was saying. "I know it's a sport, but it's got the feel of hunting. If I shoot a clay thing flying through the sky, am I supposed to imagine it's a living, breathing bird and kill it? Horrible idea. I don't want to do it."

Nick saw a way back into more familiar territory: a long-standing family game. "What if you had to choose between shooting a clay pigeon or setting fire to a wicker man?" he asked.

"Is Edward Woodward inside the wicker man?"

"He doesn't have to be."

"Shooting the clay pigeon, I suppose," conceded Tony.

"What if you had to choose between shooting a clay pigeon and stabbing a puppy in the eye?"

"Obviously I would shoot the clay pigeon—"

"What if you had to shoot a tiger that was going to kill your whole family?"

"I'd shoot the tiger! This is hardly the point, Nick. I'd like to think I would always take the less harmful option. I'd take a life to defend family, no doubt about it, but shooting for its own sake just doesn't appeal to me."

Nick drove silently for a few minutes, wondering where he'd gone so wrong. Tony ate the last of his sandwich and stared out of the window. Pickles made loud chomping noises from the back seat. Maybe they should pass the dog some bacon. Nick twisted round to take a look.

He yelped in shock: Pickles had chewed right through the back seat. There was a hole leading into the boot. The cost of repair was going to be horrendous, but that was far from Nick's biggest problem. Pickles had dragged Oz's foot through the gap and was chowing down on the heel like it was a tasty bone. Nick turned back to the road and tried to look like someone who hadn't just witnessed casual snacking on a corpse.

"Look at that view!" he exclaimed, pointing out of the window. His squeak of alarm had already given him away: Tony was staring at the back seat, trying to make sense of what he was seeing.

"Is that ... is that a foot?" he asked.

"Zombie leg chew toy," Nick stated, his brain automatically throwing down its best cards. "A new range I'm working—"

"Nick, stop treating me like an idiot," snapped Tony. "Pull the car over. Now."

Nick scanned the road ahead for a stopping place. They were coming into a village so sparsely populated it only counted as one because it has a sign. *Dalwhinnie*. He took the slip road. Almost immediately there was a long, low series of interconnected buildings.

DALWHINNIE CAFÉ AND VISITORS CENTRE
PIES, SAUSAGES, SOUVENIRS

Nick signalled and pulled into the car park. He drove to the far end, taking as long as felt politely possible to find a parking spot in the near-deserted car park. He knew what was coming next.

Tony got out and strode to the back of the car.

"Dad! Dad, just listen—" began Nick, but there was no stopping Tony.

He opened the boot and looked inside. Nick joined his father: Oz looked even more horrific than before. The enclosed atmosphere of the boot obviously wasn't great for keeping a body fresh. A strong smell rose up, rotten and sweet at the same time. It almost overpowered the smell coming off Nick's own body.

"Hell," said Tony softly.

Oz's ravaged face was dry and crusted over in places, like a day-old kebab. Did something just wriggle in one of the facial cavities? Nick looked away quickly, afraid of the answer. The body seeped a bloody, liquid mess which pooled on the carpet. The gorgeous green interior of Nick's car would never, ever be the same again. Pickles continued to make appreciative chewing noises from the back seat.

Tony shook his head, his hand still on the lid of the open boot. He opened his mouth to speak, closed it, coughed and tried again.

"Well, looks like you could be in some trouble, son."

It was so gently said, and such a fucking understatement, Nick nearly laughed. "Yes, dad."

"I can't say I'm happy you kept it from me."

"No, dad."

Tony reached out a hand to the body, thought better of it and withdrew his arm. He slowly closed the boot. He rotated deliberately to face Nick as though he was having some trouble getting the instructions from his brain to his legs.

"What's the story, Nick?"

Nick exhaled loudly. "Right. You're going to find this funny when I tell you." He glanced at Tony's face. "Or maybe you won't. No, probably not. It began with the Talisker."

"Did it?"

"It got delivered to this guy and I couldn't get him to come to the door." Nick glanced at the closed boot lid. "I suppose it's understandable really, given his condition."

"The man was like this when you went to get the parcel?"

"I'm not a killer, dad."

"But you ... what? Stole his body?"

"I couldn't get the parcel. It was driving me mad, so I ended up breaking in to his house."

Tony gave him a scathing look. "Really?"

"I told you, it was important." Nick thought about the conversation they'd just had. "I *thought* it was important." Nick heard the whine creeping into his voice. He cleared his throat. "It was a bad idea, I can see that now, but while I was in there, I found the body and sort of fell over. I got blood and, um, stuff all over me, and I left a lot of, um, footprints. I couldn't have made it look any more incriminating if I'd tried, so I decided to try and get rid of the evidence."

"How did he die?" said Tony.

Nick swallowed as he visualised the scene back at the house. "I can't imagine what went on, but I found him on one of those folding workbench things like you've got. There were a whole bunch of tools clamped on it, facing upwards, and he was slumped over them. He either flung himself on, or someone else did."

"Tools? What sort of tools? Like chisels and screwdrivers?"

"No, electric things, most of them. A couple of drills. A saw. What sort of thing looks like a cookie cutter on a spinning thing?"

"A circle hole cutter," said Tony promptly. "It's a type of drill."

"I knew you'd know. That's the thing which made his face look like that. There was one of those small whizzy tools as well, like the one you used to use for polishing the brasses."

"A Dremel?"

"Yes."

Tony tutted. "What a terrible way to treat a fine tool."

"Not what I was thinking at the time, dad."

"So what exactly were you planning to do with this?" He gestured at the body.

Nick shrugged. "Scotland, somewhere remote. Maybe the well at the cottage?"

Tony thought about it. Not for very long. "No, absolutely not. This has to end before you make it any worse. You need to come clean."

"Woah. Hold your horses, dad."

"Horses be damned! It's the only way. I don't know what kind of madness got into you, but it needs to stop."

"I would like it to stop."

"We'll turn the car around, go home and go to the police. I don't want to hear any more nonsense about getting rid of the body. You are not James Bond, you are just an idiot who's got himself into a mess."

"But I'll go to prison!" said Nick, miserably.

Tony's face tightened uncomfortably. "Probably not for long." Nick couldn't tell if his dad was lying or not. Perhaps it didn't matter. "Sometimes you just have to do what's right, even if you don't like it."

Pickles gave a small bark from the back seat.

"I suppose the dog came from this house too?" asked Tony. "Of course it did."

Nick nodded.

"Well I think Pickles probably needs a toilet break. There's a little path down there, through the trees. You go inside the café and find somewhere to get cleaned up: you smell almost as bad as this poor guy. I'll take the dog and think about how we best handle the situation."

Nick seized on the idea of getting cleaned up like a drowning man spotting a raft. If he could get rid of his appalling stink, and ease the painful chafing in his pants, he could deal with anything. He grabbed his bag off the back seat.

"Car keys," said Tony, hand out.

Nick stared at him, uncomprehending, for several seconds. "I'm not going to drive off and leave you," he said eventually. "I'm not an idiot."

"Car keys," repeated Tony.

Nick grimaced and handed them over. "Have you got poop bags?"

"Pardon?"

"Poop bags. For the dog."

Tony reached into the car for his bag. He produced a compact folding tool with a flourish. "Travel trowel. Pickles, your toilet awaits, and we can leave the blasted Scottish countryside as we found it."

Nick watched Tony saunter away with the dog. He went to look for a bathroom.

27

Adam accelerated harder, overtaking yet another car.

"We should be able to see them by now, they only had five minutes on us," he said. They crested a rise, the empty road visible for a good half mile ahead.

"There's a village or something," said Finn. "Slow down."

They approached a café and rest stop place.

DALWHINNIE CAFÉ AND VISITORS CENTRE
PIES, SAUSAGES, SOUVENIRS

Adam slowed to a crawl so they could take a look at the parking area.

"Bingo," said Finn. "They're here

"Our target is still wearing his thick coat," said Adam, steering slowly into the car park. "He must be really hot,"

"You know, if it wasn't for the coat, I can't see how that is Oz," said Finn.

"He doesn't look anywhere near old enough," Adam agreed. "Hair dye?"

"The photo we have isn't good enough for us to tell one way or the other. How important is it we get the correct heart?" she asked.

"I beg your pardon?"

"I mean, because that guy has almost certainly got a heart."

"No."

"We could take that one. Kill him first, ask questions later."

Adam turned to look at her. "I can't tell if you're joking. No, it has to be the correct heart."

"Matching blood types is it?"

"Something like that. I need to see if I can confirm his identity."

Oz headed into the building. The older guy with the dog headed off towards the tree line at the rear of the café.

"We need to ID him," said Adam.

Finn pulled the leather-sheathed blade from inside her coat.

"No," said Adam. "He's probably going to the toilets."

"Nice and quiet."

"I don't want you going into the gents and causing a scene. I'll follow him and have a chat. Why don't you disable the car or something? Like MacGyver."

"Who's MacGyver?" asked Finn, opening her door.

28

The place was essentially a motorway service station, without the motorway or much in the way of service. Nick liked motorway services. Ever since childhood, service stations held a magical charm over him. They spoke of long journeys and therefore of holidays. They were a touch of the exotic: a little town centre which had broken away and decided to go off and live by themselves in the countryside, without all those bothersome houses and other stuff which made up the rest of the town. Even now, as an adult, Nick was drawn to the service station's allure: a tiny newsagent, a tiny games arcade, and the prospect of a tiny, offensively over-priced cooked breakfast.

The place was like a proto-service station: what service stations must have been like before they metaphorically crawled out of the sea and evolved decent lungs. All the essential pieces were there. There was a shop which was very keen on selling the passing traveller its local sausages and pies, as well as the obligatory piles of travel paraphernalia: the folding chairs, ponchos, insulated mugs and neck cushions which seemed to incubate in service stations from Lands End to John O'Groats. There was a tired and uninviting café which probably offered a side dish of salmonella and misery with every main meal. And there were the toilets.

"Thank God," he breathed. He felt caked in filth from knees to waist, and never had he been so desperate to get out of a dead man's coat (although he had no other experiences with which to compare this one).

He went inside the gents and pushed open a cubicle. The floor was awash with a slurry of piss and mud. He wasn't prepared to put his bag down on that, and the toilet cistern was too slender to balance it on. He checked the other cubicles, but the piss and crud theme had been extended to all of them. He went outside to see if there might be a disabled toilet, or by some miracle, a shower. He hesitated at the door of the women's toilet, deciding he'd attracted enough anger for one day. He backtracked into the gents: the floor by the washbasins was probably clean enough.

The place was hardly busy; it was unlikely he'd be disturbed. He would just have to brazen it out if anyone came in. With some relief he peeled away the outsized, inside-out sheepskin coat. Drying blood had mixed with his sweat, making dark patches on the coat and dyeing his t-shirt an unpleasant brownish-pink.

He gagged in revulsion. As he put the coat aside, a pocket rattled. He instinctively felt inside and withdrew a bottle of tablets with a child-proof lid. The label read, *Argentum nitricum, take as directed.*

Were these the pills Oz had overdosed on before getting physical with a Black and Decker workmate? Nick didn't want to think about it. He put the tablets by the basin and wondered about dumping the coat.

The bin by the door, though entirely empty, was too small to take the bulky sheepskin. Nick hung the coat on a cubicle door, removing the bin's white liner to put his own soiled clothes in. He stripped off his t-shirt, grimacing as it unavoidably brushed his face. He pulled down his trousers.

"Ah, for f— *Jesus!*"

They were even worse than he'd imagined. The increasingly sore chafing had rubbed poo into every seam and crevice of both his trousers and skin. It was like a tribe of bored toddlers had been let loose with henna dye on his lower body. He pushed the trousers into the bin bag, taking a flannel from his travel bag. He ran the hot tap and soaked the flannel thoroughly.

Ordinarily, Nick liked to use a hot flannel as part of his shaving routine, draping it across his face to open the pores. He was never going to use this one anywhere near his face again.

He started on the relatively safe zones: his chest and arms. Blood swirled down the drain; he felt the guilt and anxiety subside as he cleaned up. He tackled his legs and groin next. The filth came away in dried flakes and clumps. Fresh wafts of Nick-stink rose from his wet body; he told himself this was just the crap waving goodbye. He washed his groin repeatedly; each time more shit came out with it. His meat and two veg had been stewing in gravy for nearly eight hours and there was seemingly no end to the stuff. Maybe he'd need to shave his pubes off to be rid of it all. He wasn't going to get lathered up and shave himself now but...

"Hang on," he said to his poor and mistreated genitals.

He went back into his bag and found his nail scissors.

"Yes!" he hissed in triumph, and attacked his befilthed man-garden. He cut savagely and threw each clump into the sink. This was aggressive deforestation, just short of a slash and burn policy.

He knew he was taking longer than he should but each step towards a cleaner body was a step towards bliss and normality. Nick went back to the flannel and sluiced himself down before getting out a towel and starting on the drying process.

Towelling himself down like a normal man – a normal man who wasn't covered in shit and didn't have a corpse in his boot – felt so wonderful, felt such a relief he let out an gigantic sigh. At that moment the door opened and another man entered the toilet. Nick tried to turn his sigh into a cough, suddenly conscious he was making semi-erotic noises while standing stark naked in a public toilet. The sigh-cough wasn't his greatest work, sounding more like a lascivious "Woof!"

The stranger, an immaculately presented young Asian man, stared at him. What should have happened was the smart young fellow stared briefly at the nakedness and the pube-filled sink before quickly backing out. Instead, he stayed immobile for an unnerving beat.

Nick gave a pointed cough: the ultimate English act of disapproval.

The man didn't flinch. With a sigh, Nick carried on. If the guy wanted to feast his eyes on his naked loveliness, then Nick was in no position to stop him. The stranger turned to the cubicles. Nick averted his eyes to the mirror above the basin and finished drying his lower half.

When he looked up he saw the stranger standing by the hanging coat, a piece of paper in his hand. The paper was crumpled, covered in handwriting and, Nick realised with a jolt, quite familiar. It was the letter he'd picked up in Oz's house, and popped into his pocket.

Had the man gone through Oz's pockets.

Nick coughed again. "Can I help you? You seem to have my letter."

"Oh," said the man. "It was on the floor."

"Uh-huh?"

"I didn't realise it was yours."

Nick gave him a look containing the right proportions of polite acquiescence and stern disbelief. He held out his hand.

"Sorry—" said the stranger, twisting his head to look at the paper, "—Oz."

Nick snatched back the letter and swept it, along with the bottle of pills, into his bag.

"That's quite all right," he said, in a tone he hoped conveyed it most certainly was not.

29

Finn tackled the car first. She'd never had to disable a Cadillac before, but it was an old model. She imagined there would be plenty of straightforward ways she could prevent them from going too much further. Sure, she could just stick something sharp in the tyres, but there was no finesse, no challenge in that.

She sauntered over, scoping out the local area for onlookers. The car park was pleasingly empty. A stiff, near-Arctic breeze ran over the place and she turned up her coat collar against the chill. She peered in at the oddly-coloured upholstery. There were blood stains on the back seat. She wondered why a top killer like Lupo would favour such an obviously old-fashioned and unreliable vehicle, even in retirement.

"Sloppy," she muttered.

She crouched by the front wheel arch and felt around inside. Her fingers brushed the smooth curve of the metal-braided brake line. She unzipped a waist pocket on her Muubaa, unfolded a multi-tool, and snipped the cable. She went to the other front wheel and repeated the process.

As she stood, she noticed a damp scuff mark on the knee of her Zara jeans. She brushed it, but the mark wouldn't lift.

"Damn."

The car wouldn't be going far now. If Oz tried it, he might just end up as an entertaining smear on a Scottish mountainside; one which she could swiftly dissect to remove its heart. As for the older looking chap: he was making a circuit around the car park on a cordoned-off trail just behind the line of the trees. He held the lead of an exuberant dog which pranced and pulled in every direction, apparently overjoyed to be outside. Finn walked directly towards them, multitool still in her hand.

As Finn got closer, the dog paused for a toilet break and the old guy produced a small trowel to bury the dog's poo. Finn was silently impressed – anyone who had a folding trowel about their person was prepared to take on the world. Her respect for Oz's nameless friend shot up, not that it would stop her killing him. She might despatch the man with his own trowel. She'd never killed anyone with a trowel before.

The man patted down the earth and turned his attentions to a large board with a *YOU ARE HERE* map on it. Finn stepped through between the trees and onto the dirt path. She took out her Polaroid and snapped a picture of the man.

"Excuse me," said the man, frowning. "Don't you know it's polite to ask if you want to take someone's picture?"

Finn made a vague head gesture, an acknowledgement of the question, not an answer. She wafted the picture dry and took out her Sharpie.

"Name?"

The man looked confused. He looked down. "Pickles."

She had written the *P* before she stopped herself. "Your name is Pickles?"

The man looked even more confused. "My name? I'm Tony. The *dog's* name is Pickles."

"Why would I want to know the dog's name?" she asked.

The man, Tony, ruffled the creature's ears. It barked happily. "She's a good girl, aren't you, Pickles? You like dogs?"

Finn wasn't sure what the answer was to that question. She'd never owned a dog. Her parents had never bought her one.

"I take it you're on holiday," said Tony, pointing at the camera.

She shook her head. "Work."

He sniffed and nodded. He gestured at the cold and mostly brown landscape around them. "Yes, I can't quite imagine why anyone would want to come here on holiday. I've been dragged up here from the south by my son."

"Oz?"

Tony laughed. "No, not that far. Birmingham. Might as well be Australia though. It has been a—" He exhaled, as though there were a lot of emotions going on beneath the surface and he was struggling to keep them in check.

Finn hoped he did. She was okay with blood and organs spilling out of people. She wasn't a fan of emotional outbursts.

"You know, travel with someone and you learn a lot about them," he said. "Or how little you know about them. You with someone?"

She nodded.

98

"Course you are," he said. "Nice girl like you." He gave her a momentarily worried look. "Didn't mean anything by that. You seem like a nice person."

"I try," she said. She looked back at the car park. No sign of Adam yet. This guy didn't appear to be the kind to hang out with a retired contract killer. He certainly didn't appear like a retired contract killer's dad.

Finn joined Tony at the map. It was a fanciful cartoon rendering of the small wood at the back of the café. It claimed a nature trail ran through the wood, featuring wildlife such as red squirrels and deer, which were illustrated on the edges of the board. Finn was fairly certain she would be able to spot any wildlife from here: it would be hard-pressed to hide in this handful of spindly trees.

"Nice trowel," she said. "May I?"

"Sure," he said and handed it over. She unfolded it and wanted to test its sharpness on the soft tissues of his neck.

"Sheffield steel," said Tony proudly. "Before everything was made in China."

She nodded. She was thinking. "I don't actually like the guy I'm travelling with," she said.

"No?"

"He wants to control everything. It's all lists and ETAs and schedules and he wants to tie me down to, you know, his plan."

Tony nodded. "I know the type. Don't tell me. He's a corporate business type."

She thought about it. "Yeah. That's it. It's all business. Flies in from Dublin with a list of instructions and bag for the—" she gestured vaguely "—the, you know. And because he's got his schedule I've got to dance to his tune. And then his handler, Col, phones up and we've got to dance to *his* tune. And that's not how the world works."

"It isn't," agreed Tony emphatically. "Some people just live in a bubble. No concept of the real world."

"Right!"

"My lad. He lives life in a dream. No, he thinks his life is a dream. He has this idealised view of how things are and how they should be and it's never going to work out that way. Oh, his heart's in the right place but... this weekend..." Tony sighed deeply. "He wants to have a so-called special weekend with me so he can put me in some metaphorical box." He chuckled without humour. "And then put me in an actual box and bury me."

She gave him a sideways look. "You're going to die?"

Tony hesitated. Maybe this wasn't the kind of conversation people had with strangers. Finn wasn't sure.

"Yes, I'm dying," he said. "I have stage four cancer."

"Stage four?"

He nodded. "Means I'm definitely dying. I'm still on my feet but that's about it."

"And you're okay with it?" she asked.

Tony opened his mouth to say one thing and then seemed to change his mind. "Of course, I'm not," he said bitterly. "I'm ... I'm fucking livid. I've not smoked a day in my life. I barely drink a drop. And certainly not whisky. I've kept myself active. I've worked hard my whole life and done everything to care for my family. And I'm dying."

"Everyone dies," said Finn.

He studied her face. "I can't work out if that's profound or the most stupidly trite thing I've heard all day. And I've spent the day in the car with my son."

She ran her fingers along the edge of the trowel and flicked crumbs of dirt away. "Everyone does die," she said. "We don't get to pick the moment. And when people die, nine times out of ten, it's in a lot of pain. Animal pain – you know what I mean?"

"I do."

"And ... how old are you?"

Tony smiled. "Old enough. I've had my allotted three score years and ten. Doesn't stop me getting angry. What's that line? *Rage against the dying of the light*? I'm dying and I want to stand on a mountain top and scream at the world. *Look at me! Really look at me! I'm here! This is who I am!* And then I can die."

Finn shrugged and took a good grip on the handle of the trowel. "We're not quite on a mountain top here, but if you want to start screaming and shouting, I can do the rest."

"Thanks for the offer," he said.

There was a movement from the car park as she drew back her arm. A police car had just pulled in. It came to a stop behind the hired BMW, blocking it from pulling out. A woman cop stepped from the police car.

Finn weighed options up in her mind. Slowly, reluctantly, she put the trowel back in Tony's hand. "Nice trowel," she said and walked away.

She took her phone out to call Adam but it was already buzzing in her hand.

"It's him," Adam whispered. "Definitely. Saw some ID. He confirmed his identity."

Finn found that surprising. Everything about the old guy Tony suggested they had been tailing the wrong people all day. "Are you sure?"

"Yes!" he hissed.

"The cops are here."

"What?"

"Out front. Looking at our car. We can't let Oz leave at all. Where are you?"

"In the toilets."

"Then keep him there."

"How?"

"Improvise," she said and ended the call.

30

Nick was half-dressed. He really wanted to get away from the creepy stranger. The guy had shut himself in a toilet cubicle and was whispering urgently to himself.

The man clearly had some interest in Nick, and Nick wasn't deluded or optimistic enough to think it was sexual. Cottaging was, as far as he understood, a dying art and, even in the wilds of Scotland, public toilet sex aficionados would draw the line at a man recently smeared in his own crap.

Maybe the man was a policeman? He seemed very interested in Oz's letter. But why hadn't he just put handcuffs on Nick and dragged him away?

Whatever the case, Nick felt the man meant him harm. He was going to have to make a run for it at some point.

The whispering conversation came to an end. The cubicle door unlocked and the stranger stepped out. He stared at Nick and went to the basins, barely pretending to wash his hands.

Nick was out of time. He decided he would go without putting his trousers back on. He was wearing pants and a T-shirt. He could leave the bin bag of filthy clothes. He just needed to pick up his bag and trousers and run. It was a rubbish plan, but it was a plan. He made a big show of rifling through his bag while discreetly sliding on his trainers. He turned to bolt for the door.

The stranger reached out and snatched his trousers, holding them up in the air, out of reach.

"Hey!"

"Just wait," said the man.

"Give them back!" demanded Nick. He had no idea whether this was a fight. Was he in a fight? He gave the man an experimental shove in the chest.

"Ow!" The other man swung Nick's trousers round. The button on the waistband caught Nick's cheek. He hissed with pain.

"Right, that's it!" Nick swung a punch at the man's face. An instant later he was nursing bruised knuckles while the other man roared and grabbed the wash basin. Oh Lord, this was the bit where he would tear the basin off the wall and smash it over Nick's head.

Nick flinched; the basin seemed to be still firmly attached to the wall.

Nick tried to dart past. The man reached out to block him.

The two stumbled together into a cleaning cart in the corner. The man grabbed the mop from the wheeled bucket and swung it at Nick. The cloth head slapped Nick across the face.

"*Plah!*" spat Nick. He grabbed a bottle from the upper tray of the trolley and squirted bright blue gloop into the man's face. The man screamed and clutched at his eyes. The stuff stank of bleach. Nick glanced at the label and saw a skull and crossbones, and the diamond symbol which meant it was poisonous to aquatic life. If it was bad for fish, it couldn't be great for eyes.

Panicked, Nick snatched back his trousers and ran for the door.

The man voiced a wild yell and blundered after him.

Nick dodged between the neck pillows and camping supplies in the shopping area. He deliberately knocked over a large display of stacked cool boxes and watched as his pursuer stumbled and fell.

"Oi! What you doin'?" yelled a shop assistant.

Nick paid no attention and ran on, trousers in hand. He saw the hi-vis uniforms of two police officers by the building entrance and skidded round into the café.

The few diners watched as Nick ran through.

"Donald, where's ya troosers?" someone shouted.

"Here!" replied Nick, breathless, waving them above his head before charging out through a fire exit.

He stumbled over a grass verge and onto a dirt path. The path! He spun round. Through the twists of the path and the obscuring cover of trees, he could see someone. A man with a dog?

"Dad," he breathed and ran on.

There was the slam of the door behind him.

A glance over his shoulder told him the other man had made it out of the building and was running blindly after him. Over to his left was the car park and, there, by the entrance some distance from his Cadillac, was a police car. Was the pocket-rummaging trouser-thief with the police? He'd hardly acted like an officer of the law.

Perhaps it didn't matter. It didn't change his course of action. Get dad, get in the car and get the hell out of Dalwhinnie. And put his trousers on at some point.

"Dad!" Nick yelled.

Tony drifted unhurriedly towards him. Pickles' lead in one hand, trowel in the other.

"Ah, at last," said Tony. "Where's your trousers?"

"Problem, dad!" hissed Nick, out of breath. "The cops! This guy!"

"Oh," said Tony, looking past Nick.

The man with the blue face and unseeing eyes ploughed along the track and launched himself in something like a rugby tackle. Before he landed on Nick he checked, half-falling. He yelped.

"Oh," repeated Tony. "I didn't mean to do that."

There was blue chemical muck all over Nick's trousers. The stranger was on his knees, clutching himself in surprise. Tony's trowel was embedded in his stomach. It had penetrated right up to the handle.

"Fuck!" said Nick.

"Language, Nick," said his father automatically.

The stranger struggled to produce any sound above a squeaking grunt. "*Gnh!* Fuck!"

"Language," said Nick automatically.

"This is terrible," said Tony and bent to help the man.

"I think he's a cop," said Nick.

The stranger gritted a laugh and pushed Tony away. "Cop? You fucking idiots!" He rolled to his feet, still gripping the trowel handle.

"You probably ought not to move," suggested Tony.

The stranger backed away, blinking hard. His eyes were blue and pink in the worst possible colour clash Nick had ever seen.

"We didn't mean any harm," said Nick.

"Fuck you both!" shouted the stranger. "You're dead! Fucking monsters! He's going to have your heart and you can't run far enough or fast enough to—!" He coughed and droplets of blood sprayed from his lips. With another strangled groan he staggered off through the trees to the car park.

"He's got my trowel," said Tony in the quiet voice of a man who couldn't quite believe what he has just witnessed.

"Come on, dad. We've got to go," said Nick.

"Do you want to put your trousers on first?"

"Come on!"

31

Finn slipped into the car park at the furthest point from the police car. The two cops had looked inside the BMW and spoken on their radio before going inside the building.

The police car had blocked in the BMW. The natural solution would have been to take the police car: it was a BMW too. Tit for tat. A very tempting option, but one which would bring a lot of additional attention with it.

There was a toot of air brakes. A refrigerated truck with *Kirkwood Farms* emblazoned along the side had pulled into the car park and braked sharply to avoid someone staggering across the tarmac. It was Adam, blue on top, red in the middle; looking like he'd fought a Slushie machine and lost.

Finn ran over. The truck driver opened his window, leaning out to speak.

"What happened?" demanded Finn.

Adam coughed blood. "He stabbed me," he spat. "He—"

"Is he all right, love?" called the truck driver.

"Where are they?" said Finn.

"Stabbed me!" whined Adam.

Across the way, the Cadillac reversed out of its parking bay, nudged a bollard, and accelerated towards the exit.

"Open the door!" Finn told the driver.

"What? Shouldn't we call an ambulance?"

Finn grabbed Adam's arm and pulled him towards the truck's cab, forcing his pitiful gargling up an octave or two. The cab was very high. She climbed right up and faced the driver; he looked surprised to see her.

"We will be your passengers," she said. "You need to drive us."

"An ambulance would be better."

She turned and dragged Adam up the same steps. He screamed in pain.

"But I got pies to deliver!" protested the driver.

"No, you need to do what I say," said Finn, pointing at the Cadillac. "Follow that car,"

"Is this a hostage situation?" asked the driver.

"If you like."

"I think I had training, but I can't remember what it said."

"It said comply with people who threaten you with physical violence," said Finn. "That's me."

"Yes! Yes it did. Righto, love." He restarted the engine and swung the massive vehicle round towards the exit.

"Need to get to the hospital," gasped Adam, tears falling. "I think I might be dying."

Finn looked at his wound. Blood and blue chemicals made interesting purple patterns on his shirt. "Quite probably," she agreed.

"There's St Vincent's Hospital up in Kingussie," suggested the driver. "'Bout twenty miles."

"You're following that car." Finn pointed at the departing Cadillac.

"Why?"

"Did they also tell you not to ask questions in hostage situations?"

"I'll be honest with you, love. I don't rightly remember."

"Follow that car."

Adam slumped against her; he was leaking all over her Muubaa jacket. It had had blood on it before, some of it even hers, and its wipe-clean surface was one of the things she liked about it. Didn't mean she wanted Adam bleeding all over it today. She pushed him into the corner by the door.

He made a mewling sound. "Get this out of me," he mumbled. "I don't want to die."

"I can't take it out. It's the only thing holding most of your insides in."

"But I'm bleeding."

"He is," agreed the driver. He indicated a compartment above Finn's head: it contained a first aid kit and other supplies. Finn rootled through the first aid kit and pulled out a reel of micropore tape, deciding it wouldn't go far enough. First aid was meant for bleeding fingers, not serious stomach wounds. She looked inside the compartment again. There was a toolkit and a reel of greasy duct-tape.

"Perfect."

She found the end and pulled it free. She tore open the front of Adam's shirt, just above the trowel. "Lean forward."

"Can't."

"Lean forward!"

He sobbed as he pushed himself away from the seat. A slither of intestine, or possibly stomach lining, slipped out of his wound: just an inch or two. Finn poked it back in with her fingers and covered it with tape. She passed the roll around Adam's abdomen, encircling him several times, above and below the trowel. It was a very neat job she decided, once she'd finished. If people ever stated having trowels sticking in them as fashion accessories, they would wear them like this.

"Fucking bastards," muttered Adam weakly.

"Yeah?" she said.

"Fucking weirdos. Hairs. Hairs everywhere. All in the sink. Pubes!"

"Is he delirious?" said the driver.

"Nah," whispered Adam. "No trousers. Man... Man's a fucking werewolf. Got the instructions here." He tried to tap his shirt pocket and missed. His eyes went wide with alarm. "The bag! My bag. S'got special solution. Double-bagging."

It was back in the BMW, and they needed it. Finn wondered what else they would need. She felt Adam's trouser pockets, forcing her fingers inside one to pull out his mobile phone. Next she peeled open the chemical-soaked shirt pocket and extracted a damp sheet of folded paper. She unfolded and scanned it.

Finn rarely exhibited surprise. Surprise was an emotion for the unprepared. A lesser person would have read the sheet and exclaimed something like, "No fucking way!" or "You've got to be bloody kidding me!" But not Finn. The paper said what the paper said. It changed everything, but there was no point getting dramatic about it.

And at least it explained the silver knife.

32

"I think we've got a tail," said Nick, glancing in his mirror. He couldn't deny he got a tiny thrill from saying those words, even though he knew they were in trouble.

"What?" said Tony. He turned round in his seat, pushed Pickles' big head out of the way, and looked back. "That massive truck?"

"It's following us."

"Surely a tail is supposed to be discreet? Hey, I think it's the girl."

"What girl?" said Nick.

"The girl I was talking to."

"And by *girl* you mean *woman*?"

"She's at least half my age. I think I can call her a girl. She took my photo. We got chatting. She's with some man who flew in from – where was it? – Dublin, she said. The man was the one with the schedules and the plans."

"What are you on about?" said Nick, gripping the wheel tighter as the truck closed in on them. "You talk nonsense sometimes."

"I'm just saying what she said. She said he had plans and a bag for – you know I think that's him."

"What is?"

"The man. The man who's got my trowel."

"What? In the truck with her?"

"There's three of them. Get down Pickles! I know, I know. You didn't like her, did you? What on earth is going on, Nick?"

"He said he was going to have our heart," said Nick. "Is that a thing?"

"I'm not at all sure I know."

"This is karma, dad. Karma giving me a kicking because I messed with the body."

"Get a grip, son," said Tony. "Karma is not a real thing. It must be something connected with what you did earlier."

Nick thought. "He seemed really interested in the letter I took from Oz's house."

"What letter?"

Nick took the next turning off the main road, hitting the bend at speed. He tapped the brakes, but they felt kind of loose: squishy.

"Hey, you didn't indicate!" said Tony.

"Dad, you do know we're in a car chase, don't you? I *want* to confuse the guy behind; hopefully give him the slip."

"No excuse for not following the Highway Code," said Tony.

33

"You need to go faster than this," said Finn to the driver. He glanced at her and accelerated very slightly. Finn sighed. It would come down to her. It always did. She leaned across and pushed open his door.

His eyes bulged in alarm. "Listen, love—!"

She unclicked his seatbelt, shoving him at the same time. He tumbled out of the cab. The seatbelt trailing out the door snapped taut. Finn had her hand on the wheel. She slid across to put her foot on the accelerator.

She reached for the swinging door. A hand reached up, grasping for the door frame. A voice was calling.

"If you could just—!"

She slammed the door shut. Even dangling from his seatbelt, the guy must have been a good six feet off the ground. In the wing mirror she saw him land on his feet, bounce, roll and stumble clown-like to his feet. Then a truck in the opposite lane roared by. When it was out of view, there was nothing but a long red mess on the road.

"I don't feel good..." said Adam, in a faint voice. "Is that my phone ringing...?"

The phone on the seat between them was alight and buzzing. Finn picked it up. The caller ID simply said *Col*. She hit the speaker.

"Col."

"Who is that?"

"It's Finn."

"Finn? Where's Adam? It's very noisy."

Adam waved at the phone. His breathing was harsh.

"Kind of busy here," said Finn.

"What's that? I can't hear you."

"Everything's in hand, Col," shouted Finn as she steered the rig round a bend, too fast. The back end swung out. It struck a helpfully positioned crash barrier and bounced back into line.

"What's happened?"

"There was an accident. Adam has a small injury to his stomach. I'm about to acquire our target. I'll make sure he gets sorted out when I'm done."

"It really hurts!" hissed Adam.

"Very good."

The car had turned onto a narrow road; more of a track, really. It was a rather obvious ploy to shake them off, assuming the truck couldn't get down there. Finn smiled and gunned the engine. Branches whacking loudly against the windscreen. If anything, the truck was doing better than the Cadillac, which was definitely not built for the wilderness. It wallowed in the potholes and bounced wildly on suspension meant for smoother roads. Finn urged the truck forward. It nudged the Cadillac's rear end.

"Gotta go, Col," said Finn. She turned her attention back to driving.

34

Nick screamed when the truck hit the back of his car.

"The car's no good on this road!" he wailed.

"Keep it together, son, you're doing great," said Tony. Pickles barked, although it wasn't clear if this was a vote of support. The truck nudged them again.

"What's he doing?" gasped Nick.

"You know it's the girl driving now, right?" said Tony conversationally, as Nick tried to get more speed out of his car.

"What, like in Terminator Three?" Nick couldn't suppress a tiny thrill at the thought he was in a real life action adventure. One strongly tempered by his suspicion the brakes weren't working half as well as they should.

"What happened to the man driver?"

"Tell you later," said Tony. He ran a hand along the chrome knobs and switches on the dashboard. "If you've got any buttons which deploy rockets or guns, this would be a good time to try them out."

"We could throw the body out," said Nick.

"How would that help?"

"They seem really interested in Oz. Let's give him to them. If we toss his body out onto the road they might stop." Nick pushed away the memory of how hard it had been to move Oz's body into the boot in the first place.

"We'd need to stop," said Tony.

"Not necessarily," said Nick. "Pickles has made a secret passage, remember?"

"So, let me get this straight. You want me to crawl through a hole into the boot, grab hold of a dead body, somehow pop the boot open, and throw it out?"

"You can make any idea sound stupid if you use that tone of voice!"

Pickles ran back and forth across the back seat, yipping excitedly. Nick steered the car around another bend. They emerged from the trees onto a track hugging a mountainside. Heather and gorse grew out of the hillside on the right hand side, stretching up out of sight. On the left was a terrifying drop. Nick gasped at the sight and tried hard to inject some nonchalance into his voice.

"Lovely views from here."

"What?"

"I'm just— Oh, hell, dad."

Nick looked in the mirror to see the truck closing in on them again. Surely the driver wouldn't try to manoeuvre along the narrow road? It was barely wide enough for the car, and that was one *huge* truck. One side of it whacked bushes and rocks loose from the mountainside and the other looked like it was halfway over the precipice.

The truck rear-ended them again. Nick fought to control the fishtailing car. He checked mirror again. For the first time he saw and recognised the *Kirkwood Farms* logo over the cab roof.

"I did a shit job on the adverts but it's hardly worth killing me for," he muttered.

"What?"

"*She always enjoys my sausage in cider.*" Nick wondered if he was getting delirious.

"*What*?!"

The truck rammed them again. This time it was catastrophic. The front end of the Cadillac slewed over the edge. Nick could feel the absence of ground beneath the nearside wheel. The world tipped. The chassis screamed as the underside of the car rode on the brink of the cliff. The car would have slowed, but the truck was right up behind it, driving forward like a plough.

"I'm so sorry I brought you to Scotland, dad!" yelled Nick, swinging the wheel randomly and pumping the dead brakes.

"I'm sorry too," said Tony, gripping the coat hook above the door with one hand and bracing himself against the dashboard with the other. "Trust me on that."

"This isn't going to end well," said Adam faintly.

"Let me handle things." Finn and kept her foot on the accelerator.

Adam's face (what was visible beneath the coating of chemical cleaner) was pale, ghostly. "Why can I smell disinfectant?" he said.

The Cadillac's nose ploughed deep into the ground. The impact braced it momentarily against the front of the truck. The car snapped up from the ground, see-sawed briefly, slid over the cliff edge and down its steep slope. Without the resistance of the car in front of it, the truck surged forward. Finn tried to counter by stamping on the brakes and spinning the steering wheel. It wasn't enough.

The truck and trailer drove off the road and powered down the slope.

The ground dropped away before the Cadillac at a ridiculous angle. The car shot forward, unchecked.

"Tree!" yelled Tony.

Nick swerved.

"Tree!"

Nick swerved again.

"Tree!"

"*It's all bloody trees!*" yelled Nick.

The world was a rumble of earth and stone: bouncing viciously off the side panels; clattering off the windscreen. Pickles turned frantic circles on the back seat and whined. Above it all was a booming, rending roar behind him.

Tony looked back.

"What?" shouted Nick, terrified. "What is it?"

"Don't look round!" shouted Tony. "And don't slow!"

Less than ten feet from Nick's door, a tall fir tree slammed into the earth. A large, single tyre bounced off it and flew, wobbling crazily, across the car's path.

"What happened to the truck?"

"Tree!"

"I can see that, d—!"

The windscreen smashed. Nick's brain froze. Some part of his consciousness was telling him to adopt the brace position. Another part was asking what the hell the brace position was. Yet another part was looking for the rock or tree which the car would ultimately hit: slamming them against the roof and into a steel-coated pancake.

The car crested a ridge. It dropped onto a lower slope. Nick was no longer driving, not even remotely. The Cadillac was tobogganing down a hill of fallen leaves and mulch. The slope was lessening, but not fast enough. Through the juddering, muck-filled haze, Nick could see a line of gorse bushes and a track running left to right in front of them.

"Brake now, son," said Tony.

"No brakes, dad."

Nick still held the steering wheel as if he exerted some control over the car's direction. Eventually, the Cadillac slewed and drifted sideways, to stop gently against a gorse bush. There was a silence which felt really strange after all the yelling and screaming of a moment earlier. The mountainside behind them was suffused with a haze of muck and dust. Trees creaked high above. There was no sign of the truck.

"Is everyone still alive?" asked Nick.

"For now," said Tony.

Pickles yipped.

"Close enough," said Nick.

37

Finn knew how to brace. She adopted the position the moment it was clear the truck was going to crash. She was dimly aware the weight of the trailer had twisted them into a roll down the mountainside. No time to shout a warning to Adam.

Finn closed her eyes tight. She felt the glass from the windscreen explode across her face. There was a weird pressure and a crunching sensation in the general vicinity of her right arm. Despite everything, she held her position until the cab came to rest.

She opened her eyes.

The cab was upright, mostly. The front was bent over, angled into the dirt. The windscreen was fifty percent earth, fifty percent sky and smoke. The seat next to her was empty. Adam was gone. Bizarrely, it made her want to laugh.

She gave a tentative, testing stretch. Her right arm would not co-operate. It was broken; somewhere between elbow and wrist. She couldn't remember the names of the bones in the forearm, even though she knew every bone in the human body. So far there was no pain.

"Adrenalin," she said to herself, her voice coming from far away. Adrenalin was good right now. It was better than what would come next.

She loosened the seat belt and slid forward against the dashboard. Something creaked from behind, in the trailer. The smoke was thickening, but she didn't hurry. Vehicles caught fire far less often than people thought, and almost never exploded.

She looked around for something to help with her arm. Somehow the duct-tape was still in its cubby hole. There was an extending wheel brace down the side of the driver's seat. She laid the brace against her lower arm as a makeshift splint, bound it up with duct-tape. One-handed she taped her arm tight to her Muubaa jacket to hold it in place.

The driver's side door wouldn't open. She climbed to the passenger side. There was blood and nuggets of broken safety glass everywhere. She dragged herself up and through the shattered windscreen, sliding feet first to the ground. She skidded on the loose earth slope. Pebbles bounced down the mountainside, raising dust against the trees.

The Cadillac was at the bottom of the slope, maybe half a mile distant. It was right way up and in one piece. She glanced back up the mountain and saw where Adam had gone. Half of him hung from a sapling about twenty yards away, the other half was underneath the cab. It was the half with the trowel in it. Finn took the trowel, dropping it as she tried to place it in her right hand. Fingers weren't responding. The adrenalin was wearing off.

After a moment's reflection she duct-taped the trowel to the end of her splint to make a fixed blade. It was Sheffield steel after all.

38

Nick stared up at the trees above them. He raised his hand against the light of the setting sun. "I think I see movement."

"I should think the whole mountainside is moving," said Tony. "Turn it over again."

Nick squinted up the mountain. "It's that woman," he said, leaning out of the car. "That crazy woman is still coming after us. I think she really might be a terminator."

"The terminator's a man, son," said Tony. "Turn it over."

"Huh?"

Tony pointed at the ignition. "Turn it over. It might work this time."

"Dad, I don't think this car should go anywhere. It needs serious attention. Don't forget it's a vintage model."

"I don't want to panic you, but I think we should consider the possibility a mentally deranged lady on the mountain is coming for us. There's no doubt she means us harm. If your car gets bust-up by us driving it, then you're just going to have to take it on the chin. We need to get out of here."

Nick turned the ignition. It grunted, roared briefly, before settling into a deeply unhappy *put-put-splutter* noise. When Nick put it into gear, it grew worse. He might be able to ignore the squealing engine, but he couldn't ignore the crunching and banging from the suspension. He'd never driven a clown car with square wheels, but guessed it would be something like this. They bounced unsteadily over the bushes and lumpy grass; it didn't get much better when they joined the dirt track. There were no brakes but it didn't matter: the car's top speed was no more than ten miles per hour as it lurched up and down.

"Classic," said Tony.

"Pardon?"

"Your car. It is, at best, a classic car. To be a vintage, it has to have been built before nineteen thirty."

"Is that so?"

"It's the precise definition. Veteran, vintage, post-vintage, classic."

"A classic, huh?" Behind them came a clunk and a crash. "What was that?"

"Bumper," said Tony. "Keep going, we can always fetch it later."

"We need to go up there to get away," said Nick, pointing right.

"There's more of a flat area if we go straight on," said Tony. "Let's go this way for now and see where we might be able to turn."

Moments later Nick's door popped open. He leaned over and pulled it shut but it responded by immediately falling off. He felt exposed as the chilly air rushed in. Pickles barked in excitement.

"We could run faster than this," said Nick. He looked at the wing mirror for signs of the woman, realised there was no wing mirror, and risked looking back out of the door gap. He couldn't see her, which was notionally a good thing, but not all that reassuring.

"There was a woman terminator," he said.

"Was there?"

"In the third film."

"There's been three terminator films?"

"Dad, there's been five."

"Really? Maybe they should have quit at number two. Good film that one. That's the one with the lava and the thumbs up as he goes down."

"In the third one the terminator's a woman," said Nick. "Looks really angry all the time. She just keeps coming until they switch on the particle accelerator, and it, um, kills her. I think. I might have fallen asleep at that point." Nick risked another glance back. "So, we have an enemy who wants to kill us but ... on the plus side, she's probably on foot now. We can talk to her. Try and explain we're nice guys really."

Tony shook his head. "She's got a funny manner, that one."

"Funny?"

"Not sure charm's going to work."

"Well then," said Nick, "she's not very big, is she? I'm pretty sure she was a good six inches shorter than me. We could restrain her if we had to. Couldn't we?"

Tony gave his son a serious look. "I think she could handle herself too. Did you see what she did to the driver of the truck?"

"No, dad. I was trying to keep the car on the road."

"She shoved him right out of the cab."

"Oh. Right."

"Into the path of another a truck," said Tony, distantly. "Smeared on the tarmac like a puddle of grease."

"Fuck," said Nick.

"Language, Nick."

"Shhh."

"You can shush me all you like. I know we're in a spot of bother but we need to keep standards up."

"No, no. *Shhh.*" He flapped his hand at his dad. "Think I can hear water."

Tony cocked an ear. "Might be a river over there on the left."

Pickles gave a sniff and a bark.

There were trees in the middle distance, but the low roar of water suggested whatever it was lay between their present position and the woods.

"If we hit a river it's going to stop us getting any further," said Nick.

"Or, to look on the bright side," said Tony, "at least we didn't crash down the mountainside, go straight into the river, and drown."

"Yes," said Nick. "That is a cheery thought indeed, dad."

"Yes, it is a river," said Tony, pointing. "I can see bulrushes over the tops of those shrubs. Just keep going steady for now."

"But it means we can't get away!"

"We'll get away. Just keep driving," said Tony.

A few minutes later the view to the left opened out. They could clearly see the rocky banks of the river. It was only about fifteen feet wide, but it was still a river.

"Look up ahead," said Tony. "There's a bridge."

There was: a high stone bridge which looked wide enough for a car. Nick approached it slowly (not that he had much choice in the clown-car Cadillac). It was broad enough for vehicles, but there were double gates and cattle grid barring the way. Nick read the sign on the gate and groaned.

"Kirkwood Farm. I don't believe it!" He banged the steering wheel in frustration.

"What's the matter?" asked Tony. "This is great, it means civilisation. Someone here can help us! Let's go and find whoever's in charge." He undid his seatbelt.

"Kirkwood is a client." Nick let out a deep sigh. "If we meet any of them, they'll probably chase me back the way I came with a pitchfork."

Tony got out of the car and approached the gates. They were constructed from welded steel and both were the size of a double bed. A padlocked chain held them shut. Tony weighed it in his hand and gave an experimental tug.

Nick glanced back along the track. "Maybe they did send a terminator back in time to kill me."

"What?" said Tony, coming back.

"I really messed up the job promoting their sausages."

"How do you mess up marketing sausage? A sausage is a sausage, surely?"

"That's sort of where the problems start," said Nick. "To stand out, a campaign needs to be bold. I was a bit too bold. Rude, if I'm honest. They didn't like it."

Tony climbed back in and shut his door. "It's a strange world you work in. I remember a time when you'd have a smiling father figure pluck a perfect sausage off the barbecue, and everyone knew those were the sausages to buy. Honest and straightforward."

Nick saw it in his mind's eye and had to concede it was better than his efforts. Certainly, if there was ever a sausage advert so bad it brought about the collapse of civilisation and forced future robots to travel back in time to kill its creator, his efforts were key candidates. It wasn't a sane or helpful thought.

"What I do know," he said, grasping for something useful to say, "is this is the site of Kirkwood's *old* operation. They moved their main production operation further south because this place gave them accessibility problems . Nobody's here full time anymore."

"Best ram the gate then," said Tony.

"We can't do that!" said Nick. "I haven't even got a bumper anymore."

"You've got one on the front, it was the back one we lost. We need to get across the river, and this is our only opportunity to do it. This place might be a bit inaccessible, but there's a good chance there's another track leading out of here. That's exactly what we want right now; so let's ram the gate."

Nick looked at the gate and weighed up the likely outcome of ramming it. Considering the state of his car, as long as they didn't end up in the river, their situation couldn't be any worse. He put the car into reverse so he could take a run up. That was a mistake. The car emitted a whole new set of tortured noises. For long moments something jammed before the car shot back.

"Here goes," he said. "Brace yourself, Pickles." He stuck it in first gear, held on tight and floored the accelerator, heading squarely at the gates. He threw in a long, loud yell in the illogical belief a warrior voice might add momentum. Tony joined in too, but perhaps that was because he hadn't had time to put his seatbelt on.

The gates groaned, buckled and folded. The car screamed. Metal ground against metal. And then they were through.

"Keep going. Keep going!" urged Tony. "Go! Go!"

Nick kept the accelerator floored. The engine revved, although ninety percent of its power was clearly going somewhere else, as their high speed getaway was little more than a geriatric stagger. Tendrils of steam rose from the radiator.

They followed the track up into the gloomy wood. Night was falling rapidly. With mountains to either side, the sun was completely gone from sight. In the woods, what little light remained was filtered by thickly-gathered fir trees. Nick automatically reached for the headlight switch.

Tony put a gently restraining hand on Nick's. "Let's not advertise our location, eh?"

Nick gave an unhappy sigh. How very practical of his dad, even in this situation, even in his dying weeks. Where did he get such amazing levels of dadness? That calm manner, the appearance he always knew what he was doing, even in moments of chaos and terror. Did they take men aside when their children were born and teach them all that stuff? Did they go to a secret Dad College where they learned to tell bad jokes, dance embarrassingly, and rewire plugs? Nick could have used some Dad College training because he never knew how to do any of that stuff. When disaster struck in his life, he just flapped and panicked, but not old Tony. Even in the darkest moments, he didn't panic. He just went into full-on dad mode.

"Hey, do you remember the time we broke mom's vase?" said Nick.

"Pardon?" said Tony, who was leaned forward and peering ahead.

"I said—"

"I'm sure I saw something moving."

Nick focused on the track ahead. Out of the corner of his eye he saw something move in the thick undergrowth. "Me too."

They both peered through the windscreen as the car crept forward.

"There!" shouted Tony, making Nick twitch the steering wheel in fright. The car veered towards a tree; Nick recovered it just in time. He looked to where his father was pointing and saw a horrific, bristled face peering from the bracken around the base of a pine tree.

"What the hell is that?" he gasped before realising he knew the answer. "Is it a wild boar?"

Tony chuckled. "It looks like a pig crossed with a toilet brush, so let's assume it is. There can't be too many of those around."

Two more stepped onto the path in front of the car, sniffing the air in curiosity. Nick decided to keep moving forward before they blocked his path. One of them snorted as they drove by.

"Kirkwood sausages are made from wild boar," said Nick. "I think these animals must belong to the farm."

"Explains the gate and the cattle grid," said Tony. "Good grief," he added in apparent delight, "they're everywhere!"

The boars were closing in from every direction. Nick's brain wasn't prepared to count them while he concentrated on keeping the car on the track, but there had to be at least twenty peering through the trees, or trotting along the track.

"Why are they all coming for us like this? They look as if they're getting ready to attack." He realised he was whispering. He wasn't sure why.

"I don't think they're aggressive," said Tony, "I think they're curious."

"Curious? Or hungry?"

"They're pigs. They're always hungry."

They approached a farmhouse with a number of outbuildings. There was no movement, no lights, and no sign of life. Some of the upper windows were boarded over.

"Keep going, keep going," said Tony. They crawled past, the car grumbling. The track began to climb again.

It became steeper, and more challenging for the wrecked Cadillac. The steam roiled from the radiator, unseen mechanical problems knocked and banged throughout the chassis. Nick ignored them all and pressed on, trying to coax gentle, steady progress out of the car by gently patting the steering wheel and singing under his breath.

"What was that?" Tony said.

"What was what?"

"It sounded like you just sang *Brave, beautiful Caddy* to the tune of *Food, Glorious Food*."

"No, no. Of course not. I was just counting the boars," said Nick.

"How many?"

"What?"

"How many boars?"

"I lost count." Nick wished his father would let him concentrate. Didn't he realise the car was on its last legs? They rounded a bend, the car grinding more and more slowly, when Nick saw the track was impassable up ahead.

"Damn," he said. He noticed Tony didn't reprimand him for his language this time. There was a huge piece of farm machinery in the road. It looked like a tractor crossed with a Moon buggy. Even if they could move the machine, there was a pile of logs on the other side. Whole tree trunks: stripped of branches and stacked in a triangle. Nick steered the car up to the machine, stopping crossways on the road so it didn't roll backwards.

"What is that thing?" asked Tony.

"Not sure. A tractory, movery sort of thing. Let's go and have a look."

A bristled snout appeared in Nick's lap through the open doorway. He screamed, batting the thing away. The boar backed off a few feet and wrinkled its nose at him. Pickles barked from the safety of the back seat.

"Those horns are freaking me out," said Nick. "It's sort of smiling, like Pumbaa in *The Lion King*."

"Who?"

"Pumbaa, isn't it? I mean it's smiling, but it's smiling *horribly*. Like it's about to make a kebab out of my innards."

Tony got out. "There's a wild boar in *The Lion King*?"

"Um. Yes?" said Nick. He wasn't so sure now he came to think about it.

"Tusks," said Tony.

"Yes, yes, I'm coming."

"No, I mean they're tusks, not horns," said Tony.

Nick slid out of his seat. When he stood he realised the gates from the bridge were on the roof of the car, still intact, still joined together by the chain.

"We carried them a distance, didn't we?" said Tony.

With the gates on top, the car looked like a battered, metallic butterfly, the gates its large silvery wings. Tony dragged them off, with little regard for what remained of the Cadillac's paintwork, dumping them by the side of the road.

Pickles jumped out of the car. Instead of barking at the suspicious boars to drive them off, she tried making friends with a protracted routine of sniffing and barking.

Nick looked at the vehicle blocking the road. It had chains on its wheels for traction in the mud of the forest and a long extending arm with a complicated-looking mechanism on the end of it.

THE MANITOBA DX HARVESTER read a plaque on the arm. "Some sort of tree-chopping-thingy?" wondered Nick.

"Could be," said Tony.

Nicked climbed up into the cab.

Finn had no difficulty following the path the car had taken, even as the light faded. There was a trail of flattened gorse bushes down the side of the mountain. Once she reached the bottom the ground was softer, so the tyre marks showed up clearly. Her broken arm was a nuisance, but Finn knew she was more than capable of finishing the mission before she worried about that.

The full Moon was visible above the woods ahead and her thoughts instantly turned to the instructions Adam had brought with him, which she now carried. They were clear and they were unambiguous.

When she'd been given the job, she had briefly wondered what Mr Argyll wanted with this Oz guy's heart. Mr Argyll was a powerful figure in organised crime, a man with connections and deals with drug lords, people traffickers, arms smugglers and terrorists of every flavour. He was also a legitimate businessman of no small order. He owned shops and hotels, car washes and nail salons on both sides of the Irish Sea. She heard he owned a private plane and two helicopters. The man was, in short, rich. If he needed a heart for a transplant then he would have been able to buy one. Tissue match or whatever, Finn was confident he could buy one from Africa or Asia, or wherever it was black market organs came from. He wouldn't need to send his top killer and a logistics nerd running around the UK after some scruffy guy in a damned Cadillac.

Oddly, with the new information gained from Adam's instructions, things made more sense, not less. Finn didn't need background information and extra motivation to get a job done; nonetheless it felt good to know the truth.

Of course, she still didn't know what Mr Argyll intended to do with the werewolf's heart once he got it.

Nick felt much safer in the logging vehicle's cab, above the boars circling with interest. Yeah, they looked all cute and cuddly – okay, not actually cuddly: cute and bristly – but he'd definitely seen a film in which a guy got eaten by wild boars. And he'd definitely heard in a film something about pigs being able to eat a man entirely in, like, ten minutes or something. Definitely pigs; not piranhas. He was certainly happier up in the cab.

"You coming to have a look, dad?" he called.

"I'll join you in a minute," shouted Tony from the car. "I want to have a look at that letter."

"What letter?"

Tony was not listening.

Nick scanned the controls in front of him. He'd never been inside a fighter plane cockpit, but he was willing to bet this thing was more complicated. Two computer screens were embedded in the dashboard, and the seat was flanked by joystick controls. An endless array of buttons covered *every* surface, including the joysticks. There were even buttons on the buttons. A big green one with *On/Off* seemed like an obvious one to try. He pressed it, just to see what would happen. He was shocked when the engine turned over with a shudder and burst into life. He gave one of the joysticks an experimental tweak: the boom in front swung across towards the pile of logs.

"Clear the logs. Drive on out," he whispered to himself.

He grabbed the other joystick: it moved the boom up and down. Nick also found a button for extending the boom arm. Maybe he could topple the pile of logs. He extended the arm as far as it would go, but the computer screen burst into life, flashing red and displaying the message AUTOMATIC CUT-OUT APPLIED. Nick sighed. He un-telescoped the boom and tried some other controls. He swung the boom into a tree, and—

"Dad! Look!"

The machine on the boom's tip clamped the tree and sawed through the trunk. One computer screen displayed a set of numbers. Nick lifted his hands away from the controls and watched in awe as the machine held an entire tree at the end of the boom.

"Wow," he murmured. It was like uprooting daisies with his fingers – using a giant robot arm instead of his fingers and a whole fir tree instead of daisy.

He wasn't entirely sure what to do next. He hesitated before trying another, smaller joystick. The entire vehicle surged forward, at something well below walking pace; probably just as well given the severed tree was still dangling from the end of the boom. Perhaps he and Tony could escape by cutting a new path through the forest. But it would take hours, and the light of day was effectively gone. He turned off the engine off and climbed down from the cab.

Tony was leaning over the roof of the car. "No good?"

"Not if we want to get through any time before dawn," said Nick. "I think we're going to have to walk round."

His dad gave him a look. "A walk? In the woods? At night in Scotland? Have you any idea what the night time temperatures are like in the Scottish Highlands?"

Nick gave the heaviest of sighs and recalled where they should have been by this time: at their little cabin on the Moray Firth. The mental image of their wonderful weekend away was more vivid and bright than the biggest HD TV in the world. The two of them, indulging in the finest hamper goodies, sipping Talisker like mature gentlemen; perhaps sat on the veranda in cosy deckchairs and looking out over the water. And, yes, in his vision, it might have been a cold night but there would have been a roaring fire. Not actually on the veranda – that wouldn't work – but in a chimenea, or the hearth inside. Or maybe even a fire pit which the two of them had dug with their manly hands or, failing that, Tony's folding trowel. Whatever, they should be having that perfect moment: two men at peace with the world and themselves; luxuriating in their perfect father-son relationship. Not stuck in a dark wood with a busted up car, no way out, a corpse in their boot, a hungry pack of boars circling them, and a psycho killer on their tail. It couldn't get much worse. There'd have to be rabid dogs or ... or zombies to make this situation worse.

"This letter," said Tony. He had a ragged sheet spread over the car roof.

"What letter?" asked Nick. He realised it was the screwed up bit of paper he'd picked up in Oz's house; the one the man in the toilets had shown such an interest in. "Is it important? I only took it to help start a fire."

"Listen. It's signed off by someone called Col. That woman mentioned someone called Col. Their *handler* or something."

"This is fascinating backstory, dad, but I think we ought to –"

"Listen, will you!" He focused on the letter. *"Dear Mr Bingley, I trust this letter finds you in good health. We've undertaken a review of the current arrangement. Our mutual employer remains grateful for the years of service you have offered, during which you have managed your condition to good effect. The comprehensive care package provided for your mother and the pension you have been given are tokens of that gratitude.*

"As you know, our employer needs to consider the issue of succession planning and has decided the time has come to recruit a suitable replacement. The new candidate will absorb your condition in the manner laid out in our discussion papers, and based on the materials your mother was kind enough to provide for us. A team will be visiting you shortly to collect the necessary materials. Your full co-operation would be appreciated, as our employer is keen that the transition should be managed smoothly." Tony passed the letter back to Nick. "Signed *Col.*"

Nick read the words himself. Nope. They still didn't make any sense.

"What do you make of it?" he asked eventually.

Tony shook his head. "I have no idea what Oz did for them. I'm guessing it wasn't good. The only thing we can really take from this is the *necessary materials* mentioned refers to Oz's heart. That's what the guy said when I ... when I stabbed him."

"You're kidding me, right?"

"There was an old woman living in that house. That would be Oz's mom. The way I read it, her care was being paid for by this *mutual employer* chap. Sounds awfully like a euphemism for a crime lord – you know: some kingpin."

"No one uses that phrase anymore, dad."

"Point is, there was a price to be paid. And it sounds to me like it was Oz's heart. From what you've told me about how you found him, it seems like he didn't want them to have it."

"Oh, wow!" Nick suddenly got it. "He threw himself on top of his entire toolkit to mess up his internal organs?"

"Worked, didn't it?"

"God, yeah," said Nick.

"These tablets must be related to the condition mentioned," said Tony, holding up the bottle. "*Argentum nitricum*. I never heard of it."

Nick pulled out his phone. "Not a great signal, but let's try a quick search." He waited long seconds for the browser to return results. "Huh. It's homeopathic silver nitrate. Used for gastric problems."

"Is homeopathy the one that's a loads of codswallop?"

"Now, don't be intolerant, dad. People put a lot of faith in homeopathy."

"People put a lot of faith in the government. Doesn't mean it's going to do them any good. I'm a rational fellow and no one's going to tell me medicine that's been diluted ten thousand times until there's nothing there but water actually works. It's up there with God, the Easter bunny and horoscopes."

"Oz obviously thought it worked," said Nick.

"Yeah. Look, we're clearly tangled up in something nasty that we don't really understand. Why don't we use your phone to call the police? We'll just have to come clean about the body in the boot."

"And the guy you stabbed in the service station," added Nick. He couldn't imagine the conversation going well. One dead body might be explained away, two looked extremely careless.

"What if there's another way?" said Tony slowly.

"Go on."

He pointed at the letter. "We've got Col's phone number there."

"We give that to the police?"

"No. What if we call him? Tell him where Oz is and ask him to call off his crazy killer woman."

Nick considered. "I mean, it couldn't make things worse, could it? They're already on our tail. We're just putting them straight on some issues."

"Exactly."

Nick dialled the number and put it on loudspeaker.

"Hello?" came an Irish accent.

"Ah, hello," said Nick, feeling the peculiar urge to drop into a cod Irish accent himself. He quashed the urged and focused on sounding as English as possible. "You don't know me, but—"

"Who is this?"

"Yes. You don't know me, but I think perhaps you've got some people chasing me because they think I'm Oz Bingley."

There was a brief pause. *"Continue,"* said the voice.

"Do you know who Oz is? Am I talking to the right person?"

There was another pause. *"I said, continue."*

"Well, what you probably don't know is: Oz is dead. I think he killed himself."

"Where's the body?"

"I have it here," said Nick. "With me."

"Where are you?"

"Well, that's the thing. I wanted to do a sort of trade." He scrunched up his face. "No – not a trade. We really don't want anything. Just to be on our way."

"We?"

"My dad and me. We're just on holiday. Well, a weekend break. But this body..."

"You have the body of Oz Bingley."

"Yes, indeed, and I'd be very happy to make it available to you. But could you please get those people to stop chasing me? You know: the woman?"

There was a pause, a long pause. Nick swiped his phone screen to check the call was still in progress and hadn't been cut off.

"Let me have your co-ordinates," the voice said eventually.

"Co-ordinates? Well, we're by the old Kirkwood sausage farm in Dalwhinnie—"

"Sausage farm? Are you pulling my feckin leg now?"

"No, no, not at all, sir. There's this farm in the wood and—"

"Co-ordinates."

"I don't have the co-ordinates. I don't have a map."

"Don't you have a smartphone? You'll be able to find your GPS co-ordinates."

Nick took a few moments to locate the right screen. He relayed the co-ordinates to Col. "Is that okay?"

"Sure," said Col. *"By the way, how did you get this number?"*

"It was on a letter Oz had," said Nick. Tony caught his eye, shaking his head and making cutting motions across his throat.

"Okay so. I'll sort everything. Don't you worry now."

"So, we're free to go when we—"

"My men will meet you at the ... sausage farm."

"Right, right, but then we're good after that? We can—"

There was click on the line and the call ended.

41

Finn maintained a steady jog alongside a river she could hear beyond a screen of trees. Her shoulder ached, tensed from holding her broken arm in place. Adam's phone vibrated in her pocket. She slowed to a walk and fished it out with her good arm. It was Col.

"Yes?"

"Finn, it's Col."

"Yes."

"I was hoping to speak with Adam."

Finn made no reply. It hadn't been a question.

"Is he there?" he asked.

"No, he's dead."

"Did you...?"

"No. There was a vehicle crash and he wasn't wearing his seatbelt."

"Jaysus. Where now?"

"In a wood. No witnesses. We're in the countryside, near a place called Dalwhinnie. I'm still tracking the target."

"Which brings me neatly to my question. How did you and Adam identify the target you're following?"

"Adam talked to the guy. Said he confirmed who he was and showed him some ID. We were having doubts before that."

"For good reason, it seems. That's not Oz you're following."

"What?"

"Oz is dead."

"Oh. Interesting," said Finn. "So, I have a question for you. Now he's dead, can you confirm Oz – codename Lupo – was a werewolf?"

"What?"

"You heard me."

"That information was not supposed to be shared with you," said Col slowly.

"Not an answer."

"No, it's not." Col fell silent a moment. *"The guy who phoned me – some gobshite called Nick who said you were chasing him – is holed up in a local farmhouse. He said he's got Oz's body. I told him I'm sending my men to collect the body, then let them go free."*

"Are we?"

"Sure, and why would we? I want you to locate these people and kill them."

"And the body?"

"Do nothing with it. This whole operation is a mess already. I'm coming to collect within the hour."

"You're nearby?"

"Nope, but we will be soon enough."

42

The car was back at the farmhouse. It hadn't so been much driven there as rolled back down the slope. It appeared to be terminally damaged, and listed at a strange angle. Remarkably, they hadn't hit any boars on the way down, in spite of them milling around in even greater numbers. Pickles ran about, yipping in excitement and dodging the wild pigs; although they seemed nervous of her. Nick discovered it was impossible to keep them all in sight. Once he was out of the car, he sidled away from those he could see; only to find others bumping the back of his knees. Nick squealed.

"You don't have to join in with the noises," said Tony.

"I wasn't."

"That woman will be here soon. We don't need to make it any easier for her to find us."

"Col said he was going to call her off."

Tony made a unconvinced noise. "I think we need to consider the possibility Col was being economical with the truth. A night-time walk through the woods is looking more and more attractive. Perhaps we should hijack that log-cutter machine."

"It was slower than a mobility scooter."

"So you will be after two hours of night-hiking. Now, let's get this body." He popped the boot.

"*Fagh!*" He wafted the smell from his nose. The dank and meaty smell, not quite rotten, but certainly not enticing to human nostrils drew the boars and the dog closer. "Let's get this over with."

"Do we need to move it?" said Nick.

"They want the body. They don't want your car. This vehicle is either coming with us, or needs disposing of."

"Disposing of?" Nick's voice rose with emotion. "You don't mean...?"

"It's just a bloody car, Nick. Now grab a hold. I'll let you choose which end."

Nick took the feet. Tony gabbed Oz by the shoulders. It was so much easier lifting Oz with two people, although Nick was certain the body had deteriorated considerably in the hours since he last saw it. The blood had dried and crusted around the wounds: they had to peel the body off the carpet.

"Oh wow," muttered Tony when the full extent of Oz's self-inflicted injuries became clear. "Power tools you say?"

"Mmmm," nodded Nick, not wanting to dwell on it.

Tony tutted. "This would not be covered under the manufacturer's guarantee."

"I don't think he was planning on taking his Bosch power drill or the scraping little buffing thing—"

"Dremel."

"—back to the shop. He really meant to do himself some harm. Best not to look, eh?"

Tony grunted in agreement. "Over there. In that outbuilding."

They staggered along a path littered in leaf-mould towards the low, functional looking building attached to the side of the house. Nick guessed with a spot of loving care and the cleansing light of day, the woodland farmhouse would look quite charming. Sadly, in the deepening dusk, with nothing but cobwebs and shadows at the windows, it looked like the setting for a cannibal hillbilly horror movie.

"You're sure this place is empty?" said Nick.

"I think someone might already have been out to greet us if it wasn't," said Tony. "It's not like we're popping round with a little housewarming gift, is it?"

Pickles jumped up and clamped her jaws around Oz's exposed ankle, forcing them to put the body down for a moment and detach the dog.

"Bad dog, Pickles!" said Nick, shooing her away.

As Pickles ran ahead to explore the outhouse, Nick realised they had another problem. One of the boars had been bold enough to step forward and investigate Oz's exposed organs. Now it was buried, snout deep, inside the corpse.

"No! Stop it! Surely boars are supposed to be vegetarians?"

"Omnivores, I think," said Tony.

"We can't let them get a taste for human flesh!"

"A taste? It's just having a snuffle."

"They'll turn on us. There's hundreds of them. Look!" Boars flanked them on every side, sniffing the air.

Tony rolled his eyes. "Come on, Nick. Bit of focus, please."

They hefted Oz up again, dislodging the boar. They continued the slow journey to the outbuilding, turning Oz around to go feet first as they approached the mildew covered door.

"I think I can get the latch with—" Nick waggled his elbow. The latch was rusty; the first try scraped his elbow. He let out a brief whimper. His stomach lurched as he saw blood drip from his elbow to the concrete apron in front of the door. "I'll probably get tetanus now!"

"This body is quite heavy," remarked Tony.

"I know, dad."

"Some of us aren't as young as we used to be."

Nick lifted the latch on the second attempt. The door swung open. They carried the body indoors. It was some sort of preparation area: with stainless steel counters and large chest freezers. Large hooks hung from the ceiling and industrial catering machines hulked in the corner like dead robots. Tony nodded to the far side of the room and they managed to lift Oz onto a counter, so the boars wouldn't be able to reach him. Happily, the boars didn't seem all that keen on crossing the threshold.

"It's an abattoir," said Nick.

"Hardly," said Tony. "A processing room of some sort. Their killing shed will be somewhere else."

"Whatever. I'm not sure this is the kind of place I want to be hanging around if there's a killer in the woods."

Tony chuckled without humour. "Hardly five star weekend accommodation."

Nick located a light switch, surprised when it worked. Kirkwood had clearly not moved out completely. It smelled a little musty but was otherwise wipe-down clean and ready for work. He looked at the rack of meat cleavers and other blades hanging on a far wall. The butchery tools sparked a worried thought.

"Dad."

"Hmm?"

"This business all seems to be about Oz's heart, yeah?"

"Right."

"Well, some parts fell out back in Birmingham."

"Fell out?"

"I'm not sure which. What if he hasn't got his heart? What if they get really mad and come after us?"

Tony sighed. "They're probably going to do that anyway. We need to cover our tracks and get out of here. Let's have a quick look and see if we can tell what's missing."

To Nick's horror, Tony approached the counter and dug his hands into Oz's abdominal cavity like a ghoulish lucky dip.

"What are you doing?" he hissed.

Tony nodded downward. "Looking."

"You didn't even put any gloves on!"

"Did I need to?"

Nick liked to pretend he didn't get squeamish easily. Even if it wasn't true, he'd been more than a little intimate with a corpse that morning: manhandling it into his boot. However, the sight of his dad having a merry shufti around Oz's innards turned his stomach. "But what about infection?" he said.

"I don't think Oz here is worried about catching anything. And I'm not going to catch anything from Oz as long as I wash my hands after." He pushed chunks of Oz-meat out of the way like an open-the-flap book for serial killers. "I think that thing there is a kidney, from the position and shape, yes?"

"Oh, Christ. We're doing *Guess the Organ* now?"

"Is it a kidney or not?"

Nick nodded. "I suppose."

"The big thing here must be the liver. Look at the colour of it, and there are teeth marks. Would it be fair to say Pickles had a hand in this?"

Not a hand, no, Nick thought. He really didn't want to barf in front of his dad. He tried hard to concentrate on something other than the grisly *Show And Tell* his dad was performing.

"If we look higher up, there's some damage, but the ribs have stopped it going too deep. See, these white bones? I think that's the heart behind them. Yes, look! It's very like a lamb's heart. Used to get those in the butchers, probably still can if you go to the right places. Your mother would know. It's not too badly damaged, apart from this blade stuck in there. We'll leave it where it is, I think. Nice blade too. Criminal waste."

"Of a life or a blade?" asked Nick.

Tony withdrew his hands. "And *now*, I wash my hands, see?"

He went to a sluicing sink and turned on the water. The nozzle sputtered before a powerful spray came out.

Nick breathed a sigh of relief. "I'm just going to get some essentials out of the car. If the boars try to eat me, I'll let you know. You know: *Oh no, dad, the boars are eating me. I told you they'd developed a taste for human flesh.*"

"Sarcasm, son."

"Well spotted, dad."

"If you're worried, you might want to distract them. Give them something to eat."

Nick stopped in his tracks. Was his father actually suggesting they should pull out some of Oz's spare organs to entice the boars away? How far would one person's innards actually go? Then he realised his father was pointing into the corner of the room at a sack labelled *FINEST QUALITY PIG PELLETS*.

"Oh. Yes," said Nick. "Great idea."

He tried lifting the sack but it was heavier than it looked, and he spilled a large pile on the floor. Instead, he filled his cupped hands with pellets and went outside to scatter them, well away from his car. He was disturbed to find one of the boars lapping at the tiny puddle of blood from his scraped elbow. He shooed it away, more convinced than ever these were man-eaters who were just biding their time.

He retrieved his bag from the car and contemplated what else to take. He had quite a few useful things in here. The first aid kit could be handy, especially for his grazed elbow. He didn't have a great many tools, but there were cans of WD40 and tyre foam. Which one would be most useful? He couldn't decide so he tucked them both under his arm.

"Pickles!" Indoors, Tony was trying to catch the dog. He stepped outside. "Damn dog, it's way too excited with all of the boars and whatever else is out in the woods. She's run off somewhere." He approached the car. "You ready to go yet? What's this?"

Nick juggled the items he'd taken from the car. "If we really have to destroy my car, there are things don't need to go up in flames."

"You know you can get more WD40 when we get out of here? We need to take the bare essentials and travel light."

"Right you are. I'll just grab the whisky," said Nick.

"Not an essential."

"Ah, but we could always use it to start a fire; or as a Molotov cocktail."

"Interesting fact. Whisky as an accelerant is ineffectual, unless you heat it first. In a Molotov cocktail it almost certainly won't work."

Nick looked at the bottle and sighed. It had caused him so much grief to get hold of it, he felt it still had a part to play. Plans. All his weekend plans had come to nothing, spectacularly so.

"Right, I'm done," he said, resigned. "Will the car explode if we, um, take off the petrol cap and put a lit rag in there?"

"I'm sure we can do better," said Tony. "Check out that plastic hopper trailer round there. I think it's red diesel."

They went to the trailer at the corner of the building. It was covered in several months' worth of forest crud, and weeds grew thickly around its wheels, but there was definitely some liquid inside it. Tony experimented briefly with the valve tap mechanism. He sniffed and nodded.

"Red diesel, or something like it. That'll do."

"Need containers," said Nick. "Maybe there are some in the abattoir place."

"It's not an abattoir."

"Whatever. There were fridges at the back and a walk-in freezer. Bet there's some tubs or something."

"Let's be quick about it. That woman can't be more than half an hour behind. If she saw which direction we went, she's bound to come here."

"And a burning car – a burning classic car – would totally pinpoint our location," sniffed Nick.

"We'll be well on our way by then."

Tony led the way back into the meat prep building, scanning the room. Oz, laid out on the container, looked surprisingly at peace. For an instant, Nick was jealous. Tony headed over to the large freezers at the back. Nick looked up at a shelf.

"Will creosote burn?" asked Nick, pulling down a tin.

142

"Creosote?"

At that moment they both heard a noise from outside. There were enough boars to account for any amount of random noise, but this was a very deliberate sound: like a stick dragged across railings. They looked to the door, knowing someone was outside.

"Hide," whispered Tony.

43

By the electric light spilling from the doorway and the glimmer of the Moon above, Finn could see a trail of blood from the car to the outbuilding. Her future victims were inside. She dragged the trowel taped to the end of her splinted arm across the rough, cracked plaster on the outside of the building, knowing they were already spooked. She smiled in the certain knowledge they would be a damned sight more by the time she'd finished.

Finn entered the outbuilding and saw the body on the counter. It was utterly mutilated. It looked like they had tried to have sex with a woodchipper. Had her two targets done this? She would ask them once they were under control.

"Oh my," she said in a loud, pantomime voice. "Where could the naughty boys be hiding?"

There were various fridges and hulking pieces of machinery in the room. Plenty of nooks and crannies to hide in. There was also what looked like a walk-in freezer. The door was open a crack. A stupid place to hide, but people were idiots at heart.

She moved forward, trowel arm at the ready, preparing to draw the silver werewolf blade Adam had given her if needed.

The old guy, Tony, stepped out from between two fridges, a meat cleaver held in both hands. "We were expecting you," he told her.

"Are you sure?" she said.

"Col told us you were coming."

"Knowing something and being prepared are two different things. It's Tony, right?"

Tony nodded warily. He pointed at the body with his cleaver. "There's Oz. That's what you came for."

Unconcerned by an old man with a blade which was too big for him, Finn looked at the corpse on the counter again. She was familiar with death, she'd seen a lot of bodies, but she was more experienced with the transitional phase: the moment between life and death, and the immediate aftermath. It was rare for her to look at a body which had given up its ghost some time ago and had time to settle; to lose any semblance of life. This thing was a riot of dried blood and sallow flesh. Beautiful in its own way; perhaps doubly so

144

in the Moonlight angling through the window above. What it didn't look like was a werewolf.

"Where's the other one?" she said.

"What?" said Tony.

"Your son. The dreamer."

"Does it matter? There's your body. You can let us go now. We were going to torch the car, destroy the evidence and then just be on our way. It would be like we were never here."

She gave him a frank look. "They say when death is approaching, when you're about to die, all illusions are stripped away and you see life as it really is."

"Do they?"

She nodded. "You're dying. Honestly, do you think you're going to walk away from this?"

Tony nervously adjusted his grip on the cleaver. "You want to know what I think? I'm thinking why has this woman taped my folding trowel to her hand?"

44

Despite his terror, Nick was thinking the same thing. Wedged into the space between some sort of industrial mincing machine and a storage unit, he watched her enter and thought this really was a terminator brought to life. She was silver from elbow to wrist with a shining blade on the end. It had taken him several terrified seconds to realise the silver was duct-tape and the blade his dad's folding trowel. It genuinely defied explanation.

The tone of her conversation with Tony was alarming from the outset. Dad had been right. She wasn't going to let them leave and, in a straight fight, cleaver-dad had little chance against trowel-lady. Nick needed to act. He knew that. But what did he have? There were no weapons within his easy reach. There was the first aid kit and the tyre foam kit on the nearby counter; neither were weapons. In his hand he still held the can of creosote. WOOD TREATMENT. PROTECTS EXTERIOR WOOD AGAINST ROT AND DAMP. DOES EXACTLY WHAT IT SAYS ON THE TIN. What it didn't say was if it could be used against homicidal woman with trowel hands. But it was heavy. Enough to stun someone. There were two of the Carver boys and only one of her...

He leapt into action before he could change his mind. He ran at her swinging and yelling. The yell was a mistake. It just advertised his presence a full second before he got to her.

The woman turned, almost lazily. Nick swung the tin at her, and she easily side-stepped. Barely needed to move. Tony gave her a shove and raised his cleaver to strike. Nick wanted to strike back, but his hand was still being carried by the momentum of the heavy can's initial swing. The woman whirled on Tony. With a cinematic metal-on-metal *ching!* she knocked the cleaver from Tony's grasp with her trowel hand, punching him in the face with her fist. Tony staggered back.

"No!" yelled Nick. He swung the tin in a return arc.

The woman spun, ready to disarm and probably disembowel Nick. What she probably wasn't ready for was being coated in pungent chemicals. The lid came off the creosote and it emptied across her chest and face, slapping around her hand in a sticky dark tidal wave of wood preservative. As she stepped back in surprise, it ran down her body, front and back.

Her eyes slitted open against the acrid chemicals, just in time to see Nick swinging the empty tin towards her face. Her nose made a horribly and wonderfully satisfying crunch as he whacked her one. Her feet skidded from beneath her. She fell onto the open sack of FINEST QUALITY PIG PELLETS. The bag of rich and meaty animal food exploded beneath her, throwing pellets and dust into the air. Despite her nearly useless tape-and-trowel arm, the woman rolled and folded and sprang to her feet. There was suddenly a knife in her left hand, her good hand.

She stepped forward and with casual ease, sticking the tip of the blade into Nick's shoulder. It was almost gentle: like she was testing a joint of meat to see if it was cooked. But – by fuck! – it hurt. Nick cried out and dropped his empty tin. She backed off, getting both Nick and Tony in her arc of vision. Tony was holding his nose, eyes woozy.

The woman dragged a sleeve across her eyes. Her biker leathers and jeans were coated in the sticky creosote, and she'd picked up a crusty coating of boar feed. Brown and knobbly. She looked like she was going to a fancy dress party as a Ferrero Rocher. A terminator dressed as a Ferrero Rocher. As images went it was confused at best, but this world of corpses and criminals was new to Nick, so what did he know?

"Enough of this!" she roared, swinging her blade between them. "Sit!"

"Sit?" said Tony.

"*Sit!*"

They sat obediently, backs against the chest freezer. Fear gripped Nick. He just knew he was going to do exactly what he was told. The woman pulled cable ties from an inside pocket and held them in front of Tony.

"You. Put this around his wrists and pull tight. Do it properly, I'm watching."

Tony tied the wrists of his son.

"Now, you do his."

Nick fumbled with his bound hands.

"Ow, that's tight," hissed Tony.

"She said to do it properly," Nick hissed back.

Satisfied, the woman put the knife down and trussed their ankles with more cable ties. "If either of you try anything..." she began.

"We really won't," said Nick.

She looked around, spotted the sluicing sink, and spent some time trying to wash the creosote from her hands and face. When she was done she had mostly succeeded but the brown gloop still covered her head and upper body. It was like a weird inverse of someone blacking up.

She regarded her jacket and sighed. "Do you know how much this Muubaa cost me?"

"Moo baa?" frowned Tony.

"The jacket," said Nick. "It's designer gear. And it looks really good on you too, miss," he added loudly.

"Ruined," she said.

"And goes well with those boots. Jimmy Choo?"

"Moncler."

"Of course."

"How do you know this stuff?" asked Tony.

"It does no harm to show an interest in quality designer clothing, dad."

The woman unzipped a pocket, trying to avoid the sticky stuff, and pulled out a Polaroid camera. The case was seriously cracked. The woman juggled it in her good hand and came in close to take a photo of Nick. He gave her his best smile although he wasn't sure why. The flash made shapes pinwheel across his vision.

"Name?" she demanded.

"What?" said Nick.

"It's Nick," said Tony.

She wrote on Nick's picture with a marker pen. "So this is the boy who has an idealised view of the world? The one who organised this *special* weekend for you?"

Nick frowned and looked at his dad. "What have you been telling her?"

"Plenty," said the woman. "He knows that this weekend is a half-arsed attempt to patch up – what? – thirty-odd years of a poor to non-existent father-son relationship."

"That's not true!" said Tony.

"Too right," said Nick. "There was nothing half-arsed about my plans for this weekend."

"Over-arsed if anything," said Tony.

"At least I'm trying," snapped Nick.

"You are that, my son."

The woman smiled. "Anyway, I'm Finn, your executioner. You should probably be grateful to me," she said to Tony. "I'm saving you from a tedious weekend with your useless offspring here and, better still, I am going to kill you quickly. Which has got to be better than waiting for the cancer to take you in slow and painful increments. You know what—" she said with sudden enthusiasm, "—we could give you a little eco funeral out here. You'd like, wouldn't you, Tony?"

"He doesn't know what he wants," said Nick. "He's never willing to discuss his funeral."

Tony sniffed. "Why should it bother me? I'm going to be dead, son. You can do what you like with me – I won't know and won't care – just roll me into a hole and bury me."

"There you go," said Finn. "Deal."

"Can I just point out we don't need to die at all," said Nick. He cleared his throat and looked at his dad. "I meant, like, not now. I haven't forgotten you're ... I was just saying—" He turned to Finn. "You can deliver Oz and his heart to your boss and let us go. There's been a simple case of mistaken identity."

Finn wandered over to the body. "You know these people believe in werewolves?"

"Who?" said Tony.

"The people who want his heart."

"And are they mad?"

Finn shrugged.

Nick was confused. "You mean werewolf as in werewolf? Not...?"

"Not what?" said Tony.

"Not like ... into animal spirits and wearing T-shirts with wolves on and listening to too much Celtic folk music."

"Hippies," said Tony.

"Gangsters," said Finn.

"We're talking about actual werewolves?" said Tony.

Finn took a damp and crumpled sheet out of her pocket. It was slimed with blood, blue chemicals, and now creosote. "The reason they want this guy's heart is because eating it is supposed to make you a werewolf. According to Ma Bingley's instructions."

"Can I just check," said Nick, "none of this has anything to do with the marketing campaign for Kirkwood sausages?"

"No." She looked at him like he was an idiot (which was rather unfair since she was the one talking about werewolves.) "Did you think this was about sausages?"

"No," said Nick, "but it's nice to have it confirmed."

"You know werewolves don't exist, don't you?" asked Tony.

Finn shrugged. "That's what I thought, but the people who are *paying* me believe they exist, and that's the main thing." She looked into the dead man's chest cavity and pulled out a few bits of remaining material, including a jigsaw blade, a drill bit and a small but expensive-looking knife, more ornamental than a tool.

Finn weighed the knife in her hand. "Silver. Seems Oz believed it too. I guess he believed it enough to lock himself in a cage, last place he lived."

"The silver homeopathy tablets," murmured Tony.

Nick was thinking about the extra dog basket back at Oz's mom's place. The bars on the windows. It was the sort of practical detail you'd need in your life if you believed in werewolves. If you believed *you* were a werewolf and needed locking in once in every blue Moon. Not blue Moon, he told himself; full Moon. He idly wondered how large a demographic werewolves represented. It would be a terrible thing to die on the cusp of discovering an untapped market. It would be a terrible thing to die anyway.

Finn leaned over the body and took a Polaroid picture. In the camera flash, the body seemed to twitch. Nick suspected it was a trick of the light. Or he suspected it wasn't a trick of the light, and hoped it was.

"That silver knife," he said.

Finn looked at him, picked up the blade and effortlessly balanced it on the end of her finger. "Yes?"

"Did you perhaps take it from his heart?"

"Does it matter?"

Nick made a faint, lightly panicked noise. "You see, as a marketing guy, I know all about the customer's journey. I know narratives."

"Are we going back to the sausage thing?" muttered Tony.

"No, it's more about me knowing what should happen in certain situations. The narrative flow."

"Tony, if it's all the same to you, I'm going to kill your son first," said Finn.

"And if there's a werewolf – *if* there's a werewolf – with a silver blade in its heart, and someone takes it out..."

"For the last time," said Tony, "there's no such thing as—"

There was a loud growling noise from the thing on the counter.

"Fuck!" said Finn.

"Language!" said Tony. "It's just the body settling, expelling gases and— *Fuck!*"

On the counter, Oz sat up.

"Put it back! The knife! Put it back!" squealed Nick.

Oz's eyes opened. Yellow animal eyes turned on Nick.

"Or not," whimpered Nick.

Something was happening to the gaping holes gouged into Oz's chest. They were sealing up. Tissue fibres re-weaved themselves together. It was like watching a time lapse video of an autopsy in reverse. Blood flaked away. Loops of intestine and blobs of organs slipped back into position and waited for the skin and tissue pixies to come by and make good the surface layer.

"Hair!" yelled Tony, transfixed.

He wasn't wrong. There was suddenly more hair. A lot more.

A hideous change rippled across Oz. Limbs noisily elongated, flinging his shoes away and making dog pads of his toes. He opened his mouth and ran a tongue across his new, terrifying fangs.

"Wolf!" yelled Tony.

"Fucking werewolf," breathed Nick.

Oz's throat vibrated with a beastly growl. He slipped onto the floor, two feet taller than he had been as a man. While much of Nick's mind was flailing around in madness and terror, an unnecessarily analytic part of it was trying to comprehend what he was seeing. It had a wolf's head but not precisely a wolf's head. It had an elongated snout and the ears had shifted round and up and the teeth... Oh, God, the teeth. That jaw was massive. It looked like it could swallow Nick whole. He was prey and it was a predator – *the* predator – and those off-white fangs... Nick knew, just knew, those teeth would soon be coming for him, tearing into his flesh.

The Oz-wolf roared at them all. Nick couldn't be sure, but Oz had to be raging against the undignified manhandling his corpse had received. If he had super powers as a werewolf, that would surely include an enhanced sense of smell. It wouldn't take him long before he tracked the shitty smears on his shirt to Nick, who was working hard not to fill his pants again. He knew he was in big trouble. They were all in big trouble, but Oz had particular reason to be angry at Nick.

Pickles ran in through the open door. Nick had hoped the dog was somewhere far away from harm. He'd even entertained a brief hope she might turn out to be a wonder dog who would run across the countryside and get help from strangers. No, she had to back and most likely to get killed alongside the rest of them. Pickles yapped up at Oz in excitement. Did she recognise her former master, or did she just see a massive dog standing on its hind legs?

The Oz-wolf was distracted for a moment. Finn took the opportunity to lunge at it with the blade so recently removed from its heart. She grazed its chest, but the knife didn't find its target. Oz spun out of the blade's path and came back at her with a claw-fisted punch which knocked the knife from her hand and sent her flying against another counter.

Pickles barked and danced around. Something exciting was clearly going on but Pickles couldn't work out what, so she did the dog thing of jumping about and making noise. A small group of boars had entered the building too. Whether they were drawn by the noise or the smells was uncertain. Whatever, they were entirely unfazed by the werewolf and several seemed much more interested in the food pellets glued all over Finn's body.

The Oz-wolf, surrounded an excited dog, milling boars and three mostly prone humans, roared his dominance. In that instant, Nick realised he had been totally cured of his fear of boars. All it took was the appearance of a fucking werewolf to terrify him so thoroughly there was no room for fear of anything else.

Finn rolled, punched a nosy boar on the snout and got to her feet.

"They weren't lying then," she said. She dug inside her jacket and pulled out a sheathed knife. With a wrist flick she cast off the sheath to reveal a long, surgery-sharp knife.

The Oz-wolf clearly recognised the blade for what it was, and growled angrily.

"Knife," whispered Tony.

"I can see it's a knife," Nick whispered back.

"No. Knife!" He pointed with his bound hands at the one Finn had dropped.

Nick was closest to it. He tried an experimental roll sideways.

"Who do you think they had picked out as your successor?" Finn said to the beast. "Think it might be me?"

The Oz-wolf had no witty comebacks apart from snarls. Finn beckoned it closer, trowel and knife ready for it.

Nick writhed across the floor towards the dropped blade, well aware he was not being subtle. A boar leg appeared by his face and he bit it without a second thought. The boar moved, but another replaced in moments later. Nick registered Oz leaping down on top of Finn but pressed forward in his mission to get the knife. The growling, grunting and barking reached a crescendo as Oz raked powerful claws across Finn's chest.

She screamed, crashing down on the floor between Nick and the knife. She snorted in pain, spraying bubbles of blood from her crushed nose. For a man with less mobility than a slug, Nick managed to spring back out of the way very quickly. He glanced back at Tony. Somehow his father had his wrists free and was making his way over to help.

Tony held up a piece of jagged plastic. "I think she broke her camera."

As Tony sawed through the cable tie holding Nick's wrists, the Oz-wolf dragged Finn upright. She pummelled the beast with a one-two: knife then trowel. The werewolf recoiled for a moment only, lunging forward and clamping its jaws over the woman's arm.

"That jacket will definitely be ruined now," Nick heard someone say. He realised it was him.

"This way," said Tony. Nick let himself be pulled backward, feet still bound together. Nick snatched at precious items as he was pulled through a door. They were in the walk-in freezer, a windowless cubicle of a room. Tony grabbed a metal hook off an overhead bar and jammed it into the latch mechanism. "That should hold it."

Outside, Finn bellowed. Nick was very much a live and let live kind of guy. He liked to think one of the reasons he worked in marketing and advertising was because he was always ready to see things from the other person's perspective. People, on all sides of any conflict, had their own personal motivations, and no one viewpoint was anymore valid than another. People were just people. No one was good or bad; it was all just different flavours of humanity. That said, if someone was going to be ripped apart by a vicious seven foot werewolf, he couldn't think of anyone more deserving than the trowel-handed and creosote-dipped killer, Finn.

He let out a ragged sigh. Just for a moment he could fool himself they were safe. He might have a little cry in a bit though. He could feel it coming on.

"How are you holding up, son?" asked Tony.

Nick let out another long sigh. Turns out he had a lot of sigh in him. "All things considered... You?"

"Yeah fine. Apart from the fact we're trapped in here while a hired killer and a werewolf slug it out before they kill us."

"Yeah. Things got a bit weird, didn't they?" said Nick.

"I don't think *a bit weird* quite covers it."

Nick laughed, which was better than crying. He shuffled around and found a box to sit on. "How did a simple trip to Scotland get so messed up?"

"Do you really want to analyse that now?" said Tony and knelt to saw through the cable ties around Nick's ankles.

"So this is my fault, is it?" said Nick. Just because he was almost certainly going to die didn't stop him being instantly defensive.

"I don't know anyone else who would have made some of the choices you've made," said Tony.

"Oh, you really *do* think it's my fault!"

"It's not a straightforward right or wrong thing. You come up with choices that nobody else would even dream of. What have you even got there?"

Nick looked at the *precious items* he had grabbed before hiding in the walk-in freezer. He had the first aid box, the tyre foam kit and the bottle of Talisker whisky.

"I had to think on my feet," said Nick.

"Any kind of thinking would have been good," said Tony.

"You just don't appreciate that I think outside the box a bit."

"And where has thinking outside the box got us. Maybe the box is there for a reason, did you ever think of that?"

Nick tried to respond, but wasn't sure how. Somehow the box analogy had got out of hand. He put his hands on the door. It was cold but not sub-zero; the freezer wasn't turned on. He pressed his ear to the door to listen.

"Hear anything?" said Tony.

"I think they're done," said Nick. "Or they've moved on." He listened longer. There was no point rushing back into the fray. "You know, there's a reason I am how I am. A dreamer. I can't do the things you do."

"What things?" said Tony.

"Stuff. Repair a toilet cistern. Put up shelves. Talk to blokes in pubs. I can't do the things you do, or think about things the way you do. You never showed me how."

"What?" Tony made a noise halfway between amusement and outrage. "Are you saying I was a bad father?"

"I was just—"

"No, this is great timing, son. Take your dying father on a weekend away and..." The words died apoplectically in his throat. "You know, I always made sure you had everything you needed."

"I'm not saying you were a bad father."

"Really? That's not what I heard."

"It's just, you were never around. You worked hard, I know that," he added quickly. "Maybe you worked a bit too hard. I wouldn't have minded not having stuff, sometimes, if, you'd ... you know?"

"No. What?"

"If you could have been round more. We could have done stuff."

Tony made an exasperated noise and stalked away as far as the walk-in freezer would allow; which was wasn't far enough so Tony did some angry little laps.

"What stuff?" he demanded eventually.

"What stuff?" said Nick.

"Yes. What stuff? What was it you wanted to do so desperately that I was too cold and distant to do with you?"

"I didn't call you cold and distant." Nick shook his head and thought. "Nothing specific."

"So, I wasn't a good enough dad because I didn't give you my time, but you can't say what it is I should have taught you in that time."

"Nothing specific," repeated Nick. "Not actual lessons, just like being a team."

"A team? Well if we're going to get out of this we're going to have to be a team," said Tony.

"Yes, that's right," said Nick, happy to latch onto something practical rather than persist with the amateur soul-searching and vague recriminations. "What do we need to do?"

"First of all we need to take stock," said Tony. "What's our situation? What do we have?"

Nick looked at his meagre haul: first aid kit, foam tyre kit, and whisky bottle. "I think you've already poo-pooed my items. I've got my phone." He took it out. "No signal and almost no battery. What about you?"

Tony dug in his pockets. He produced his house keys, Oz's *argentum nitricum* tablets, a little Nokia brick phone and his tobacco tin.

"What's in the tin?" said Nick. It was sure to be something amazing. Something to get them out of this mess.

"Nothing useful," said Tony. "What's here in the freezer?" He explored the shelves and tested the hooks and chains on the hanging rail.

Nick looked at the tyre foam kit. He'd been given it following his last engine service but never read the instructions. He roughly understood the principle. It was basically an aerosol canister full of expanding foam which, if squirted into a punctured tyre, would inflate it and harden enough to make the tyre drivable until the next garage. Nick had taken it as freebie without any intention of using it. There seemed little point in faffing about with foam and tyres when he had full cover from the AA.

"Maybe," he said thoughtfully. "Maybe we could spray this stuff at whoever's out there, and then you whack them with one of those hooks."

"A bit violent and definitely short-sighted," said Tony. "If that thing really is a werewolf."

"I think we can be certain it is."

"Then I doubt a surprise attack with foamy spray and a metal hook will cause it much grief."

"No," said Nick. "No, you're probably right."

45

Finn sat at the base of a tree.

She wasn't sure how she had got there.

She just needed a few minutes to get her head straight and everything would be fine.

She tried to recall what had happened.

The werewolf – Oz – had slammed her into the wall. Her leg was definitely broken in the struggle. There was a bit of blur after that. There had been some running. Or maybe some crawling. Or was it dragging?

Yes, she remembered her arm being in the creature's mouth, it hauling her out across the yard towards the trees; and then it must have let go. No, it hadn't let her go. She remembered now. She looked down at herself. Blood glistened in the Moonlight.

She just needed a few minutes to tend to her wounds and then everything would be fine. The most immediate concern was the amount of blood she was losing. Her Muubaa was shredded, and the werewolf had bitten off her right arm. It was the broken arm, though, so she could at least apply a tourniquet if she could get the duct-tape out of her pocket. She still had one good arm; she need no more than that. Presumably the right arm was around somewhere but she'd find it later.

Her breath was ragged, and she felt very light-headed.

She'd told the old guy – Tony, that was his name – that nine out of ten people died in pain, animal pain, but she couldn't feel any at all. That wasn't necessarily a good sign.

"Duct-tape," she said. She groped for her pocket. Nothing was where it should be, as her jacket hung in tatters, or maybe the shock and blood loss had made her disoriented. Her fingers closed around the stiff edges of her photo collection. She pulled them out and they spilled across her lap. She closed her eyes for a moment, she opened them again.

Squat shadows had gathered in the dark around her. The dead had come for her, she thought, head woozy. Her victims gathering at the end. One of the shadows snorted and stepped forward. The boar snuffled at her Moncler boots and nibbled at the crumbs of pig feed stuck there.

"Piss off," she said and waggled her foot to shoo it away.

She used her good hand to turn all of the photos the right way up. It became increasingly difficult – her hand just wouldn't do what she wanted, and felt very distant. As though it belonged to someone else. When did she last count these photos? There were dozens. A life's work in pictures. She closed her eyes again. It was just too hard to keep them open.

She just needed a few minutes to rest and then – what? – she struggled to recall. Something about her wounds. Something about the pictures.

Another boar came forward and grazed on the nuggets of food pasted to her jeans.

Finn had seen enough people die to know what it looked like. But she'd met a werewolf – fought a werewolf even – and that was cool.

Something nibbled at the fingers of her good hand, her left hand, and still there was no pain. There was no feeling of any sort.

She just needed a few minutes and then she'd do something about that...

46

In the walk-in freezer, the Carver men wracked their brains for what they could do about the werewolf.

"We could drive a stake through its heart," said Tony.

"I think that's for vampires," said Nick. "We need some silver. What about a coin? I might have a fifty pee."

"You know it's not made of actual silver, don't you? I have got this, though."

"What?"

"It's my St Christopher."

Tony hooked his fingers under his shirt collar and pulled out a chain and a thin medallion, no larger than a fifty pee.

"You have a St Christopher?" said Nick. "I'm surprised."

"Why?"

"For a start, I know you're not a fan of jewellery on men."

"I don't think I've ever said that," said Tony.

Nick looked at him levelly. "When I told you I was thinking of getting my ear pierced, you told me the only men who wore earrings were poofs and pirates."

"That was twenty years ago."

"And a bit homophobic."

"That word hadn't been invented then! Next, you'll tell me it's piratephobic too."

"Besides, you're not religious," said Nick. "Half the arguments you have with mom about funeral plans are because you don't believe in anything."

"I believe in lots of things!"

"Like what?"

"Measure twice, cut once."

"That's not a belief!"

"And you don't have to be religious to carry a St Christopher."

"You do if you think it's going to protect you on journeys. Clearly St Christopher hasn't been looking over us this weekend."

"It's just a lucky charm."

"Pah!"

"And maybe just the act of wearing it reminds me to put on my seatbelt, to not stand too close to the platform edge, hmmm?

Maybe it's just the little things which carry memories and meaning—" Tony sighed. "It was your grandad's."

Nick's miserable sniping attitude stopped dead. "Grandad?"

"This St Christopher got him through the war, he said. Here, there and everywhere, dodging Hitler's bombs."

Nick had no idea what it would have been like to fight in the war, but he'd seen *Saving Private Ryan* at the cinema. The first twenty minutes of violence and gore on the Normandy beaches had been so shocking he'd dropped his Ben and Jerry's ice-cream. And those ice-creams weren't cheap. He remembered something else. "Grandad didn't fight in the war."

"No," said Tony.

"He was the foreman at the munitions factory at the end of the road."

"And every day he'd walk there and walk back. I'm sure he told you what it was like during the air raids in Birmingham."

Nick's grandad had told him nothing of the sort. By the time Nick had reached an age to start paying attention, the old man had become a very old man, with little interest in anything except the horse-racing on the telly. He had been happy to watch Scooby Doo cartoons on TV with young Nick, though. The only thing Nick could remember his grandad saying with any clarity was "Look at their little legs go!", although he couldn't recall if it was while watching Scooby Doo or the horses.

"It's the only thing of his I have," Tony was saying. "That and the old tobacco tin," he added, patting his pocket.

"The tin was his?"

"Have you ever seen me smoke? It's all I've got to remember him by. I ... I don't think I really ever got to know him. Apart from the broad facts and a few memories there's not a lot I could tell you. I don't know why he had a St Christopher. He wasn't a religious man. He and your grandma were married in All Saints' Church but I don't think they were churchgoers at all." Tony turned the St Christopher over in his hands. "He was just ... dad. You know?"

"Oh, I know," said Nick.

Tony shrugged. "Strong. Dependable. Clever with his hands. Never ever wrong. What's the word? Infallible. Morning 'til night. I guess I thought that's how a dad was supposed to be."

"Then you certainly succeeded. You never once struck me as fallible."

Tony chuckled. "Oh, I made plenty of errors raising you."

"Messed up the firstborn and ironed out the kinks in raising the second, huh?"

The look Tony gave him was mildly wounded. "No, son. We did the same number on you both. Your mom and I are equally proud of our two sons."

"Really?" said Nick, genuinely surprised. "Me, who can't even sell sausages, versus Super Simon the globetrotting planet-saver with the Scandawegian girlfriend?"

"Huh," grunted Tony. "Your mom and I like *your* girlfriend."

Nick opened his mouth to protest Abigail was technically no longer his girlfriend. Tony waved him into silence.

"Yes, yes. You're under the illusion you've split with her. That's soon fixed. At least Abigail doesn't refuse to eat your mother's lamb curry because it's cultural appropriation, or the lamb's from New Zealand, or it's got too many air miles or whatever she got so aerated about. *And*, at least when people ask, I have half a chance of being able to explain what you do for a living."

Nick didn't know what to say. He didn't want to hear his dad bad-mouthing his baby brother, but it was the nicest thing Tony had said to him in— Since Nick could remember.

"Sooo," he said eventually. "The St Christopher. It's made of silver, is it?"

"Yes. I'm certain," said Tony.

"It's not very big."

"No."

"If we got close enough to scratch him with that, he'd rip our heads off."

"I know what we can do." Tony pulled away a support strut from one of the wall shelves. "This piece has a split in it. I'll wedge the medal inside and make an axe."

"An axe?"

"I don't know a better word. Do you?"

Nick thought for a moment. They needed an optimistic frame of mind. Insanely optimistic, even for a weapon which had zero chance of helping. "Right. Axe it is then."

Tony jammed the little medallion into the crack and looped the chain once over the length of wood. "Let's go."

"Now?" said Nick.

"Is there a better time?"

Nick put his ear to the door again. Hearing nothing, he slid the hook out of the latch mechanism and cautiously opened the door. The food prep room was empty, apart from smears of blood, creosote and boar food pellets across the floor. They proceeded carefully: Nick carrying a useless bottle of Talisker in one hand and an equally useless foam tyre canister in the other. Tony hefted his St Christopher axe. The weapon looked ridiculous, but Nick tried to picture it splitting the skull of the werewolf. The power of positive thinking would get them through.

"Is there anything else we can—"

Something fell over in the corner. Nick squealed in fear and swung his foam tyre kit at it.

Pickles bounded out of the dark, tongue lolling.

"Pickles! For fuck's sake!" Nick gasped.

"Language, son," said Tony, crouching to ruffle the dog's ears.

Nick put his hand to pounding heart. "I nearly crapped myself in fright."

"Don't exaggerate," said Tony. "No one actually does that."

"Actually, dad—" Nick was about to point out he had done exactly that, when he heard a sound from outside.

It was low, intense grumbling. It was a very *busy* animal sound. Nick tapped his dad's arm, put his finger to his lips for quiet (nearly poking himself in the eye with the tyre foam kit) and beckoned him towards the exterior door.

163

47

Finn lifted her head. Somehow she was still alive. She hadn't been expecting that.

She felt far from all right though. A strange vibration ran through her in rhythm with her beating heart; a shuddering, not unpleasant quiver: like her blood cells were throwing shapes at a rave. Was this what it felt like when a heart gave its last few beats? Some sort of hyper-consciousness? The stump of her arm prickled with heat; perhaps nerve endings leapt into overdrive near death? A last-minute adrenalin rush. It was probably one of life's many cruel jokes.

Or maybe it was like that thing – Finn was dazed and woozy and struggled to find the words and concepts – there was that thing which happened to zebras or antelopes or whatever, when the lion dragged them down. She was sure she'd seen it on a David Attenborough documentary or something. When a lion took the zebra down and it knew its number was up, a chemical or hormone or something flooded the zebra's brain, and it went into a blissed-out calm. A morphine blast to take the edge off its final moments.

She found the thought of lions taking down zebras peculiarly arousing. The mental image of teeth locking around a throat, pulling and rending and dragging down to the ground, gave her a shudder of pleasure which matched the throb in her blood.

She looked up and saw the Moon, shining clearly through the trees. She was wrong about the strange vibration. It wasn't the beating of her heart, it was in time with the rhythm of the Moon. How had she never noticed before? How had she never realised how energising it was?

The Moon was pale and huge and she was, for the first time in her life, keenly aware of how unfairly distant it was. Its glow, its love, was enough to call her to her feet, but not enough to sustain her. The Moon was an indifferent and unloving parent; Finn knew all about those.

She stood. Her leg was still broken and she made sure she put as little weight on it as possible. Somehow it didn't seem to matter anyway.

Shapes snuffled in the darkness. Finn forced her eyes to focus: the forest floor was abruptly brighter and clearer. The sustaining Moon gave her more than enough light by which to see. Three boars stood at a short distance, caught between caution and curiosity. Finn looked down at her feet. There were deep teeth marks in the toe of one boot where a boar them had nibbled it.

"You know how much these cost?" she said, coughing through her dry throat.

The boars were unapologetic.

Finn walked towards them. Walking on a broken leg was easier than she thought it would be. She just had to keep telling it who was boss; listen to the rhythm of the Moon in her blood instead of the pain in her bones.

The boars stepped unhurriedly away as she neared. One of them snorted and continued nosing the earth for food. She lunged. It tried to bolt but was far too late. She was far too quick. It squealed, long and high, as she rolled it in the earth, exposing its round belly and fleshy neck. Finn rammed her strong fingernails into its throat, ripping, opening it like a birthday present. The squeal died in a spray of arterial blood. Trotters kicked and thrashed. She ignored them and buried her face in its bloody neck.

Lions and zebras. That's all the world was.

48

As they crept outside to investigate the sounds, Nick stayed closed to his dad.

The world untouched by the light thrown from the door and window was black and impenetrable. The full Moon, scudding over wispy clouds, gave definition to the treetops and the looming mountains, but nothing more. Nick was acutely aware that beyond the farmhouse was a landscape of dark woods and unfriendly mountains. Having been given living proof of the existence of werewolves, he was prepared to believe in all manner of ghosties and ghoulies and flesh-eating beasties living in such woods. But thinking of werewolves...

The Oz-wolf squatted in the square of land made by encircling outbuildings. It had its back to the house. Light glistened on its spiky, oily coat. It was making those worrying, grumbling sounds as it worked on whatever it held in its front claws.

Tony looked at it and raised his axe questioningly. Nick held out a restraining hand and gestured towards the car and the track. Nick was of the opinion they should just try to sneak away. Tony shook his head and, with a complex but surprisingly communicative series of gestures, pointed out they should attack it now, rather than be attacked when stumbling around in the dark.

Pickles brushed past Nick's legs. He bent to grab her collar. She looked up at him with an open-mouthed dog smile. Nick put his fingers to his lips, which was daft he knew, unless she had been taught some rather unlikely visual commands.

Tony jerked his head towards the Oz-wolf. Clearly it was time to take the fight to the werewolf. Nick was not ready.

There was an engine roar, rising out of the background white noise of the wind and the nearby river. It rose rapidly in volume. A wide beam of light and the outline of a helicopter flew over, so loud it couldn't have been more than a hundred feet above them. For a moment, the werewolf and the square of wasteland were picked out in bright, ugly light. The Oz-wolf stood automatically, gazing up.

As the helicopter searchlight passed, the werewolf took a step to follow it. Nick could have punched the air. Yes, go follow the pretty light. Run off and play. If it chased after the helicopter (mountain rescue? The police? That Col character they'd spoken to on the phone? It didn't matter), if the werewolf ran off in pursuit, maybe he and Tony could just slope off into the night.

He held out a hand to hold his dad back again. The werewolf took another step. Its arms flexed and Nick saw what it had been gnawing on: a length of duct-taped arm with a trowel jammed in the end. Where there should have been a hand, the werewolf had chewed away four fingers, leaving just an upright thumb giving a jauntily inappropriate approval to proceedings.

A whispered "Fuck!" of surprise escaped Nick's lips.

The werewolf turned, saw them and roared, rearing up to its full, terrifying height. Nick screamed. In his mind he had planned to keep his cool and lure the thing into range of Tony's weapon. He had failed to factor in the bowel-loosening terror the thing induced. He stood there like the useless one in a teen horror movie, and screamed.

Tony moved across the ground at an angle. "Distract it," he whispered.

The werewolf stepped towards Nick. In a moment of terrified clarity, he saw the shreds of duct-tape and black jacket leather wedged between the werewolf's teeth. He screamed again. The wolf charged.

Tony swung his shelf support St Christopher axe. It grazed the top of the werewolf's shoulder. It gave a gratifying howl of pain, reaching around to clutch where the medallion had touched. Tony swung again and caught the werewolf across its chest. It fell backwards onto the ground. Even in its pain it was fast: it rolled, it bounced, and knocked the weapon from Tony's hand.

Nick ran at it. His feet were clearly braver than his brain.

The Oz-wolf reared to bring its claws to bear. Nick swung with the bottle of Talisker. It made a dull *clonk* against the beast's head, rattling Nick's wrist. The werewolf's jaws widened in surprise and anger. It lunged down at him. Nick raised the tyre foam kit to block the attack. Muscular jaws and powerful teeth ground at the canister shoved into its mouth. It tried to rear back but, scared beyond reason of that mouth getting a grip on him, Nick pushed it as deep and as far as it would go.

"Run, dad!" he yelled.

Tony grabbed his rubbish axe and pulled at Nick, hauling him away. Pickles bounded about and barked. It was half a second's worth of distraction, and the father-son team stumbled back to the door of the outbuilding.

Tony tried to close the door the moment were through, but the werewolf barged it and him aside. It charged inside, still gargling and chewing the foam canister like a cartoon cigar. As he fell back, Tony swung blindly with his weapon. It whacked the monster's snout, and the end of the cannister.

Like rabid saliva, expanding tyre-repairing foam bubbled from the werewolf's jaws. It reared back in surprise, thrashed its arms and legs. Panicked, it tried to rip the can from its mouth. It roared a weird, gurgling roar.

Its yellow eyes widened. Foam shot out of its nostrils like jets of silly string. Foam which hardened on contact with air and fell in noodle-y loops to the floor. The werewolf descended into mindless panic: spinning round and round, waving its arms to dispel the choking gloop. Nick was irresistibly reminded of one of those inflatable wavy-armed men used outside car dealerships or carpet shops: wiggling and waving their limbs as air was forced through them.

In its last moments, the Oz-wolf made some attempts to roll over and spit the stuff out, but the foam was drying to a toffee thickness. Mouth and noise and—

"Oh, my God," said Nick. "Is it coming out of its ears?"

"Eustachian tubes," said Tony, fighting to get his breath back.

The werewolf writhed its last on the floor, and fell still.

"I thought we needed silver," said Nick.

"I guess werewolves still need to breathe," said Tony.

Pickles barked and licked the dead thing's nose.

49

Finn belched. Wild boar tasted good.

What had the idiot target been blathering about? Something to do with advertisements for sausages? She had an advertisement for him right here: her grinning face covered in delicious and tangy pig's blood.

"Picture," she said and patted her pockets. Yes, her camera was still in her Muubaa pocket.

As she unzipped it and took the camera out, she remembered and saw the photographs she had scattered about her as she lay dying.

They had been very important to her not so long ago yet, right now, those images of lives she had taken seemed entirely unmoving. She had the music of the Moon in her veins and a fresh outlook on life; Polaroid images of the dead seemed silly and juvenile in retrospect. They were like a childhood scrapbook: important and precious in the moment, but something to be set aside upon reaching adulthood.

She held up the camera, struggling with it one handed, giving a broad smile. The picture was almost completely developed by the time the flash's afterimage cleared from her eyes. She gave it a final waft and a blow.

Finn looked upon herself. She had certainly changed. There was a new, powerful line to her jaw – a nice strong jaw. And her teeth ... they'd grown too. Had her ears shifted round a bit? Her hairline had moved down, that much was certain. There was a new hairiness around her cheeks, a not unfeminine hairiness. It was sleek, beautiful and predatory, and definitely matched the new yellow of her eyes. Blood drenched her lower face.

"There's your advert," she said. "Eat sausages. Because meat is fucking tasty."

She frowned at the picture. Her nose was a bloody mess. It had been smashed flat in the fight and it ached as she'd gorged on fresh wild boar. And there was the business with her missing arm, ripped away at the elbow.

This new vitality she was feeling deserved a whole body; a complete body. She felt so pepped up she imagined she could regrow a new arm and hand if she put her mind to it. She wanted two strong arms. She wanted claws.

She stumbled on. She was sure her broken leg was healing with every step. Ahead of her was a building. The farmhouse. She had been here before, but that had been the old Finn; the Finn whose body didn't sing with moonshine. The Moon reflected on a closed door. The lock gave way after a single shove.

It was a kitchen. It smelled of dust and abandonment. There was no light on, yet she could see perfectly. She rooted through stiff wooden drawers and ransacked cupboards. There were knives, but none of them said *claw* to her. Then, in the back of an upper cupboard, she found it. The perfect arm replacement. Her new claw. It was even battery operated.

50

Nick and Tony stared at the dead Oz-wolf.

"We can't be sure it will stay dead," said Nick. "He carved himself like a Halloween pumpkin and came back."

"I wasn't planning on cleaning out its airways and giving it mouth to mouth," said Tony.

"They say you shouldn't do that these days anyway," said Nick.

"Give werewolves mouth to mouth?"

"Anyone."

"Oh," said Tony. "That makes sense. Otherwise it would be oddly specific. We should dismember it."

"What?" said Nick.

His dad looked at him. "Dismember it. Butcher it. Take out the heart."

"I thought we were going to leave it well alone."

"It's like you said: we can't take any chances. Also, those people – the gangsters – they still want its heart."

Nick nodded, wishing his dad didn't have to be right so often.

"Well, let's get on with it." Tony clapped his hands together. "We need some tools. I saw a big old logging saw leaning up against the wall outside."

"You don't want to use the things which are already here?" Nick pointed at the cleavers and knives hanging in the room.

"Butchering and jointing an animal isn't easy," said Tony. "It's an art. And a saw will be quicker."

They went outside. As Tony had said, there was a huge double-handled saw. The blade was brown with rust, but Tony assured Nick it would work well. They carried it back indoors. Working it back and forth between them, they sawed Oz's body in half.

Nick couldn't help think they looked like a pair of low-rent magicians performing the sawing the lady in half trick. He had to fight down the nutty urge to cry out, "And for my next trick...!"

Gore, blood and bone spilled across the floor. They kept going until the two pieces could be separated. They put the lower half in the walk-in freezer, shutting the door for good measure. Next they sawed across the shoulders. Nick found himself falling into the rhythm of the task.

It felt so good to be working as a team it was almost possible to overlook what a disgusting task they were undertaking. They used the saw to crack the ribs and dragged the heart out by hand.

"Let's put it in one of the boxes from the freezer," suggested Tony.

As they packaged the heart, Pickles crowded in, licking at the blood and scraps of flesh on the floor.

"Stop that, girl," said Nick. "It's unsanitary."

Pickles ignored him and selected a pulpy gobbet of flesh. She ran outside, its edges trailing on the floor. Nick sighed. If he ever got out of here, that dog would need some obedience classes.

51

Finn regarded the battery-powered stick blender and the three sharply-angled blades at its tip. She tried the button and it burst into life, blades whirling.

"This is the weapon for me," she said.

She found the duct-tape in her pocket and bound the stump, although it was no longer bleeding. She used more tape to fasten the stick blender on. She smiled. She needed to be ready in case she met the werewolf again. She had several vulnerabilities and needed to take the opportunity to protect them. Her smashed nose was minor, but she spotted an excellent way to prevent further pain.

A metal funnel on the side, possibly part of some jam-making kit or something, looked like it could have been custom-made for the job of protecting her broken nose, it fitted so perfectly. She held it to her face and wound duct-tape round the back of her head to hold it in place.

As she finished she saw hairs – the thickest and blackest hairs – growing from the back of her hands. She considered she was hallucinating due to blood loss, but dismissed the idea at once. There was a far more obvious explanation, although she couldn't quite put a name to it. A new temporary arm and claw in place, a protective funnel over her still-healing nose, she went back outside.

The Moon called to her with powerful, throbbing energy. She felt an urge to call to it, biting down on the impulse. She didn't want to alert others to her presence; not yet. Even through the funnel over her nose she could scent blood on the air. Wolf blood. Man blood. It called to her as much as the Moon. It was coming from the outbuilding just round the corner: the one with the light on.

She sprinted on feet that ached to be free of encumbering and constricting shoes. Even with the ridiculous boots on her feet, she found silence easy. She crept forward, alert for any sign of the werewolf. She stepped into the doorway and was staggered to see the werewolf, her target – her *kin!* – lying dead, mutilated almost beyond recognition, reduced to an upper torso and a pile of offal.

The dog looked up from its delicate nibbling at the remains, saw Finn and then went back to its meal. It had food and was in a live-and-let-live kind of mood. The two human targets stood nearby, soaked in blood to their elbows, placing a slightly larger than fist-sized organ into a plastic box.

It was Oz's heart! This was excellent.

52

"So, we take it with us," said Tony.

"We might need it for bargaining with these lunatics," agreed Nick.

"Right. But if we get out of here alive, we burn it, or bury it."

"Absolutely. Is that a tooth mark?" Nick jiggled the Tupperware box.

"We might have caught it with the knife," said Tony. "But it's not like anyone wants it for a transplant organ."

Nick looked up at the open doorway.

"Holy crap."

His brain took a moment to process what he was seeing. The woman was back, and she looked like a cyborg. A cyborg which had been run over by a lawnmower. Run over by a lawnmower and stuffed in a gorilla costume. Her face had some sort of metal beak strapped to it and her arm had been replaced with a food mixer: one of those handheld devices Nick saw the pros using on *Saturday Morning Kitchen*. Her clothes hung off her in rags, still coated in food pellets in places. The skin which he could see sprouted thick black hairs. She looked ridiculous – like she was trying to audition for the roles of Tin Man, Cowardly Lion and Toto simultaneously – but she was every inch the predator. Her eyes blazed with malevolence. As her mouth opened in a smile, she displayed fangs dripping a mixture of drool and blood.

"Perfect!" she growled. "I'll take that box."

She approached Tony and slashed lazily down his chest with her remaining arm, and the three-inch claws where her fingernails had been. Tony's chest split into a set of gaping, parallel wounds. She caught the box as he fell: Nick's attention was solely on his dad. He grabbed hold of Tony and cushioned his weight as he collapsed to the floor.

There was a helicopter buzz overhead. Searchlight beams swept across the room. Another helicopter? Or was it the same one, circling?

The Finn-wolf raised her head as though listening. "Too soon," she growled. "I don't need any help!"

She looked at Nick. Her eyes locked with his. Her claw hand twitched. The stationery blades of the food mixer wavered. She looked like she was struggling with a decision.

"I don't need any help!" She ran, howling, into the night.

Tony laid by Nick's side. Blood was pumping out of him at a terrifying rate, pooling on his chest, soaking through his no-nonsense shirt and wouldn't-suffer-fools-gladly raincoat.

"Shit, dad! What do I do?"

Tony's eyes fixed on him. He was incapable of speech. Nick wavered in distress. He should know what to do: he'd watched enough episodes of *Casualty* and *Holby City*. Something about applying pressure? Maybe a tourniquet. Nick grabbed the bundled remains of Oz's trousers (which had exploded off him in the transformation into werewolf) and pressed them against his dad's chest. Tony groaned.

"I don't know..." muttered Nick.

He fished for his phone and dialled 999. Pickles licked the top of Tony's head with a long, red tongue, and nudged Nick, hard. Nick shoved the stupid creature away.

His phone made a crackle, produced a single phone ring and then made the *bleep bloop* sound signifying a dead battery. Nick stared at the black screen before throwing his phone away as hard as possible. It smashed against the far wall.

"*Fuck!*"

Tony's face was pale and he was blinking like a bewildered frog. His hand flapped against Nick's.

"Dad. I'm not ready..." said Nick. "I don't know what it is I'm saying. You're a good dad – no, you're a great dad and—"

Pickles nudged Nick again.

"Pickles!" Nick was ready to punch the dog but he saw there was something different about the mutt. Pickles looked— "Pickles, have you grown *bigger*?"

The dog opened her huge mouth. It was filled with giant fangs, her tongue lolled over them in a goofy, yet slightly threatening manner.

"Jesus, Pickles! Not you as well?"

The most unhinged and half-formed plan slammed into Nick's brain.

"Oh, God, let's do this," he said. He looked around at the bloody carnage remaining from their impromptu butchering of Oz. The gaping hole in what remained of the torso seemed a good place to start. Nick delved in and pulled out shreds of remaining gore. He looked in disgust at the red morsels. "They've never done this on *Casualty*…"

With bloody fingers, Nick parted Tony's lips and put a sliver of meat into his mouth.

The old man – and he did look old now: old and worn and as close to being done in as any human could without actually being dead – the old man looked at Nick, blinking and staring. Staring and blinking.

"Come on," said Nick. "Chew."

There was a weak movement in Tony's mouth. Just a reflex, or a memory of eating, perhaps. Nick repeated the manoeuvre, murmuring encouragement, trying not to think about what he was doing. If there was any chance he could save his dad, he would take it, even if it meant…

He glanced at Pickles. The dog had definitely changed. A nibble on the Oz-wolf corpse, heart or not, and the dog had been transformed. Nick had seen with his own eyes the magical repairs worked on Oz's body when man became were-beast.

When he looked back at his dad, he was clearly getting weaker. What was Nick supposed to do? Moving injured people was a bad thing, he was certain of that. He was even more certain leaving people lying there when a confirmed serial killer (now with super powers and a worse attitude) was planning to return was a *very* bad thing. Could he even move his dad, though? He looked around to see what he could use. There was a latticed basket on a shelf, the sort used by bakers to deliver bread. He left his dad's side for a moment, dragged it over, and sort of half-scooped Tony into it.

Tony moaned softly.

"Sorry, dad, sorry. Just need to move us out of the way."

Nick backed out of the outbuilding, convinced he would be attacked from behind as he hauled the breadbasket across the floor. He was nudged by boars, but he ignored them, shoving them out of the way with knees and elbows as necessary. He made his way past the red diesel tanker and across the square of scrubland to where he'd spotted a possible hiding place. It was either an old Wendy house or a former log store. He really didn't care either way. He managed to drag Tony inside and close the door.

Tony moaned again as Nick lowered the makeshift stretcher bed. The moonlight was incredibly bright outside, but in the shed there were only deep shadows, the sole illumination coming from a grimy Perspex window. He felt around and found a garden lounger, mouldering in a corner. Nick grabbed the mildewed cushions, folded and squeezed them under his dad's head and shoulders.

There was a noise outside. After a few seconds Nick realised it was the helicopter, circling again.

"It's not going to be mountain rescue, is it?" he said bitterly.

There was a barely audible response from Tony. Nick wasn't at all sure what to do. Nothing in life had prepared him for any of this. His dad was going to die. Nick couldn't even begin to process the idea. He would keep his dad going. Keep him talking for now.

53

Finn watched the helicopter swing over the forests to the south, temporarily blotting out the Moon. That interruption, the breaking of her sacred communion with the energy-giving Moon, angered her in a way and for reasons she couldn't define. But it gave her a chance to see the helicopter's silhouette. It was a civilian craft, a Eurocopter or similar. That meant it wasn't the police or any of the armed forces. Which meant Col, and the forces Mr Argyll was able to bring to bear on the situation.

The helicopter was descending, somewhere on the far side of the river. It was time for her to go meet them.

She made her way through the trees. The scent of Scots pine, rowan, aspen and juniper filled her nostrils; she knew these trees like never before. She knew them in her blood. She could smell the animals too: squirrels, pine martens, badgers, the passing trails of red deer and, of course, the boars. Boars pestered her as she loped down the slope. They were attracted to the pellets clinging to her remaining clothes. She pressed the button on the stick blender and its high-pitched whine made the boars back off slightly. She thrust it towards them, blades catching the ends of a couple of snouts and they retreated, angry and afraid.

Angry and afraid. That was how she wanted the rest of the world to be.

She wondered what kind of a person Col would turn out to be. What could she surmise? Mr Argyll's organisation had clawed its way to the top by being utterly ruthless. That wasn't in doubt. Was it likely they had absorbed former paramilitaries, possibly from both sides, who found themselves at a loose end after the peace accord? It was extremely likely. She had spoken to Mr Argyll when he first called upon her services. She was English and, for various reasons, Mr Argyll did not want to use Irish men and women for all of his dirty work. There was some benefit in using killers with a different background and skillset to those former bombers and assassins left over from the Troubles.

Mr Argyll had founded his empire on brutality, extortion and death, moving steadily and surely towards respectability and legitimacy. In their phone conversation, he had made it clear ninety five percent of his business was honest and above board, and she should disregard anything she'd heard about his past. Obviously, she belonged in the other five percent, along with Col. In Col, she was about to meet someone cut from similar cloth to herself; the thought was simultaneously interesting and annoying. Well, one thing was for certain: Col would probably have two functioning arms instead of a stick blender. She whizzed the motor a couple of times and pressed on across the river to where the chopper had landed.

54

In the darkness, Nick took his father's hand.

"You know," he said softly, "I said you always struck me as infallible. That's not precisely true. There was that time with the vase. Do you remember? Possibly one of my favourite days with you ever. You remember?"

Nick felt the slightest tremor in his dad's hand so he pressed on.

"How old was I at the time? Eight? Nine? I'm not sure. It was just the two of us in the house, all day for some reason, and we had fishcakes for lunch. No, that's not the good part, but we definitely had fishcakes. You weren't a good cook. Mom always said you could burn water. Bit of an unreconstructed male in that regard. That's not the fallible bit either. The thing was, I broke mom's vase. Her favourite one with the swirly glass. You know the one. I think she bought it when were on holiday on the Isle of Wight."

Tony blood-slicked fingers twitched against Nick's hand.

"I know you think I kicked a football at it. I had just joined the mini-league club on Saturday mornings. I hated it but you seemed keen on me doing it so I went anyway. You'd bought me a new football and assumed I'd kicked it in the living room, but I hadn't. I broke it while I was trying to see if I could draw around the top to make an interesting shape. It was when I had my Spirograph. It broke. You came running.

"Maybe you were in the kitchen, scraping burnt fish cakes off the oven tray. I don't know. But the look of panic in your eyes. I don't think I'd ever seen that before. I was terrified. I thought you were going to be so angry, but you were just worried about what mom would say and you snapped into Action Dad mode.

"Anyway, you said we could go out and find a replacement for the vase, so she wouldn't get mad. Do you remember? It was brilliant. We went to fifteen different shops. We were like detectives, following any lead. We found one which was the right shape but the wrong colour, and then a lady in a shop tried to sell us one which was completely different but she kept insisting it was the same. We ended up going in a place you called a flea pit: one of those antique shops with the scruffy bit out the back, with boxes of junk. You were really panicking by this point. I don't know if you were scared of what mom would say or just didn't want to see her unhappy.

"There were loads of vases and knick-knacks in the back. I think by that point you were suffering with vase-blindness, couldn't tell one from the other. I found one that was *exactly* the same! We were so excited the man charged us two pounds for it, even though it was in a fifty pence box, and we didn't care! You said he charged us more because my poker face needed some work and the man knew we really wanted it.

"We rushed home and we swept up all the little bits of glass. All the chunky shards. We put the replacement vase on the window sill and you looked at me like I'd just saved the house from burning down or something, when it was really my fault in the first place."

Nick paused, completely lost in the memory. He became aware Tony was squeezing his hand, very gently. "You do remember," he said.

Tony unhooked his fingers and moved his hand, trying to reach for something. A few moments later, he pulled the tobacco tin from a pocket with his fingertips. The moment the box was free, his hand fell away, as if the effort had exhausted him.

"You need something?" said Nick.

This was bad. It spoke of something very final. Reluctantly, Nick thumbed the lid off. He angled it towards the window, to pick up the moonlight from outside.

"Oh. Oh wow."

Nick lifted the shard of glass from its bed of cotton wool. The tin held nothing else but a thick triangular piece of glass from a broken vase.

"You kept it?" Nick felt his voice thicken with emotion. "You kept it."

He picked up his father's hand again. Whatever life had been in it before was lacking now.

"Dad?"

Nick felt for a pulse, but there was nothing.

55

The helicopter landed on a shale-covered patch of land on the far side of the river. Finn loped across the high road bridge. Nearly a dozen men had clambered out of the chopper and were spreading out in defensive circle: black camos, submachine guns at the ready, holstered pistols, night vision goggles, body armour. A couple of them even carried grenade belts. It was laughable overkill. They looked more like Special Ops cosplayers than mercenaries. Maybe it was a reflection of how dearly Mr Argyll wanted the werewolf's heart.

"Sir!" yelled one of the mercs nearest the bridge, taking a knee to aim as Finn approached.

She slowed. No need to get shot, even with the Moon's healing rays beating down on her.

She counted the number of weapons aimed at her. Nine men on the ground and what looked like a tenth still in the cockpit.

"Hi Col," she shouted. At least it's what she tried to shout. It sounded like a barely coherent growl; her mouth seemed to be crowded with extra teeth.

A man stepped from beneath the still-spinning blades of the chopper. As he approached he touched his fingers to a throat mic and said something she didn't hear. No one shot her, so it was a good thing.

"And who the feck will you be?" shouted Col, aiming his weapon.

Col wasn't a young man, but he was lean and wiry. He had sandy-coloured hair and pale eyes. He was also shorter than she'd expected, or perhaps she'd grown. She was trying hard to keep a lid on whatever was sweeping through her, but it was becoming more difficult with every minute spent under the Moon's throbbing siren call. She pointed at his submachine gun.

"An MP9. Bold choish. Mosht would prefer the Ushi." Damn the lisp she'd developed!

"Tell me now who the feck you are," said Col, "or I'll have them ID your corpse."

"It'sh Finn." She waved dismissively at her appearance. "I did a little firsht aid."

Her tongue lolled out of her mouth when she tried to smile. She decided to avoid smiling.

"Jesus Christ, Finn," said Col. "Duct-tape, yeah, I get that. I have no idea what kind of first aider applies – creosote is it?"

"It wash an acshident."

He sneered at her. "Sure it feckin was. As for the tin-man face thing, that's just weird."

She'd seen that expression on men's faces often enough to know it wasn't just her appearance offended him. Some men couldn't cope with women in the business.

"I'm shtill shtanding, that'sh the main thing," Finn said.

"I'm not sure how," said Col.

"Let'sh talk bushinesh," said Finn.

Col's eyes flicked to the plastic box in her hands. His MP9 was still aimed – casually, but it was aimed – at her chest. "That's it?"

She nodded. "I get the job done."

Col laughed. "Are you trying to feckin kid me? Finn, if only your fucked-up appearance was the worst of your failures. Do you know how I found you, now? Any idea how this helicopter happens to have landed *right where you are*?"

Finn tilted her head, pushing down on the anger surging through her.

"I'll tell you," said Col. "It's because I've had your target on the phone! Your. Target. On. The. Feckin. Phone!"

Finn's gaze flicked left and right. She could see two of the bastards taking up flanking positions on either side. They needed to practice a bit more: they were a gnat's whisker away from each other's firing arcs.

"Let that sink in for a moment, Finn," said Col. "I've had more actual contact with the target than I have with you the whole time. Maybe you'll recall you and Adam spent the entire day following the wrong person, eh? Where is Adam, now?"

Finn was trying hard to retain control, but her rising anger was making it difficult.

Col waved away his own question. "Have you killed the two targets since we spoke?"

"No, but—"

"Okay so," he said loudly, "to summarise. You've fucked-up on every level. You chased the wrong people, got Adam killed, and you haven't even taken out a pair of idiots who just happen to be in the wrong place at the wrong time." He turned to a man behind him. "Stefan. Take three of the lads to the house we saw. Anyone you meet is a target."

"There'sh no one there but the old man and his shon," said Finn. "And I shaw to the old man before I came down here."

"There's no fecker for ten miles," yelled Col as the four men jogged off towards the bridge. "Be as loud as you like, lads! You can celebrate Guy Fawkes, Chinese New Year and Cinco de feckin Mayo for all I care." His parting grin faded as his attention returned to Finn.

"I didn't need your help," she said.

"You're a hopeless mess," said Col, sneering again. "Look at the state of you."

"I've got the heart," said Finn, holding up the box.

Col shrugged. "Well, and at least that's something."

56

Nick sat in the shadowy darkness of the shed, trying hard to ignore the situation. There were so many things he ought to be doing. He ought to find a way of getting to safety. He ought to think how best to alert the authorities. He ought to work out what he was going to tell his mom if he ever got out alive. He chose not to dwell on any of those questions and sat with his head in his hands instead.

"What's that smell?" asked Tony.

Nick's head snapped up. Tony was lifting himself up onto his elbow.

"Dad?"

"From outside, can you smell it?"

"Dad, I thought you were dead!"

"Did you? I certainly felt a bit winded for a bit."

"Wounded, not winded! Let's look at your chest." Nick ran a hand down Tony's chest. Maybe it was because the light was poor, but it looked very much as if his torn shirt was stained with congealing blood while the flesh below it was healed.

"It's a miracle," he whispered, tears pricking his eyes.

"I probably just needed a rest."

"Can you sit up? Is your breathing all right?"

"My breathing's fine. Never better, in fact," said Tony. He realised the tobacco tin was resting on his chest. With an oddly guilty look at his son, he shoved it away. "Look at the Moon! Glorious, isn't it?"

The Moon was a greasy smudge of white in the Perspex window. "It's just the Moon, dad."

"We should go and have a look at it."

"Dad, I'm pretty sure you died. More than sure. You stopped breathing and everything."

Tony gave him a look as he stood up, stretching. "You're not a doctor, son. It's not always clear-cut." He sniffed the air. "I can definitely smell something outside. It's a friend."

"You smell a friend?"

"Yes."

"That's not a normal thing to be able to smell," Nick pointed out. "What does a friend smell like?"

Tony opened the door. "Pickles. Come on in."

Pickles bowled through the door, nearly knocking Tony over, but his dad laughed, ruffling the dog's ears.

"Dad, look at the size of Pickles. She's grown loads."

"Hath she?"

Nick peered at his father. Why was he lisping? Were those fangs?

"Ohh, I'm not sure I can handle this..." said Nick despite knowing (fearing more than knowing) exactly what was going on. He had been forced to accept there were werewolves in the world, and they confirmed many of the Hollywood clichés. He just needed to go one step further and accept his dad was turning into one too. He didn't like the prospect of his dad going the full hair-and-claws. "Wait, I know what to do." Nick fumbled around in pockets. "Take one of these. In fact, take two." He handed Tony the bottle of homeopathic silver.

Tony gave him a look. "Washa matter? Oh." Tony swallowed the pills and ran a tongue round his teeth. "Picklesh and I are werewolvesh now? Intereshting development."

Nick nodded. "Although, to be fair, Pickles must be something else."

"A weredog?" suggested Tony.

"Isn't the *were* bit the man? She's a sort of a dogwolf. Dog squared? She doesn't seem at all bothered by it."

"No," said Tony, bending over the dog and stroking her face while she licked his hands. "She's more bothered by that dreadful woman. Did you know she's hurt some of the boars? Pickles is friends with those boars."

"Dad," said Nick slowly. "Can you speak dog now?"

"Um. Yes," said Tony, as though he'd always been able to do it. Nick thought perhaps Tony's fangs had shrunk a little bit. Certainly his diction had improved. "I can't think how I couldn't understand it before," said Tony. "It's as clear as day. You could probably do it too, if you put your mind to it."

"No, dad, I think it's the werewolf thing, I really do. So can Pickles talk human?"

187

Tony fixed him with a look. "No, of course not. That would be ridiculous."

"Yep. *That* would be ridiculous."

Nick tried to absorb the fact his father and his new dog were now werewolves. He really wasn't sure how to proceed. Having his father alive was a definite improvement, but would he thoughtlessly eviscerate everyone if he got carried away with the whole werewolf thing? If Pickles' behaviour was anything to go by, it was possible to be a good-natured were ... whatever. She capered around the tiny shed space like a Shetland pony sized puppy. She made odd whiffling noises as she nudged Tony. "What's she saying?"

Tony nodded at Pickles. "She says the bad woman has gone to meet the big noisy flying thing – oh, the helicopter!"

"I'm guessing that's Col," said Nick.

"Probably with backup," Tony agreed. "So, to recap: Finn is now a werewolf, she has the werewolf heart in a box, a helicopter full of gangster types who want to capture the heart has arrived, and they think *we've* got it."

"Yes," said Nick. "Sounds about right. You missed the part about you two being werewolves, though. Although, it looks as though those silver pills have done the trick with your fangs."

Tony prodded his teeth. "Maybe."

"We need to get out of here."

"We don't have the heart to negotiate with anymore," Tony pointed out.

"Then we just need to make a run for it. You up to it?"

Tony breathed in deeply and patted his chest. "You know, I don't think I've felt this good in a long while." He started to open the door again.

"Careful," said Nick. "They could be out there."

Together, they cracked the door open an inch. Apart from the dozen or so wild boars milling about, the square of pathetic garden between the farmhouse and outbuildings appeared deserted.

"Seems fine," said Nick.

"You mean apart from the two men creeping round the house," whispered Tony.

"Where?"

Tony pointed.

"I can't see anything," said Nick.

"In the shadows. Armed. They're like the SAS about to storm the Libyan embassy. They've got them goggle things with the green glass in."

Nick squinted and then looked at his dad. "By any chance, has your eyesight improved all of a sudden."

"Funny you should say that." There was definitely a golden tinge to his pupils.

"We have to get past them," said Nick.

"Hmmm. It will be tricky."

Pickles give a snort and a sniffle.

"What's that?" said Tony. He was paying close attention to Pickles. Small yipping sounds passed between them.

"Are you seriously consulting the dog for ideas?" Nick hissed.

"It could work," Tony said to Pickles. "Let's do it."

The dog slipped out the crack in the door and into the night.

"Where's she off to?" asked Nick.

"Rounding up boars," said Tony. "We get down on our hands and knees and crawl out amongst them. We'll show up on the night vision goggles, but they will think we're boars."

Nick's mouth gaped. He wasn't sure which was more appalling. The plan itself, or the fact it had been suggested by a dog. Or, worst of all, the fact it appeared to be their only option.

A few minutes later they heard mass snuffling and trampling noises from outside. Nick peered outside. There were several dozen boars, milling around. They were doing an excellent job of looking casual, given the situation.

"Hey, something over there!"

Nick shrank back at the shout from near the house.

"Bleeding pigs!" another voice called back.

"Never mind that. I've found the motor. Let me get a light on this."

Nick couldn't see the men, but he could sense the voices moving away.

"Right, I think it's time to go," said Tony.

Nick got down on his hands and knees beside his dad and padded out of the door, into the crowd of boars. The animals were either possessed of a collective intelligence, or were being expertly

189

herded by Pickles. It wasn't clear. Whatever was driving them, they kept up the pretence of casual mingling while simultaneously shielding the interlopers and moving away from the shed.

"If we can just get to that fuel trailer," said Tony, "we can sneak round the far side of the house and up the logging track."

"That way, boars," whispered Nick, blindly shuffling among the bristly bodies towards the house and diesel container.

"You hear that?" whispered Tony at his elbow.

"What?" said Nick.

"He's radioing your licence number to base or whatever."

Nick was about to ask why when the answers tumbled into his head. If they had a licence number they'd soon have his name and address; if they had those, did it matter if he and his dad got away today? Gangsters, bad men with long reaches, would be able to find and silence them at their leisure. And not just them. With the word out, they could have someone on his mom's doorstep before they even got out of the woods.

"What do we do?" said Nick.

"One thing at a time, son."

A boar trod on Nick's hand and he gave an *ow!* of surprise.

"*Hey!*" shouted a voice. There was the sound of running feet and the snap and clatter of weapons.

"Faster boars, faster," urged Nick.

"You! You two! We can see you!"

Tony gave an experimental and frankly optimistic oink but the ruse was up.

"Get up now or we open fire!"

Nick looked to his dad and wished he could see in the dark, gauge any kind of expression or suggestion, but he didn't have wolf-vision.

"We surrender," said Tony and nudged Nick. Together they rose from the mud, backs to the tanker trailer, boars still milling about them.

The armed men had opened the boot to the Cadillac and the automatic interior light was enough to give them silhouettes. There were four in all.

"Is one of you Col?" asked Nick.

"Hands on your heads!" one shouted, which was no answer. There were all carrying guns. Nick's knowledge of weapons began and ended with Hollywood action movies and broadly fell into the categories of AK47, Uzi 9mm, Walther PPK and .44 Magnum. Maybe these were Uzis or something similar. Nick wasn't going to spend his last moments on earth worrying about it. But the one doing most of the shouting had grenades hooked onto his flak jacket which was kind of cool in a *would be cool if he wasn't intent on killing me* kind of way.

"I said, hands on heads!" he bellowed.

Nick obeyed. From his peripheral vision he saw Tony do the same. Grenade man walked forward, pushing through the boar herd, while his colleagues held back.

57

Col tapped his ear and put his fingers to a throat mic.

"You found them? Alive?" He glanced at Finn, his eyes twinkling with amusement. "Both of them? Finn here said she'd killed one of—" He paused and then shrugged. "Then she's a feckin liar, isn't she? Or incompetent." He listened at length. "That's grand, Stefan, but I thought I was clear. Cinco de fucking Mayo, I said. That's – yeah, the one where they all fire into the air. Yeah. Mexicans. The—" He raised his gun to mime a little celebratory gunfire. "Yeah. That one. Tell me when it's done."

He dropped his fingers from the throat mic and looked at Finn. "You said you saw to the old man."

"I did."

"You see, where I come from *see to* would mean to kill. Does it perhaps mean something different in your retarded little country?"

"I got the heart," Finn reminded him.

"Whoop-de-feckin-doo," said Col. "Next time I need something from the butcher's I'll know who to call."

Finn decided it was time to smile. She pulled back her lips to reveal the fangs crowding her mouth. She bared them in an unholy grimace and let the change melt across the rest of her body. Her muscles rippled with power, and the last of her clothes split under the pressure. She flexed and grunted, the food mixer prosthetic snapped away as a fresh, clawed forearm burst forth from her stump of an arm. It hurt but felt orgasmically good. The new arm was covered in thick black fur, wet with the slime of its own afterbirth.

"Fuck me!" swore one of the mercs.

Finn admired the sheen of her new pelt as it shone in the moonlight. Maybe she wouldn't miss the Muubaa after all. Fur was definitely back in fashion.

Col took a step back. "Don't go making this any feckin worse," he growled.

"Catch," she said and threw the heart in a box. Col's face lifted to track it, one hand raised to catch it. She'd thrown it too hard and too far. It arced up and over onto the still spinning blades of the helicopter.

Col yelled something. The heart vanished into the roar of the blades, chopped so finely there was only a fine mist of blood. As attentions were diverted, Finn leapt to the side, landing on one of Col's men. She lashed out with a clawed hand, rammed it under his body armour and rib cage, and felt for his heart. Her claws closed over it and dragged it out, noting the look of surprise on his face.

She turned to the others.

"Fuck you, Col!" she roared, threw the heart at his feet, before bounding away with a howl.

"It's fine!" Col yelled after, with what sounded like a laugh. "I don't need Oz's heart any more. I can just take yours. It will do the job perfectly."

They opened fire as she ran for the bridge.

58

When he first heard gunfire, Nick flinched, but it was in the distance, muffled by the night and forest. It sounded like rain on a metal roof.

The man nearest to Nick and Tony smiled. "Loose ends," he said.

He settled his gun's stock against his shoulder and aimed. Nick tried to think of something to say and found nothing forthcoming at all.

"Hold on, Stefan, what's this?" called a man by the car.

Frozen with terror yet instinctively curious, Nick peered over. Pickles had walked out from the shadows of the house. This was regular-size Pickles: shrunk down to a modest, almost pitiful size. She held up a paw, limping painfully.

"It's just a dog," said Stefan. "Jesus."

Pickles approached the men at the car with wide eyes and a whimper.

"Aw, wassup, buddy?" said the nearest man. He knelt to inspect her.

"Don't interact with it," sighed Stefan. "We're not animal bloody rescue."

"He's got a problem with his paw," said the nearest man. "Let me have a look at—"

Pickles erupted into full wolf form, inflating to pumped-up-on-steroid proportions mid-leap. She buried her teeth in his throat. Blood fountained an arterial spray which caught another man in the eyes. His shout joined the first's gurgled cries. As the two recoiled, one in pain, one in shock, someone opened fire.

Boars screamed. Bullets struck the plastic diesel trailer behind Nick's head with hollow, drum-like thuds. Something splashed on him. A moment later his dad rugby tackled him, throwing him to the ground.

Stefan yelled, "Don't shoot me you— *Nnnh!*"

Nick momentarily had a face full of dirt. Stinking diesel was pouring onto the ground around him. He didn't want to be around when it caught fire. In the movies, fuel and guns always equalled a giant *kaboom*. Somewhere, one of the men was still shooting wildly. Nick followed Tony as he scrambled away.

"It's getting away!" someone shouted.

"Right you bastard!" another yelled. Nick thought it was the one named Stefan.

Nick turned to check. Stefan, stumbling and wounded, snatched a grenade from his belt, pulled the pin. "Damned dog!" He lobbed his grenade.

"No!" shouted one of the men by the car. "We're—!"

Nick heard the grenade bounce off the boot lid and into the car.

"Get down," hissed Tony.

"My car!" wailed Nick.

There was a yellow flash, and a bang which was far too loud. Seconds later, pieces of Cadillac rained out the sky.

"Oh my God! My beautiful car."

The boars were all screaming and running as one. Stampeding, thought Nick. That was the word.

A little bonnet flag, burning along one edge, drifted in the wind.

59

On the bridge, Finn ducked under the cover of one of the wall struts as Col's men advanced. They were firing haphazardly but still had her somewhat pinned down. Maybe pissing them off to their faces wasn't the best combat tactic; fun though. Now, she needed to get to the cover of the woods where she could pick them off individually. Unfortunately, the woods were at one end of the bridge and the men at the other. Wolf-speed or not, they'd have too much time to shoot her down.

She could jump over the side, but it looked around a thirty foot drop, and there were leg-snapping rocks at the bottom. Bullet wounds and broken legs might be temporary upsets to a werewolf in the fullness of her power but she didn't want to injure herself unnecessarily. Not while she was having fun.

She looked down at the water. It reflected the moonlight. She held out a hand, feeling the Moon's power as an almost tangible thing. She wanted to revel in it. She crouched low: Col's men were moving into position on the bridge.

She looked towards the forest. There had definitely been an explosion from that side of the bridge. As she listened carefully, she picked up another sound: something growing, rumbling, punctuated by terrified squeals. Blobs of orange fire flicked between the trees.

"Sir!" called one of the mercs. He sounded worried. Finn reckoned he ought to be worried: it was the sound of a hundred charging boars.

She smiled; she was always adaptable. With her new skills, she was more than ready to take advantage of whatever came next.

The mass of boars hit the far end of the bridge. The mercs, perhaps realising they were trapped in a bottleneck with a hundred tons of porky death bearing down on them, opened fire. One mook ran forward and took up a position not five feet from where Finn crouched.

These boars were not for turning. They had a surging crowd at their backs. Some of them were on fire. On actual fucking fire. The mercs were going to be trampled to death.

It was time for Finn to leave the scene. An idea had popped into her head, and she wanted to try it out. She grabbed the man nearest to her, swatting his weapon away, and raked a deadly incision across his stomach. As his mouth froze in denial, she pulled out a loop of his intestine.

"The gut ish shaid to be around twenty feet long," she said. She pulled him close to the bridge wall. "Hold on."

She dived over the wall, clutching the intestine. The man automatically braced himself as she dropped, his guts unravelling en route. As she reached the end, she felt the briefest tug of elastic resistance. The man's brief scream became a terminal *erk!* His internal organs tore free, and she dropped the few feet to the water below.

60

Nick and Tony sheltered against a farm building wall, away from the remains of the burning car and the as yet unlit pool of spreading diesel.

Nick panted, hands on knees. "Did we just kill two of the bad guys?" he asked.

"At least that," said Tony. He raised a hand.

Nick looked at it. "What?"

"High five?" said Tony.

"You want to high five?"

"Is it not appropriate to congratulate ourselves for taking down villains?"

Nick shrugged. "I just thought you'd think high fives were too ... *urban* for your tastes."

"Urban? You'd rather we gave each other a hearty handshake."

Nick shook his head and high fived his dad. Strangely he felt a surge of happiness, even though they were still in big trouble.

"And now we run away," said Nick.

Tony was shaking his head. "We can't. They've got your registration number."

"So we need to warn mom, call the cops."

Tony pointed at the surrounding mountains, above the moonlit trees. "If we're lucky, they'll not yet have been able to get a signal out. Not until they leave in that chopper of theirs. If we take them all down before then maybe – maybe – we'll be safe."

Nick stared at his dad long and hard. "Has becoming a werewolf suddenly made you reckless and a little bit, you know, Die Hard?"

"I liked that movie," said Tony. "Although the last one, with the riddles and the bombs was good too."

Nick thought for a moment. "That wasn't the last one. There's been five Die Hards. That was only number three."

"Really? Surely Bruce whatisface is knocking on a bit now. It's a tad unbelievable having geriatric action heroes running around, taking out bad guys."

Nick coughed meaningfully and looked at his seventy-something year old dad.

Tony sniffed. "I think we've been pushed around enough by these people," he said. "We need to take them down."

Nick realised he was grinning. He felt more than a little light-headed. He wondered if he'd been shot without noticing and was losing blood. He checked himself.

"You did say you wanted to spend some father-son time together," said Tony.

"Yeah." Nick laughed. "Take them down,".

"It's a plan?"

Nick clapped Tony on the shoulder. "It's an awful plan, dad, but, yeah, let's do it."

"We'll need to find some equipment."

"I don't want to go crawling around in the dark looking for equipment."

"Dark?" said Tony. He tutted and tapped the corner of his golden eyes. "I forgot. Wait here."

Before Nick could complain, Tony disappeared into the shadows. He was back within thirty second, although thirty seconds in the nerve-wracking, bladder-clenching darkness on the edge of a firefight felt a hell of a lot longer.

"Here," said Tony. "Put these on."

Nick felt the contours of the night vision goggles. "Oh, cool." He slipped them on. Suddenly the world was picked out in a washed out but clearer green. His dad nodded approvingly.

A thought came to Nick. "You stole these off a dead bloke, didn't you?"

"He didn't need them. Accidentally shot by his own men. Friendly fire. Here." Tony handed over an earpiece. "We can keep a track of what they're saying. And this." Tony passed him a handgun.

Nick almost dropped it. It was surprisingly heavy. "What am I meant to do with this?"

"I think the general plan is to shoot people," said Tony, straight-faced.

"Yes, but..." Nick held the weapon gingerly. "I've never used a gun before."

"You were the one who wanted to go shooting this weekend." Tony chuckled. "Funny how things turn out."

"Funny. Yes." It wasn't the term Nick would have used. "I just have no experience with guns. I don't know how to cock them. I mean, do you even cock modern guns?"

"You've watched enough films. What do they do?"

Nick thought. He gripped the gun in both hands. He prodded the little levers and buttons on the side. He pulled at the slide on the top. It made a satisfying mechanical sound when he did. "And then I think you—"

The gun went off. It was very loud and it nearly snapped his hand off at the wrist. He stared in numb pain.

"That seemed to work," said Tony.

"Ow," said Nick, not sure if what had just happened was super-cool or utterly terrifying.

"And now let's go get our equipment," said Tony.

On the bridge, men and boars screamed.

The river was cold. Finn gloried in the sensation and swam to the shore. She felt a surge of joy at the sinewy power of her physique as she emerged onto the dusty bank.

She used all four limbs to run – it made perfect sense to her. She ran into the edge of the woods, swung on one arm from a tree and launched herself into a cluster of boars which hadn't joined the stampede. They squealed and grunted in fear and pain as she rampaged through them.

She crushed the life out of one just because it felt good to feel its deflating body shriek like a giant, tortured whoopee cushion.

Death was beautiful in all its varieties.

Finn climbed to the highest boughs of a birch tree and howled at the glorious Moon. She knew she should be down on the forest floor, creating death and havoc. Tonight was all about sending a message to Mr Argyll. There was only one werewolf contract killer in the business: Finn. And if he wanted her services, it was going to cost.

Tonight it was going to cost him the lives of ten men.

Nick and Tony crouched amongst the trees. Each of them had scavenged what they could from the outbuildings, while keeping out of the sights of the surviving gunmen. They reconvened with a Pickles who had jaws slathered with blood and an idiotically happy look on her face. While Tony took an inventory of their haul, Nick tried to listen in on the radio chatter.

Col had ordered his men to sound off over the comms. The best Nick could tell in the confusion, there were around six left. Some were down by the helicopter on the far side of the river. Others were in the woods. Nick wasn't sure where. It didn't sound like the men were sure either.

"Where's Stefan?" said Col.

"They got him," came a reply.

"They?"

"There was shooting. One of his grenades went off."

"Feck!"

"We're just mopping up the last of the pigs on the bridge," came another voice.

"Is pigs one of our feckin targets?" said Col.

"They killed Fitzpatrick and Dempsey, sir."

"No, they didn't," said another voice.

"Dempsey?"

"Aye. I'm up in the trees. I think I've got eyes on the woman—"

There was a pause. Both in his earpiece and out in the distance, Nick heard the sound of gunfire.

"Dempsey?"

There was no reply.

"That feckin bitch!"

"What's going on?" asked Tony.

"I think the woman and her boss have fallen out," said Nick. "We've got six or so armed men out there, and one very angry werewolf." He picked up a meat cleaver he had added to their haul. He gave it an experimental swish through the air. It didn't feel like much of a match against the big automatics the men carried. "We're seriously outnumbered and outgunned."

Tony held up a spool of wire. "We need to be sneakier than them. Sneakier and a little bit smarter. Watch."

Tony looped the wire around a twig. It looked to Nick like the crappiest twig in the whole forest. If they were relying on a twig to save their lives then this was not the one to choose. He swallowed the urge to voice his assessment and watched.

"So we twist the wire back round itself to make it nice and secure. There."

The twig snapped. Tony held up the wire. "See? A nice secure eye for the trap we're going to make." Clearly the twig had just been a tool to form the little circle.

"We're making a trap?" said Nick.

"Not just one. We're going to make a whole bunch of them. Now, we thread the wire through the eye we made, and we have a loop snare that will tighten around something – a man's ankle, hopefully. If we spring load it, with a bent sapling, then all sorts of cool things become possible. Ready?"

Nick didn't bother to suppress the huge grin on his face. "Oh, yes. Let's make traps, dad."

Nick soon found a sapling of the right height and whip-like flexibility. Tony showed him how to suspend their wire loop on a nicely breakable frame, constructed from more crappy twigs. If someone trod in the right place, their foot would go right through.

"Right, let's notch these branches to control the spring mechanism. We carve a little piece out, make it like a tent peg."

Nick wondered where Tony's casual reference to camping and survival techniques had come from. It seemed a bit advanced for Enid Blyton.

"Where did you get all this from dad? Were you in the scouts?"

"No. Off the telly, son. There are cable channels with no end of this stuff."

"Cool." Nick watched as Tony dragged the sapling into place and tested the hook which would fasten it down to the snare. Once he was satisfied, he joined up the pieces. Nick was in awe of its simplicity.

"Can I make the next one?" he asked.

"Give it a try."

Pickles ran up and gave a little bark. Tony looked earnestly into the dog's eyes and made some low yipping sounds. Pickles looked very excited and leaped up into the air.

"She says all but one of the men are downhill from here," said Tony. "Between us and the river."

"Oh, good," said Nick, trying not to sound sarcastic.

"I've also told her about the traps. We don't want her getting caught. If we make a line of them, on the far side of this path, we might get a few gunmen as they come up here."

Nick nodded and set to work. They were on a path through the trees which looked well-used by the boars, with lots of churned-up mud. Despite the slippery conditions, Nick soon finished his own trap and presented it for his dad's inspection.

"Great work," said Tony, slapping him on the shoulder. "To the next one. I reckon Pickles can probably get some of the men to walk into them, either by chasing them or doing the poorly paw routine."

Nick nodded, bemused. He dared to hope they might just make it out of here, though he wondered how on earth they were going to explain to his mom how Tony was fluent in dog language.

"Pickles also told me the boars trampled a couple of the men on the bridge," said Tony. "So that's good news."

"Before the men slaughtered them all," said Nick.

Tony grunted. "Don't like the idea of boars getting shot, but you're happy to eat the sausages?"

"I can be a meat-eater and believe in animal welfare, dad."

Tony tested the tensile strength of the latest trap. "There's not going to be much in the way of human welfare when those boys run into our traps."

"Hey, you know what we need to do?" Nick said. "It'll be perfect, really make us look the part."

Tony gave him a narrow-eyed look. "Look the part?"

Nick reached down and rubbed his fingers in the mud and then smeared it down his cheeks and across his forehead.

Tony smiled. "Rambo! Now there's a narrative I can relate to." He marked up his own face to match. There was bracken growing low to the ground. Nick shoved some into the end of his sleeves to

204

camouflage his hands, immediately found it was quite irritating so he pulled it straight back out again.

"Spikes," he said.

"What?"

"In one of the Rambo films, he makes traps in the wood with spikes on."

"That's the first film," said Tony confidently.

"Are you sure?"

"It's a fifty-fifty guess. Unless you want to tell me they made more than two Rambo films."

"*First Blood*, parts one and two," said Nick.

"That's right."

"Then *Rambo III*."

"Oh."

"And then *Rambo*."

"*Rambo IV*?"

"I think it's just called *Rambo*."

"Even though it's the fourth one?"

"I don't make the rules, dad."

"It's just messing about if you don't number your films properly."

"I was going to say," said Nick, "this path is really slippery. If we make it slippier, do you think it would be enough to send them skidding? Maybe put some spikes at the bottom there for when they lose their grip."

"And how do we make it slippier?"

"Another tin of creosote might do the trick."

Tony grinned. "Great idea."

In short order, the Carver men set several traps. The meat cleaver proved very effective at whittling dead branches into foot-long spikes to be set into the bank at the bottom of the slippery path.

"How's that for teamwork?" said Tony with no small amount of amusement.

"This might yet trump the vase-hunt as my favourite father-son activity."

Tony wedged the final spike into place. "This one certainly has a higher body count."

"Only because mom never found out about the broken vase," grinned Nick.

Even through the graininess of night-vision goggles, Nick could see Tony's dark expression.

"Hey," he said, squeezing his dad's arm. "We'll get out of this. We'll see her soon enough. She's expecting us back on Sunday, and we'll be back on Sunday."

An odd barking sound came through the trees. Nick looked up, startled. "Is that Finn?"

"No, that was Pickles," said Tony. "We've got bad guys heading our way."

They'd discussed whether there was any point in trying to hide if the men had night vision goggles. They scuttled into a hidey-hole halfway up the path and ducked into the bushes. Nick pulled himself into the most boar-like shape he could manage, regretting it after a few uncomfortable minutes. He was about to relax into something more normal when he heard someone tramping along the trail. For them to have got this far, one of the snares must have failed to trigger. There were more. Plus, they had a backup plan for anyone who got to this point. Tony caught his eye.

On three he mimed.

Nick's first thought was to launch into the *Is that* on *three or* after *three?* routine (which would lead to a discussion on which *Lethal Weapon* film it came from, and the his dad's inevitable surprise at how many *Lethal Weapon* films there were). He pushed it from his mind and concentrated hard on the approaching footsteps. Tony held up one finger, then another and, as he raised the third finger, they both pulled on the length of wire lying between them, across the path. It worked perfectly. The tripwire sent their victim stumbling to the ground. By chance his chin slipped into one of the snares; the loop closed around his face. He was whipped straight back up again at great speed. He slid free of the snare as it reached its zenith, but the force had clearly broken his neck. He flopped lifelessly to the ground.

"Frank?" hissed a voice nearby. "Frank, is that you?"

"I've got the scent of him," whispered Tony with a nod. "He's over there." He made a brief whimpering noise. "Pickles will help. She's got quite a mean streak, if I'm honest."

Nick crept forward and looked down the path. The second man was twenty feet away, his back to them. A shape slunk toward him: the unmistakeable outline of a dog. It bounded up and leapt, shoving him over. Pickles pushed the man onto their mud-flume; judging by the speed with which he sped away, it had worked a treat. There was a scream of intense pain.

"I think we got him," hissed Nick.

They hurried through the trees to take a look over the ridge and the spike-lined bank below. The man was indeed impaled. Both feet had spikes jutting through his boots, sticking up through the tops. He writhed in pain, screaming continuously. Nick looked on in dismay. Somehow it was worse to injure someone in such a gruesome and agonising way than to actually kill them.

"I'm not sure I'm a fan of this violence malarkey," he said. "Do we help him?"

"We walk away," said Tony. "If we get out we can always send help later. Right now we just rejoice there's one less bad guy on our tail."

Nick was slightly unhappy about the situation, but they moved away into the trees, while the man hollered. At some point, he remembered his radio. Nick got the shouting at full volume in his earpiece.

"I'm coming to your position," said Col.

"Ah, Jesus, but I'm hurt, Col!"

"I'm coming to your position!" Col repeated.

"Col's coming to us," said Nick. "Are you ready?"

Tony nudged his son with his shoulder. "Would it be inappropriate to say I'm really starting to enjoy myself?"

Nick gave his dad a look. "Well," he said, generously, "that's what this weekend's meant to be about."

63

Finn crouched in the boughs of a high tree for a long time, watching Col direct his men. It amused her to see how quickly a team of ten had been reduced to less than a handful by bad tactics, accidents and a little light intervention by herself. Col clearly wanted to locate and kill any residual threat before he lost any more, but she was having too much fun. She had spent fifteen minutes distributing the innards of a stupid sod called Taylor around the tops of a fir tree. It didn't look much now but she was sure, come the dawn, her grisly Christmas tree decorating skills would give the authorities something to admire and puzzle over.

She'd momentarily lost Col. His scent went somewhere over the river and up toward the farm house, but exactly where wasn't clear. There was another merc right nearby though, stinking of nervousness and making as much noise as a drunk in tap shoes. Apart from Col, he might be the last man on the ground. By the smell of him, he probably knew it.

She swung down silently - she only had the use of her left hand: her right hand was full – but she descended silently nonetheless. She landed two feet behind the man and he still didn't hear her.

She coughed politely.

He whirled, raising his MP9, but he was too close. Finn grabbed the barrel and pushed it aside he fired. She wrenched it from his grip, smashed him in the face with the stock, and kicked him to the ground. If it wasn't for his body armour, her toe claws would have disembowelled him. He went down hard, scrabbling for a handgun on his belt. She took that away from him too.

"Don't ... don't..." he whimpered, squirming among the muck and pine needles. With trembling fingers, he reached for his throat mic. "Man down. Man down. Anybody—"

Finn ripped away his mic and earpiece. She also ripped most of his ear and a fleshy part from his cheek. She was still getting used to having claws.

He screamed. She put a foot on his chest to keep him still and shushed him. "Sshut up. I'm not going to kill you."

The words, mangled though they were by fangs, cut through his pain and fear. He looked up at her. She suddenly wanted to see his eyes and tore away his goggles.

"There," she said. "I can shee you properly now." His eyes were wide, panicked, blinking with tears and trickles of mud. "I won't kill you if you do azh I ashk. Hand."

"What?" he said.

"Hold out your hand."

Trembling, he held it out. Finn leaned down and placed the heart she was carrying in his open palm. He flinched at the touch. She didn't let him let go.

"It's jusht a heart," she said. "Boar'zh heart."

"Yes," he said.

"What'sh your name?"

"Ciamh."

"Kweeve?"

"Ciamh."

"What kind of shtupid name ish that?"

"The one me mam gave me," he said and gave a sudden sob. "I'm sorry. I just want to go home."

"Eat up, Ciamh," she said.

"What?"

"Eat." She nudged his heart-holding hand with her hairy knee. "Eat up. It'sh good for you."

Seeing surprise on a man's face in pitch darkness was a beautiful thing. Robbed of light, blinded, there was an extra level of honesty in the expression.

"Eat it and you'll let me go?" he said.

"Eat."

His lips trembled as he brought the heart close. "It's still warm."

"Shertain tribezh ushed to eat the heartsh of their defeated enemiezh," she said, smiling as he took the first tentative nibble. "Shome think there'zh shpecial power in the heart. Your bossh doezh."

Ciamh swallowed the first sliver and then took a larger, more desperate bite.

"It'sh jusht mushle really," she said. "Nothing shpecial. It'sh not the sheat of conshioushnesh – shit, that'sh not eazhy to shay with a mouth full of fangzh. You don't feel nothing with your heart."

"No," said Ciamh, ripping another chunk with his incisors.

"But we shay *he wazh big-hearted* or *she's a heartlesh bitch* like it actually meanzh shomething."

Ciamh gulped. Blood smeared his chin.

"Shometimezh," Finn said, "I wonder if we are thinking creaturezh at all." She crouched over him. "At momentsh like thezhe I try to connect with people, get a glimpshe of the person within, you know?"

She waved a claw in front of his eyes even though he couldn't see it. He was just an animal chewing and gulping and thinking of nothing at all but his slim chances of getting out of this alive.

"I think I might be the only real pershon in the world," she said. "I can't find a glimmer of real thought, real feeling, in any of the people I kill. They're jusht like robotsh. You take them apart, looking for the real them... They're jusht imagezh of people. Photographsh. You know what I mean?"

"I feel sick," said Ciamh, putting blood-slicked fingers to his mouth.

"I don't think you feel anything. Animalzh, people. There'zh no difference."

Ciamh gulped for air, gagging on the last of the heart.

She leaned in close. "You think you would be able to tell the difference between a boar'zh heart and a human heart?"

The look in his eyes sent a thrill through her. "Oh, God," he grunted, retching. "Oh, God..."

She ripped out his throat with her teeth. He spasmed beneath her as he died.

"Nice chat," she said and stood up. "Ciamh with the shtupid fucking name."

With ill-suited claw-hands, she pushed Ciamh's radio earpiece into her cavernous wolf's ear.

"Col," she said, tapping the mic button. "Col."

"Who..." The voice on the line paused. "Finn. Still alive there, now?"

"Guessh sho."

"And which of my boys did you steal the radio from?"

"Ciamh. He wasn't using it."

"Uh-huh." He tried to sound casual, but there was frustration in his voice.

"Izh it jusht you and me now?" she said.

He forced a laugh. *"Hardly. The feckin gang's all here, Finn. We're just getting started."*

"Liar."

"And I've realised something, too," said Col.

"What?"

"I don't need your feckin heart, Finn. I don't need your heart at all."

64

"What does he mean by that?" said Nick, listening in.

"What does who mean by what?" said Tony.

"Ssh, he's coming."

There was a rustle in the far off undergrowth and the man with spiked feet stopped crying and moaning. "Thank fuck you're here, mate," he said.

"How are you now?" asked Col.

"I need evac. I can't walk."

A single shot rang out. The injured man made no further sound.

Nick and Tony slid back and stood silently. "Shit, that's cold," hissed Nick. "One of his own men!"

"You're never going to properly motivate your workforce if that's how you treat them," said Tony.

"Not exactly what I was thinking, dad."

"Come on, we're going to have to deal with Col."

Nick peered out. "Can't see any sign of him." Nick felt very exposed. He might have been carrying a stolen handgun in his belt but it did nothing to add to his confidence.

"Is Col going down the path with all the traps?" he whispered, fingers crossed.

"Should be." Tony stepped out beside his son. Nick was having a lot of trouble not making much noise, and marvelled at how lightly Tony trod. Was it a werewolf thing? Or a dad thing?

"Can't see him," said Nick.

"I can smell him," said Tony.

"Where?"

"How about behind you, you feckin eejits," said Col. "Turn slowly."

Nick and Tony turned slowly. The man stood six feet away, his submachine gun pointed straight at Nick's belly. He was a pale, slender man. He didn't look like a soldier; more like the shifty kind of guy you saw in the corners of pubs. The ones Nick instinctively knew to steer clear of if a fight broke out.

"No sudden moves, Tony," said Col. "Or I'll shoot young Nick here."

Tony was already raising his hands. For a moment Nick thought about going for the handgun stashed in his belt before common sense took over.

"You've been busy here," said Col. "Doing your little wilderness trap thing. Grand pair of little Rambos with your war paint and everything." He smirked. "You should learn to hide your traps better though, else a man with a keen eye might walk round them all and sneak up on you from behind."

Nick looked at Col's feet. Either the man was supremely confident or he had failed to notice his foot was inches away from one of the first two traps they had set.

"Now, you boys owe me a heart," said Col.

"We had it," said Nick.

"We lost it," said Tony.

"She took it."

"She destroyed it," said Col.

"She what...?"

Col nodded. "So you owe me a heart, a werewolf's heart." He smiled a little. "Tony, you look like you've been through the mill tonight. All the blood on your nice shirt there, and not a scratch on your body. How might a thing like that come about, now?"

"You're not touching my dad," said Nick.

"We'll do it humane, like," said Col. "Nice hospital. Pretty nurses. The whole feckin Bupa thing." His gun didn't waver a millimetre as he tapped his throat mic. "Walshe, bring the chopper over. Outside the farmhouse. Two to pick up. Me and old Tony here."

"*Roger that*," said a voice in Nick's earpiece.

"If you have any fond farewells to make, Nick," Col said. "Now would be the time."

213

65

Finn heard the helicopter take off. It came in low over the trees, searchlight cutting narrow beams through the trees, its light a pale mockery of the Moon. So, Col was planning on taking the old man's heart: he'd picked up the gift too, apparently. Had she done that when he attacked him? Had he been converted by the werewolf's bite, like her?

Part of her was filled with excitement at the prospect of meeting another of her kind. She had known Oz as a wolf only very briefly, back when she had been a mere human. She very much wanted to meet this new wolfman and discover if she was a lone wolf or a pack animal.

Another, more coldly rational part of her, knew there was a decided advantage to being the only werewolf in existence. To be a lone wolf was to hold a monopoly. There was no point sending out her calling card to Mr Argyll, festooned with humiliated corpses and treetop intestinal bunting, if he had a pet wolf of his own. No way could she let Col whisk Tony away before she could meet him and, after a familial reunion, kill him.

The helicopter searchlight beam momentarily picked her out among the trees. She growled and leapt on, tree branch to ground to tree branch, racing ahead of it. No one was getting choppered out of here tonight.

She had to take it down. She had to disable it. Werewolf body or not, she had few weapons to use against a helicopter. She roared in delight: these were the moments she lived for. Whether it was a hand in a toaster, a corkscrew in the carotid or a bungee cord made of guts, she loved improvisation.

Finn bounded to the top of a rise where two boars stood, staring at the helicopter. The rise offered a vantage point which would, for a few seconds, give Finn an unobstructed view. She grabbed a boar by the leg and, before it could even squeal, she hoisted it up.

She spun – one footstep, two – and hurled the fat piggy skyward like a discus.

66

There was a burst of static over the radio.

"There's something – pig! Incoming pig!"

Nick, Tony and Col all looked up. The helicopter searchlight wavered.

On the radio there was the sound of smashing glass and a sudden violent, two-tone scream.

"It's a fucking pig! A fu—!"

The chopper listed violently and dropped. It pulled up sharp and sudden, clipping the treetops. Wooden debris rained down. Nick tried to cover his dad's head as the helicopter howled directly overhead. It cannoned against something and—

"The farmhouse," whispered Tony.

The explosion shook the floor of the forest. A fierce glow erupted through the trees.

Nick realised he was the only one standing. Col was crouched, staring at the fireball which was his ride out of here. Nick groped for the handgun in his belt. It was still there.

Col looked at him. He shook his head, almost amused, as he stood.

Nick pointed the gun at him. "I will shoot," he said, as Col considered his own lowered weapon.

"You will so?" said Col with grim smugness. "I don't think you even know how to fire the thing. You've never even held a gun before."

"We were going to do some clay pigeon shooting this weekend," said Tony.

"If you'd come tomorrow instead of today it would have been a totally different story," said Nick.

Col shrugged. "Take your best shot them."

Nick thought about what he'd done the first time he'd fired the pistol. He'd pressed – or was it depressed? – this button *here*, did something with the little lever on the side *there*, gripped the slide on the top and—

The pistol went off, jolting violently out of his hand. There was a puff of leaves and dirt an inch from Col's feet.

"You stupid fecker!" He raised his submachine gun, stepping back. "You nearly had my feckin toes off there—!"

Col stepped into the snare just behind his left foot. It snapped up with not quite enough force to hoist him from the ground. Col hopped awkwardly for a couple of seconds before his right foot found another nearby snare. He was whipped upside down, a loop of wire around each ankle, each straining to pull him in a different direction. The submachine gun slipped from Col's hand, fell out of reach. Nick winced at the sight of the man: it looked as if he would be torn in half at any moment.

Col twisted in vicious fury, every action hauling his ankles further apart. "You murdering bastards!" he yelled.

Nick thought that was a bit rich, given Col had clearly demonstrated what kind of murdering bastard he was willing to be.

"Who the fuck do you think you are?" Col demanded.

"Us?" said Nick. "We're just a couple of regular guys."

"Having a weekend away together in Scotland," added Tony.

"Enjoying the countryside."

"The wildlife."

"Spot of shooting."

"A walk in the woods."

"Traditional father-son activities," said Nick.

Col made an angry gargling noise. With effort he folded at the waist. Grunting, he strained up to grab a gun from an ankle holster. Tony elbowed Nick. His son agreed: time to make a speedy exit. They ran over the nearest bank and ducked through the trees before Col opened fire. Nick heard the constant hammer of gunfire; none of the bullets seemed to be coming anywhere close.

They moved towards the fiery glow of the downed helicopter. Nick looked at it between the silhouetted trees. It had just missed the farmhouse, clipping one of the outbuildings. Some of the smaller buildings were on fire. The farmhouse windows had been blown in but it appeared otherwise intact. The bullet-punctured diesel tanker in the yard somehow remained unexploded. Nick was sure any self-respecting fuel container should have exploded spectacularly by now. It seemed almost churlish not to.

"Crisis meeting," said Nick. "Let's figure out a few things."

They hunkered down at the edge of the trees and spoke in low tones.

"We're doing great, son," said Tony. You know that? We've taken down nearly all of the bad guys."

"Yeah, but the one left is the very worst," said Nick.

"Which one?"

"Finn. The terminator woman."

"The werewolf woman."

"Right. I don't even know how we can kill her. She's not going to get caught in a trap for more than a second, then she'll just rip our heads off."

"Well," said Tony, "maybe we need to use your *thinking out of the box* skills."

"Yeah," said Nick. "Not sure about that. Look where it got me with Kirkwood saus—" Nick stifled a squeak of excitement. "I might actually have an idea. Dad, you're going to love this!"

He led the way round to the food prep outbuilding. The fire raging in the outbuildings had so far left the farmhouse untouched. The lights still worked and, apart from Oz's messily disembowelled corpse and the mess from the creosote and pig pellets, the place was intact. Nick indicated the butchery equipment pushed against the back wall.

"*Ta dah!*"

Tony inspected it, looking at the huge hopper and the grinding teeth within. "And this is...?"

"A giant mincer. I'd like to see a werewolf heal itself after being put through that."

Tony examined the controls. "Well, it looks like a great piece of equipment, and I agree it would probably do the trick. I do have one question though."

"Yes?"

"How on earth do we get her into it? We could put up a sign saying *free hugs this way* but I don't think she's the hugging type."

"That's the part I haven't worked out yet," said Nick with a sigh. "How do you suppose the farmer gets a side of meat in there when it needs mincing?"

Tony looked up at the ceiling. "Pulley system. I feel the need to point out it very much depends on the meat *not* fighting back."

"Hm." Nick counted things off on his fingers. "So, number one, we need to hide the mincer, so it's not an obvious trap. Yeah?"

Tony nodded.

"Then we need to trick her into being higher up somehow," Nick continued, waving at the high roof for emphasis. "On one of those beams, maybe. And finally, we need to push or drop her in there while it's running."

"Yeah." Tony looked around. His face betrayed the hopelessness of the plan; then he gave a small thoughtful node. "I guess the way to hide the mincer would be to surround it with these fridges. They'd look a bit out of place, but let's go with it."

"Yeah!" said Nick, excited his dad was running with his plan. "Then what?"

"Well, we'd need bait," said Tony. "Something she'll want to go after."

Nick grinned. "Yeah! Oh. Right." His grin faded as he realised what the bait was going to be.

67

The Moon was high in the sky. It filled Finn with so much energy she wanted to run fast and far to truly exercise her sleek new form. Her legs carried her and her nose led. Through the shadowed forest, up a rise to the place where Col swung between two saplings, his legs pulled apart in painful splits.

He squirmed and twisted as the dogwolf, Pickles, nipped playfully and hungrily at his dangling arms.

Finn was undecided on the dog. It was obvious it didn't like her. She entertained the idea it could be disciplined to obey her. She wasn't sure how, but it might be a useful tool. Dogs were reputed to be intelligent and loyal, and this one was as clearly in tune with the Moon as she was herself. A human companion was as out of the question as it had ever been, but could she picture a dog at her side? She had decided to kill all the humans, but the dog could be spared, perhaps.

Col saw her and fixed her with a furious glare.

"You look shtupid," she lisped.

He did. He looked like something dangling in a butcher's window. All the blood had run to his face. His gear hung awkwardly on his upside down body.

"Least I'm not a feckin monster!" he managed to say, trying to swat Pickles' overgrown mouth aside.

"I wazh a monshter long before thish. Shtill think you can take my heart, Col?"

"Just give me the chance," he spat.

She stepped forward, grabbed his front to steady him and pulled a hunting knife from the sheath hanging off his belt.

"Here'sh your chance, boyo." She put the knife in his hand. The words were barely out of her mouth before he lunged at her. She bent out of range, danced aside, and let him have at her again. Every thrust made him swing more violently and the grunts of effort became grunts of pain as his tendons and muscles gave way to the green strength of young trees.

"Feckin, feckin ... *fecker!*"

Finn laughed, let him have one last pathetic stab before knocking the knife from his hand. She slashed at his defenceless groin. Tendons flew apart like violin strings beneath her razor-edged claws. Col's last, screamed *"Feck!"* rose up through the octaves. The remaining connective tissues gave into the forces pulling at him.

A severed leg flew into the air. Breaking free of its snare, it spun away like a boomerang into the woods. Pickles barked in excitement and ran after it. The rest of Col's body sprang up, bungeed back down, and swung in front of her like a bloody piñata. Col, barely conscious, groped for his bleeding stump, crooning in pain and misery.

There was a grenade hanging from his belt: a phosphorous grenade. Principally used as smoke grenades, white phosphorous burned at over two thousand degrees centigrade and did the most wonderful things when in contact with human flesh.

"Perfect." Finn grabbed it and held him still. She pulled the pin and, leaving the grenade on the belt, loped to a safe distance.

Col was too far gone to scream when the white phosphorous ignited. For an instant, the woods were transformed in a world of searing white light and perfect black shadows. Almost as quickly, it went out.

Finn panted in excited approval. The dog, Pickles, reappeared. It had shreds of Col's clothing hanging from its mouth.

"I'm not done killing," Finn told it.

Pickles growled, understanding perfectly, and ran off.

"Sho be it," said Finn. She sprinted towards the house, and her last two victims of the night.

Her nose was her guide. The enhanced sense of smell was an amazing gift. She could smell everything: a boar which had just taken a shit a hundred yards away, the sharp tang of burning from the farmhouse, the cloying aroma of spilled diesel, the pathetic stink of father and son. None of the smells were repulsive to her, there were no good smells and bad smells any more: everything held promise and fascination.

The smell of Nick and Tony led clearly back up to the farm buildings. She bounded towards them, unhurried. Once they were dead she had the rest of the night to run and play in the moonlight, before presenting herself to Mr Argyll.

The fire around the farmyard had lost its initial intensity. It still sent powerful blasts of heat through the night air, along with the occasional crash of sparks as the outbuildings' roofs collapsed piece by piece. There was another sound: a subdued rattling from the food prep room. Finn slipped through the door. The room looked different. Fridge units had been bunched together in the centre of the room.

Tony's scent was fainter, as though he was hiding, but the fearful stench of the son, Nick, was bold and bright. Besides, the whimpering sound was unmistakeable. Nick was standing on a cross beam, just below the skylight. He looked very unhappy. He positively radiated fear.

She had no idea why he was up there. Perhaps Tony had lost patience with his whining and put him out of the way. Perhaps he'd pushed the fridges over there to try and climb to the skylight, and the roof. Height equalled safety? Well, not in this case.

"Going shomewhere, Nick?" she said.

Nick looked down. "You can't get me!" he shouted.

Finn prepared to jump up onto the beam before spotting an easier option. She scooped up a bottle lying among the muck and dust.

"Talishker wishky. Exshpenshive shtuff."

"You have no idea," said Nick with heartfelt sorrow.

She hurled it at him. Terror gave him speed and he ducked. The bottle smashed against the ceiling, golden spirits trickled down the wall.

"Missed," he gasped, more in amazement.

She sprang onto the beam in a single leap. She bore down on him with her most predatory smile. He surprised her though. Instead of quailing or pleading for his life, he whipped out a knife from his coat: a silver knife. He swung. She dodged. She looked down and saw the trap: the whirring toothed rollers directly below her.

"You dare?" she snarled.

"Oh, fuck," he whispered.

She punched him. Her claws encountered something hard beneath his chest, a metal food tray. Armour wouldn't protect him. Another punch: he stumbled and pitched from the beam. He swung like a drunken clown, teetering but not falling. Only then did she see the loop of wire running under his arms and up to the skylight.

That was clever. Infuriating, but clever.

There was a fizzing, sparking sound. The splashed whisky had dribbled down the wall and hit a plug socket. Another spark and the spirits ignited. Blue-yellow alcohol flames exploded up the wall. Finn stepped back in momentary alarm.

Nick kicked her in the shins and gave her a whole-body shove. She plunged off the beam towards the maw of the machine. Nick would have tumbled with him but for the wire holding him up. She raked for the beam as she fell, but she couldn't quite reach.

The plug socket spat, the lights went out and Finn landed feet first in the mincer.

Nick looked down at her.

The mincer had stopped: the power cut.

"Bollocks," said Nick.

"Language," said another voice – one she remembered.

"Foolsh!" She climbed up out of the machine. "You thought you could minshe me?"

"To be fair," said Nick. "It would have worked if the power hadn't gone off."

"I have finally come into my power. I am unshtoppable."

"Unshtoppable?" said Tony, leaning in from the skylight and offering a hand to help his son up.

"Don't mock me!" she roared. "Azh a werewolf I will reign shupreme."

"Shupreme?"

Finn howled.

"Why antagonise the psycho?" Nick climbed through the skylight.

"Distraction," grunted Tony, pulling him through.

"You said whisky wouldn't burn."

"I'm wondering where you ordered that stuff from."

There was a clatter of roof tiles, a wiggle of feet and they were gone.

Idiots! Didn't they know she could locate them in a heartbeat?

She stalked outside. Their scent was marginally clouded by the puddles of diesel fuel all around, but they were easy enough to hear – jumping onto the plastic tanker, to the ground – and easy enough to spot – running off like frightened rabbits, focused on getting away, no concern for where they were going.

She followed behind them and let out a deliberately bloodcurdling howl. A memory flashed into her mind.

Don't play with your food, Finella!

Well her mother wasn't in any position to tell her what to do any more and she was having fun. She swung through the trees, making sure Nick and Tony could see her silhouetted against the Moon as she circled them.

68

"Where are we?" panted Nick.

"The logging road," said Tony, pointing ahead.

They had arrived at the massive pile of logs and the monster tree-felling machine. If they could keep following the track it would lead them out to somewhere eventually but Nick had seen how easily Finn ran rings around them. Literally.

"She's just playing with us," he said.

"She is," agreed Tony.

"I dropped the silver knife. I don't know what else works against werewolves."

"Another werewolf probably," said Tony.

Nick thought of the homeopathic silver tablets he had fed Tony. "We could use another werewolf right now," he agreed.

Tony doubled over and retched.

"Dad?"

"It's okay," said Tony. "I'm just..."

He put his fingers in his throat and retched again.

"Oh, Jesus," said Nick.

In all the craziness, Nick had forgotten how poorly his dad was. This was no place for a man to die, whether it was from cancer or werewolf. He climbed up on the steps of the logging machine, the Manitoba DX Harvester.

"We're driving out in this thing."

"What?"

"The Harvester."

"Too slow," mumbled Tony and threw up noisily. "Ha!" he said, pointing at the puddle of sick.

"What?" said Nick.

"The tablets."

Nick stared. How much homeopathic silver had already entered his bloodstream? Would it make a difference?

The Finn-wolf creature dropped out of the trees beside them. "Feeling shick, Tony?" she said.

"Feeling better actually," said Tony, straightening up.

"It'sh shilly to keep going, knowing you're a dead man walking."

Tony wiped his mouth and stretched. Nick squinted. Did his dad just grow three inches?

"It's better to keep going than to give up."

Nick watched Tony carefully. Was his face getting just a little bit fiercer-looking or was it anger at Finn's taunts? Nick glanced at the logging machine next to him and wondered how much protection the cab would offer him.

Finn grunted. "If I wazh feeling kind, I'd kill you firsht. I'm not shure I *am* feeling kind though. Maybe I'll make you watch while I shtake your shon out on the ground, peel his shkin off and get the boarzh to feasht on his mosht tender partsh. How would you like that?"

A low growling came from Tony's throat and morphed into a roar. "Don't you dare touch my shon!"

Tony sprang at Finn and pushed her to the ground.

"My dad's a werewolf," said Nick, unable to believe the evidence of his senses, and scrambled into the Harvester's cab. He shut the door behind him. With a bit of luck, the door handle would be too delicate for Finn's giant claws.

He peered ahead at the pile of logs and started the engine. The boom arm, currently holding an entire tree in its grip looked ideal for knocking aside the log pile, but the last time he tried it had cut out with a proximity warning. He ignored the boom arm and moved the whole Harvester forward. He reckoned the weight of the machine might be enough to topple the logs.

He glanced down. Tony was almost the same size as Finn, and bristled with newly-sprouted hair and teeth. They circled each other, snarling and raking the air with their claws. It had all the passion and showmanship of WWE wrestling. He was thrilled to see Pickles had joined the fight: transformed into full were-dog mode. She chomped down on Finn's leg.

"Just keep her busy," Nicked muttered.

The Harvester struck the base of the pile, the entire machine jolted violently. He steadied himself and ramped up the throttle. Nothing. An unstoppable force against an immovable object.

"Come on! Work with me!"

He wasn't entirely sure how this plan was going to help, but he had faith in the powers of chaos. A giant avalanche of logs might provide enough of a distraction for his dad to get the upper hand as he slugged it out with Finn.

Nick risked another glance and was dismayed. Tony was on the floor, clutching an injured leg. He shook his head at Nick, a resigned weariness in his eyes. Blood poured from his thigh. Pickles still harangued Finn, but without Tony to distract her, she grabbed the wolfdog by her rear legs, upending and pinning her to the floor, ready to disembowel.

Nick forgot the log pile. He thumped the horn.

Finn glared into the Harvester's head lights. Nick grabbed the boom arm controller and swung it round, tree held in the mechanical cutting claw like a club.

"Get away from her, you bitch!"

Finn bared her teeth and snarled.

Nick swung the arm like a baseball player winding up to hit one out of the park.

The upper branches of the tree snagged the wood pile, dislodging some key log. The pile sagged, something shifted and toppled. Once the pile started to give way, it created an avalanche of trees. As they rolled past, the Finn-wolf danced aside. Pickles sprang up and bounded away. Tons of lumber bounced, spun and slid off the roadside, taking down smaller trees and anything else in its path.

There was something awe-inspiring about destruction on this scale. Nick took the battle to Finn, tree-wielding claw like a raised sword leading his charge. If they could defeat her, or at least slow her down, they could make their escape in this vehicle. He no longer cared if it was slow: it was a protected space, that was the main thing.

Glass smashed; he screamed. A moment later he was being hauled down from the cab. So much for his faith in the complexity of the door catch; he should have known Finn was a blunt instrument, unbothered by such trivial concerns when she could simply kick the door in.

"Family reunion!" she crowed and threw him into the dirt next to his dad.

The Harvester sputtered to a halt and stalled, vertical tree-club poised on high.

Winded and aching, Nick rolled over to his dad.

"Shorry, shon," said the increasingly wolfish Tony. "Guesh you can't teach an old dog new tricksh."

Despite the grim situation, Nick groaned. "Dad jokes. At a time like this?"

Tony peeled a paw-hand away from his leg. It was sticky with oozing blood. He lifted his head and made weak yipping sounds. Probably warning Pickles to run while she still could. There was certainly no sign of the dog.

"I'm sure if I jusht have a minute, I'll be fine," said Tony. "The moonlight izh very..." He sighed. "Izhn't it?"

From the edges of the trees, boars emerged.

The Finn-wolf laughed. "I've been watching thezhe boarzh. They have the table mannerzh of giant ratsh. Looksh like Tony izh going to be the firsht courshe. When they eat him from the inside out, they will be meshy, but effishient. Very shtrong jawzh. You'll get to shee it all closhe up."

The scent of blood seemed to be truly drawing them closer.

"Back off you hairy bastards!" Nicked yelled. "That's my dad! Touch him and ... and I'll turn you into sausages."

Shouting had no effect. These boars had seen explosions, murders, gunfights and dismemberings in their usually tranquil wood; perhaps it was no surprise they were more than a little over-excited. The nearest snuzzled at Tony's leg and licked. Nick batted it away; it nipped at his fingers.

"Shee how the boarzh have the shcent of blood in their shnoutsh? Maybe I won't even have to peel your shkin to pershuade them to eat you."

Finn laid a huge claw across Nick's chest and pressed him to the ground. She bent and whispered into his ear. A stage whisper, loud enough for Tony to hear. "The thing izh, I *want* to peel your shkin off. I *want* to hear your shcreams. I *want* to exshpozhe your flesh."

Nick looked up at her. Very little of her looked human. Duct-tape hung off bristly muscle. Unrecognisable scraps of clothing hung off her, like she was some grungy nineties rock star. Her tongue lolled from her mouth as she contemplated her plans.

"A different shity for each full Moon. Nobody will ever catch me, becauzhe in between I can shtroll the world as an innoshent." She paused for a moment, thinking. "People never shushpect women. I'm a role model for shtrong women. Doezh that make me a feminisht?"

"It makesh you a twat."

Tony's voice made Finn look up. She started to chuckle; it died quickly. The Tony-wolf had hauled himself a fair distance away, claw over claw. Blood trailed in the muck behind him, the greediest boars lapping it up. He was halfway to the Harvester, looking back at her from under the umbrella of tree roots dangling from the machine's claw.

"No running out now, Tony," Finn called after him. "I need you to watch thish."

"No, thanksh," he grunted. He dragged himself further away, making more yipping noises.

Finn huffed and followed him. She lowered her head to follow him under the uprooted tree. "Come watch your shon die, Tony. And then we'll short you out. I promised you a shimple eco funeral. No fush."

"Huh," he said, dragging himself free of the roots. "I'm beginning to shee the attraction of a big fanshy funeral. After thish, I dezherve it. *Yip, ruf, rwaaaar!*"

There was an answering bark from the Manitoba DX Harvester. Pickles was in the cab, a doggy grin on her face.

"Hell, yes," said Nick.

Her paw pushed firmly against a joystick. The boom arm creaked. Finn looked up. There was a rush of air as hydraulics ploughed into action. The tree clamped in the machine's boom rammed into the earth, like a fencepost sledgehammered into the ground.

Mud, bark and soggy bits of werewolf sprayed out from the impact crater. Most of Finn's body was an invisible, presumably messy pancake, six feet under. Boars shrieked and fled into the forest.

Nick scrambled to his feet. He dashed around the newly replanted tree, kicking aside a severed Finn-wolf claw en route. He dropped to his knees beside Tony.

"Dad!"

Tony rolled onto his back, exhausted. "She's a good girl."

"She's a dead girl," said Nick before realising who his dad meant. "Oh. Pickles. Yeah. She did a brilliant job."

"And they shay you should never work with children or animalzh."

Pickles barked proudly, and howled for good measure.

Nick looked at Tony's injuries. "I still don't know what to do, dad."

"Welcome to adult life, shon," said Tony. "You do know mosht of it izh jusht pretending you know what you're doing."

"But you do it so well."

Tony coughed, in evident pain. He shuffled until he could reach the pocket of his shredded jacket to retrieve the tobacco tin. He held it on his chest like a dead knight clutching a sword. "I've had a lot of practishe, Nick. Now, shomeone mentioned getting a ride out of here..."

Nick slid an arm under Tony's shoulder. Together they crab-walked over to the Harvester. "Budge over, Pickles," said Nick.

With a lot of grunting and regrettable pain for Tony, Nick got him into the cab and into the driver's seat. Nick squeezed in next, perching himself on the edge of the seat. He started the Harvester up again. They began the walking pace drive out of the woods.

"We'll be home soon," said Nick, knowing it to be a lie.

Tony gave an almighty deflating sigh. Nick looked back. His dad was slumped to one side, using Pickle's shoulder as a pillow. His eyes were closed.

Without opening them he murmured, "We do make an amazing team," and started to snore.

69

Two hours or more down the road, when Nick wasn't watching, the Tony-wolf reverted to craggy old Tony Carver. Pickles also lost whatever wolfiness she had picked up in the night. Shortly after, the first light of dawn appeared over the mountains ahead.

Nick looked at both man and dog. They were very still. Dog-tired, he thought.

He carefully peeled back the blood-caked cloth pressed against Tony's leg wound. The skin underneath was healed, entirely unmarked. Nick smiled.

Tony slowly opened his eyes. "You know when you said that thing to the woman."

"What thing?"

"You said, 'Get away from her, you bitch!'."

"Yeah. Language. Sorry about that."

"It was a line from that film. *Alien*."

"*Aliens*. The second one."

"Good film," said Tony. "Now, I *know* there were definitely three of those films."

"Er..."

"Come on. She died in the third one."

Nick tallied mentally. "There's been six. Eight if you count the Predator crossovers."

"What?" Tony shook himself in irritation, waking Pickles. "But she *died* in the third one!"

"You of all people should know death doesn't have to be the end."

"Hmmm," grumbled Tony. "Let's not jump to conclusions." He nodded ahead. "Sun's coming up. Everything's back to normal for now."

"For now," agreed Nick. "Oh, wow."

"What?"

They'd crested a shallow hill. A cattle grid ahead, near where the trees thinned, marked the edge of the Kirkwood estate.

"It's an actual road. Look, actual tarmacked road," said Nick. "Left or right?"

Tony gave a large, contented sigh. "Well, I can see a pub in the distance, down there to the right. I'd really like a fried breakfast. A fried breakfast with twice the recommended daily dose of bacony-meaty goodness."

"With black pudding on the side."

"Nice."

"Might even be white pudding. We're in Scotland, remember."

"White pudding sounds even better," said Tony. With a bark and some lip licking, Pickles indicated she was prepared to help out with any unwanted or possibly unattended meat products.

"Although, if you ask me," said Tony, "you just can't beat a good sausage. Ha! You should stick that on your advertisement poster."

"Maybe I will," said Nick. "Let's go."

The Authors

Heide Goody and Iain Grant are married, but not to each other.

Heide lives in North Warwickshire with her husband and children.

Iain lives in south Birmingham with his wife and children.